QUEST FOR A BABE

QUEST
FOR A BABE

Frances Mary Hendry

illustrated by Linda Herd

CANONGATE

First published in 1990
by Canongate Publishing Limited
16 Frederick Street, Edinburgh

British Library Cataloguing in Publication Data
Hendry, Frances
Quest for a babe.
I. Title
823.914 [J]
ISBN 0–86241–319–2

The publisher acknowledges subsidy of the
Scottish Arts Council towards the publication
of this volume.

Typeset in Garamond
by Speedspools, Edinburgh.
Printed and bound in Great Britain
by Billings & Sons Ltd, Worcester.

Contents

Glossary

Some of the Gaelic spelling has been anglicised for easier pronunciation.

Aluinn—lovely.
bairn—child.
ban—white, white-haired.
bard—poet, musician.
beg—small.
ben—mountain.
birlinn—half-decked galley.
borb—fierce.
breac—speckled, multi-coloured.
breacan-feile—great plaid, ceremonial kilt, no longer worn.
brogans—rawhide moccasins.
cattanach—rough.
cerecloth—cloth dipped in wax, in which a body was wrapped before burial.
clachan—village.
Clan Diarmaid—Clan Campbell.
Clan Gillian—Clan Maclean.
clarsach—Highland harp.
crubach—lame.
dallta—foster-brother.
dempster—lawyer, judge, arbitrator.
Dhia—God.
filabeg—small plaid; approximately the modern kilt and plaid combined.
firestones—round stones, heated in fire, then dropped in liquid to boil it.
ghillie—servant.
glic—wise.

gloaming—twilight.
gorach—foolish.
gralloch—gut.
grieve—estate manager.
grinn—neat.
luath—swift.
luch—mouse.
lykewake—mourning feast, between death and burial.
lymphad—decked galley
moid—extraordinary clan meeting.
mor—large, great.
neas—weasel.
odhar—dun-coloured, yellow-brown.
og—young.
plaid—shawl, cloth, especially tartan cloth.
reamhar—fat.
reiver—raider.
roisin—rose.
rua—red.
sennachie—keeper of clan records, usually in his memory alone.
sett—pattern of coloured threads in tartan, linked with one clan.
shielings—temporary huts by summer pastures.
sowens—thin porridge made of oat husks.
traipse—wander.
whin—gorse bush.

From the Author

I've done a dreadful thing; I've telescoped history. I've taken several things which probably happened about twenty years apart and mixed them all together to make a better story. Mind you, the records of the times are often missing, and sometimes contradict each other, so I might be more correct than I think I am.

Eachuinn, pronounced Ochin, is the Gaelic form of Hector. I gave the old chief and his grandson different versions to make it easier to understand.

There is some doubt, according to some authors, about exactly who followed whom as chief of the Macleans round about the end of the 15th century. It is known, though, that in October 1497 there was a moid, or meeting, of the Clan Maclean, to legitimate Lachlan Cattanach, son of Eachuinn Odhar Maclean, Lord of Duart. Lachlan married two ladies: by handfasting, Marion Maclean of Treshnish, by whom he had a son Alan, later a notable pirate; and by church law, Elizabeth or Catherine Campbell, who gave him two sons, Eachuinn and Patrick. Eachuinn followed his father as chief of the Macleans.

Elizabeth's brother John, third son of Archibald Campbell, Earl of Argyll, kidnapped Marion, Muriel, or Muriella, heiress of the last Thane of Cawdor, when she was about ten years old, and married her. That's a wild story in itself! In 1524 he accused Lachlan Maclean of Duart of trying to drown Elizabeth, his wife, by leaving her on a rock at low tide.

So much is probably fact. From there on, we're on our own ... Lots of stories have been written about it, to which I have added this one.

I hope you enjoy reading the book as much as I have enjoyed writing it.

Luch

She was invisible.

Well, nearly. She was a dim, brownish, nothing child, silent and not very clever. Folk aye missed her unless she moved or spoke, or they fell over her. Small, slim, dull of mousy hair and olive skin, her best features were her large dark eyes shadowed by long lashes, but since she seldom looked up they went unnoticed. Even when she ran, and she could run very fast, she was rather less conspicuous than a mouse on the moor. So they called her Luch, the mouse; till even her mother could no longer remember her christened name.

It had its bad points. For instance, her mother often passed over her at mealtimes. Even when she was a baby, she was never fed till she cried. Then her mother, irritated and guilty to have forgotten her, would follow the faint, almost apologetic whimper to find the baby lying unnoticed for hours in some quiet corner. She would feed her, lay her down, and not think of her again till the next time. And when Luch was older, if she wasn't at hand when the food was ready, she didn't get fed. That was one thing she learned early.

But she was also often missed when her mother was ordering work around the house, the spinning or carding wool or fish gutting or minding the babies—there was aye a baby underfoot in the cottage. Her elder sisters were first set to any task, and Luch slipped off alone to bring in driftwood or peats or hay, collect strands of wool whin-pulled from the wild little sheep, trap hares and birds, dig cockles and crabs for bait and food, or gather plants or mosses for dyeing. Though she was solitary she was never an idle lass.

The May when she was about eleven the men hit a huge shoal of haddock late one afternoon. The weather was so good that they stayed at it, and came home exhausted in the black midnight. The women hauled up the coracles and boats and then covered the fish safe from rats and gulls, to be gutted and smoked next morning, while the men collapsed on their beds.

For once Luch's mother remembered her, in the grey first light before next day's dawn. 'Luch, my dear, see to the house and the bairns, eh, while we get on with the fish? You'll be looking after the babies for me, my dear, and seeing no harm comes to them. I'm heart sure I can trust you with them.' She smiled absently back at her daughter as she followed the elder girls stooping out the door, blinking at the early sunlight after the dark of the tiny house, her mind already turned to the long day's work ahead.

Luch checked that the wooden bowl of oat sowens for the noon meal was steeping by the hearth, set a couple of firestones into the heart of the fire to heat for the cooking, and carefully packed the fire with slow-smouldering seaweed. Then she stopped to consider slowly. Wee Dougal, a sturdy two years old and into everything, was tugging determinedly at the corner of the brushwood door. Well. Why not? That way he'd not waken father. She'd get a pot of livers and roes for the dinner. She could grind the meal later. It only took a second to tie his tether round the bairn's middle, and slip her hand through the end loop. She wrapped baby Kirsty in her brown shawl and heaved her up onto her hip, picked up a big bowl, and they went out after the others.

Not yet outside the fence, of course. There hadn't been a raid for some years, but Iain Gorm the head man of the little clachan knew his duty. The palisade was kept in good repair, and a watchman by the gate. No, they couldn't go far while the mist still lay like pearl on the loch and the thin fields. But they could slip down to the beach and watch the gutting. Dougal liked it when she made the fish heads gape and pretend to bite him.

As soon as they were out in the deep passages between the thatched houses, their pigsties and garden patches walled high against wind and wandering animals, the wee lad started to tug, and Luch staggered. If the paths had been wide and even it would have been easier to walk; but it was unsure footing among the broken, uneven stones, scarcely smoothed by the passage of feet. The narrow tracks twisted between the higgledy walls, and every corner was snared with tangles of weeds, briars, rubbish.

They stopped to let the black cows of the clachan pass by, the herd laddies yawning as they called the beasts up in slow, heavy procession from their byres in the house-ends. They were going up the hill tomorrow for the summer grazing, and the older lads and lasses with them to make the cheese and enjoy life in the shielings out of the sight of their parents.

As soon as they were past, Dougal started to tug again, his solid weight nearly jerking Luch off her feet. Scared she'd drop the pot, or the baby, she decided to take Dougal first, tether him at the shore, and come back for the wee one. Kirsty was sound asleep after her morning feed. Luch pulled a flap of the shawl up over the baby's face to keep the sun from her eyes, tucked her into a sheltered corner between old Ailsa's door jamb and the wall of her pigsty, and trotted down with Dougal to the gate, the big wooden bowl under her arm. It was only a few steps, anyway, though her house was farthest from the beach; only a dozen houses crouched inside the clachan's wooden stockade.

Outside the gate that led down to the loch shore, the women were settling happily to the piles and baskets of haddock, their knives flashing, the first poles of split fish already up on the racks to dry in the mild breeze and the fires started in the smokehouse. It had been a lucky catch for this time of year. Screaming gulls were already swooping through the mist. As Luch paused at the gate before stepping down across the shingle to the water's edge, she glanced up to the birds and saw the swirling shadow over the oil-smooth water.

But surely all the boats were in? Yes, there they were, beached in the sheltered angle of the rocky shore, the cobles tilted help-lessly, the light cowhide coracles upturned like round black boul-ders. Luch wondered vaguely for a long moment who this might be in the two big boats driving out of the mist, men standing in the bows waiting to leap out into the shallows as the galleys roared up the beach? The thought that there was something wrong here stirred and started to rise in her slow mind like a salmon in a deep pool.

One of the women straightened to ease her back, caught sight of Dougal and then of Luch staring, and glanced to see what was so interesting out on the loch. She froze for a heartbeat, and then screamed. 'Reivers!'

In a breath the women dropped their fish and ran. Most raced away along the shore, yelling to drive the cows up into the woods, but some headed back inside the baile, screeching and crying for their menfolk to wake. The warning horn sounded as old Donal jumped from his yawning to his duty.

The rush of women jostled Luch back in and behind the gate-post, clutching wee Dougal to her chest, dropping her bowl as she fell. As the last women scrambled through the gateway, they turned to slam and bar the heavy gate. But the wooden bowl had landed exactly where it would jam the swinging gate and bounce it back open again. Just a second's delay before it was kicked aside, but in that second the first raiders had reached the gate and were shouldering in, yelling delightedly, their swords and spears and huge double axes swinging red in the early sun.

The men wakened and hurtled out to fight beside their women-folk. Luch's mother tried to defend the gate, her gutting knife in her hand. One of the raiders ran right onto it. They fell each with a blade in the other's chest. He was the only man of the raiders that died that day, though another man was stabbed in the gut with a fish spear, one lost four teeth from a thrown firestone, and others had bruised and broken heads and ribs before the last villagers that could escaped over the stockade. Most got away. Not all.

Luch just sat still, numb with horror, sheltered by a broom bush and a clump of nettles, calming and holding wee Dougal, watching. Because of her stillness the lad stayed silent, quiet at last with shock, keeping hidden as the folk ran about yelling.

4

Even when their mother fell they didn't move, and went unseen, hidden in the invisibility that was Luch's gift.

Even before the fighting was over the reivers' leader was yelling at his men not to burn the place, to get everything down to the beach right away. They paid him little heed, being occupied in doing just that.

No-one would notice Luch or her brother, if they kept quiet. But what about wee Kirsty, lying in the corner of the wall? 'I'm trusting you to look after them,' her mother had said. It ran over and over in her mind. She must, she must get the babe to safety. It was all she could think of; they were her trust, Kirsty and Dougal both. She could not just sit there and leave the baby.

Hushing Dougal to stay still, absolutely still and soundless, she checked that he was hidden; yes, the nettles and broom covered him completely. 'I trust you with the babe . . .' She slipped away to find Kirsty. She could not stop to weep as she crept past her mother's body. She couldn't even look; her mind shut out the horror and guilt and grief, set itself on the one thing she could do; must do. Save the baby.

Yes, there was the wee one, wakened by the din, kicking and wriggling in her brown shawl. But thanks be to God, no-one had noticed the movement in the deep morning shadow, nor the small crying among the piglets' squeals. Luch stepped out quietly behind a reiver staggering out of the sty under the carcase of the sow, and drifted unheeded as always towards the babe.

A man lurched out of the house, swearing blackly, a hand to his forehead that was dripping blood where Ailsa's son had half-stunned him. Not seeing clear, he bumped into the man with the pig. Luch froze as they both staggered aside, and the reiver with the hurt head trod back onto the little bundle by the door. The baby screamed. The man jumped and his axe swept down, almost of itself, towards the sound. The noise stopped. He shook his head, blinking sticky eyelids, peered down, poked again irritably with his axehead, dismissed whatever-it-was as harmless and not worth bothering about, and put a rather unsteady shoulder under the pig to help his friend with it.

There was a long dent in the shawled bundle. It was quite silent, floppy, stirring not at all as Luch lifted it gently. She didn't unwrap it, but carried it quietly, quickly back to the gate.

Dougal was gone.

She stood silent where he had been, seeking the child. There he was, down by his mother's body, tugging at it, calling, 'Mother! Mother! Wake up!' Then a group of reivers dragged a woman past, Luch's eldest sister, screaming and struggling. When they were by, Dougal was lying motionless on the path.

Luch crouched down beside the gate again, the little brown bundle clutched tight, tight to her chest, dark stains spreading slowly on the brown wool.

'Look after the babies . . . I can trust you to see no harm comes to them . . . I'm trusting you . . . My babies . . .'

She sat still, watching motionless as the raiders dragged out every worn sheepskin, every knife, every horn cup; her aunt's thin silver neckchain; the squealing piglets, the hens, the geese; deerskin cloaks, lengths of homespun cloth, the headman's iron cooking pot and his wife's necklace of three magic coral beads on a leather thong; the last of the black and white puddings; the near-empty wooden tubs of oatmeal, that had been to keep them all till the harvest; the coins, two silver and eleven copper, that were the wealth of the village; the ale and, with a whoop of triumph, a few leather bottles of whisky.

The leader was standing on the shore with a cloth held to his left eye. One of the men called out laughing to him, complaining, 'Iain Og, it's scarce worth the raiding here, for all they've got!' The girl he was dragging sobbed bitterly; casually he slapped her on the side of the head till she was quiet.

The young man smiled rather thinly under the cloth. 'Aye, Calum? You've not done so bad, I see, and we've not taken that much harm either, except for Neil there, damn the wife! Kick that body out of Donald's way, man, before he trips. Are we done? Right, come on, then!'

It took no more than an hour, from their first appearance in the mist, past the murder and the jeering search, the empty destruction of drying frames, fences and boats, the final vicious hurling of the firebrands up onto the thatch, until they trickled off down to the boats. In almost the last group to go, carrying the body of the dead man, one of the bearers tripped, bumped into the gatepost and fell. Climbing to his knees, cursing the nettles, he found himself nose to nose with Luch and yelled in startlement. With one gasp of terror she leapt up and ran out, her baby in her arm, down onto the sand.

Men were shouting all round her, behind her, on either side. The only way out was down to the water's edge, and as they pursued her with no great keenness, she scuttled amazingly fast across the sand, past the wrecked boats, to where the ripples were licking at the smallest of the coracles, upside-down, its black hide hump blending with the rocks around it. It hadn't been noticed, and was undamaged. With desperate strength she hauled at it one-handed, heaved it up and over into the water, splashed out beside it and scrambled in. She set her precious burden down on the woven branches of the bottom of the boat, seized the paddle that was tied to the rim, and balancing wildly on her knees she drove the shallow saucer tilting out into the loch.

One of the men by the galleys, laughing all the time, raised a bow, aimed and loosed. The arrow climbed smoothly, and swooped to pierce Luch's arm to the bone. She snatched at it and tugged in a frenzy. The shaft tore loose. She threw it aside and desperately paddled on, in her panic scarce noticing the pain. The man who had shot her cursed at the loss of his arrow, but then turned back with his friends to their ship, ignoring her. In a few minutes she was far out on the loch, half-hidden by. the mist. She struggled on and on, round the point, safe at last from a pursuit which never came.

The reivers cared nothing for her escape. Soon they had finished loading, shoved the galleys off the beach, splashed aboard, with much shouting rattled the oars clumsily into the rowlocks and slowly carried their laughter and weeping and singing away down the loch.

Luch didn't hear them. She still paddled on and on, farther and farther, slowing, tearing a strip off her ragged skirt to bind the wound when at last she had time to become aware of the bleeding. She sometimes had to stop paddling to bail, for though it was almost a flat calm the ripples tipped and jostled the tiny shell of a boat, and threatened to flood or upset it. When in the end from weariness she had to stop, she had no idea where she was. She curled up on her side in the bottom of the coracle, nursing her baby, tired and wretched, till in the gloaming the tide brought her close to a shore. There was no-one about; when the coracle bumped, she stepped into the thin foam and waded in over the mussel-sharp rocks. Freed of her weight, the coracle floated away behind her. She didn't look back for it.

She might not be safe yet. Her baby wasn't safe. She clutched the shawled bundle and walked on, and on, and on; stopping to drink at a stream; collapsing at the root of a huge tree for an hour or three in the dark of the night; staggering among the clumps of grass and heather, falling and rising again; dragging herself on. Until in the end she could go no farther, and simply lay still, drained of courage as of blood, letting the black wave swamp her; never ever letting go of her baby, her charge, her care, her heart's duty.

And there the young men found her.

Eachuinn Mac Lachlan Maclean, called Eachuinn Odhar for his brown hair when young, though what was left of it was grey now, ruled Clan Gillian from the great black castle on the Duart cliffs above the Sound of Mull. His wife had but the one son, who had married, and had a son of his own before he died. Hector Luath, the swift one, the lad was called, for he could run nearly as fast as a deerhound. Tall and slender he was, vital and alert, rather darker than his grandfather had ever been, but, at twenty, more quiet and peaceable.

But after his wife had died, Eachuinn Odhar had been comforted by a lass of the clan, and had another son, Lachlan, born out of wedlock. Lachlan Cattanach, the rough one. Rough indeed he was, red in his looks and his ways, bullying all the lads of the clan till his father, proud at first of the boy's spirit, ended up trying to restrain his outrageous furies, and failing. Many a fine Eachuinn Odhar paid at the dempster's bidding to compensate the victims of Lachlan's jealousy that it was his nephew Hector would be chief of the clan, not himself. At last his grandfather sent the young man off to Ireland, to work off his temper with his Irish cousins in their fights among themselves or against the English sent by Henry VII, and win his own place in the world. He had gone on to fight Moors in Spain, and Danes in Germany. But last year he had returned for a visit, and stayed on. The Marshal of Duart, captain of the castle, had recently died, and Lachlan took his post; and, at twenty-seven, he fell in love.

Hector Luath and Lachlan were out hunting with their foster-brothers and a handful of ghillies at dawn that May morning. As the custom was, the two lads had been given to women of the clan to rear with their own baby sons, so that each had a dallta, or fosterbrother—friend, privileged critic, servant, adviser, body-guard faithful to death. Lachlan's dallta was Farquhar Neas; Farquhar the Weasel, his grin twisted like his nature. He had saved Lachlan's life more than once, and his dirk was even readier than his milk-brother's. Hector had been reared by the mother of Ewan Beg, called Small Ewan in jest for even at fourteen he'd been the second largest man in the clan.

Before two hours or ten miles went by, the hunters found their quarry; a dozen red deer, feeding quietly up on the far slope of a corrie.

'There! That hind on the right! She's barren—no fawn to drag her down. She'll make good eating,' Hector whispered, flat behind a bracken clump.

As usual, Lachlan disagreed. 'A hind! That's never a man's target! Better take the stag. Look at the head on him—a twelve-pointer!'

Hector shook his head. 'The female's better fleshed. But you do as you like, Lachlan. Don't you always, eh?' He grinned at his young uncle.

Lachlan grinned back, friendly, and turned to his fosterbrother crouched behind them. 'See them, Farquhar? Can you come round behind them with the hounds and run them this way for us, without them getting your scent?'

Farquhar sneered. 'Can an eagle soar? Wait you here, Lachlan Cattanach, and the arrow ready on your bowstring!' He melted away over the brow of the hill to where the other men waited, and lifted the leashes of the two couples of tall deerhounds. Alone as usual, he loped off along the slope, going wide, wide round the deer, the hounds eager but silent beside him.

Silently too, Hector and Lachlan waited, nearly invisible in their dark hunting kilts and brown skin. Hector's dallta crawled up with their bows. As Farquhar had advised, each set an arrow to the string, and others ready to hand in the heather. 'Lie still there, Ewan Beg. Ewan Ben!' Hector whispered. 'We could be doing with a mountain to hide behind!'

The big lad made a face at his beloved milk-brother. He'd forgive Hector anything, not only the teasing; the tie between them was far stronger than if they had been full brothers. He slid away as silently as he had come, for like many big men he could move quietly when he wanted to.

One of the deer raised its head and stared away from them up the far slope of the corrie. 'My heart, Farquhar!' exulted Lachlan in a whisper as the animals, wary but not in any great alarm, started to drift down towards them. 'See there! One of the hounds —Borb, is it? No, Grinn—see her sneaking along there beyond them! But they'll scent her in a minute. Ready?'

Suddenly a swirl of wind brought Grinn's scent to the deer. They reared round to head up the hill, but there were Farquhar and two more hounds to turn them. Downhill the wisest of the hounds, Glic, was waiting. In panic they fled straight across the corrie, leaping the burn towards the men standing now, bows drawn, loosing with a melodious harp twang and stooping in the same moment for another arrow from the heather.

At fifty yards' range, Hector's arrow pierced the chest of the hind. She took three more steps and fell, crashing among the rocks.

Lachlan's first arrow at the stag was by chance struck aside by its antlers. In a fury he snatched another as the deer leaped aside and raced away, and at near a hundred yards his second shot sank deep into the beast's neck. It staggered on, but in a few seconds the hounds had caught it and borne it down. He raced up to the heaving mass of animals, drawing his long dirk as he ran, cheering in triumph, to dive in through the flashing sweep of antlers that could easily have gutted him, haul up the stag's head and finish it off.

In five minutes the beasts were gralloched and the men washing off the blood from their hands in the burn. The legs of the stag were tied to a spear for two men to carry home, and big Ewan picked up the carcase of the hind as easily as a plaid and slung it over his shoulder.

'Is that it, then, Ewan? It's not too heavy for you?' asked Hector.

The huge lad scowled in mock anger. 'Away with you, Hector Luath. Go and try your speed as usual, and don't be insulting your betters.'

'Betters!' Hector howled in mock anger, leaping to his feet. 'I'll teach you respect for your next chief, Ewan Beg! Put down that beast and I'll—'

'Away, what would you do? Wrestle me?' Grinning at the threat, Ewan hefted the carcase casually to ease it to a more comfortable spot. 'You couldn't throw me. You and Lachlan Cattanach together couldn't throw me. One hand tied behind me, you couldn't. Away to your play, so, and leave me to be at getting this beast home. I've no time for bairns' games just this minute.' The ghillies were grinning too, enjoying the back-chat.

Lachlan straightened from washing the stag's blood off his hairy chest. 'Mind your tongue, Ewan Beg! You're far too—'

His nephew swung round. 'Too what?' The good humour had quite gone from Hector's face. 'Go on, uncle. Too what? If I choose to jest with my dallta, is it any business of yours, then? Mind now, Lachlan Cattanach, I'm not that lad in Craignure you half-killed last month.'

Lachlan stiffened. For a moment there was blind rage in his eyes, and the watching men stilled. They came nearer to blows every time . . . Farquhar tensed, hand near the black hilt of the long dirk in his belt.

'Here, now!' Big Ewan stepped down like a jovial avalanche between the two as they bristled. 'Is this any way to behave? Duart will be whipping the two of you like brawling laddies. Have sense, will you! You'll have Farquhar and myself in tears with laughter at you, fighting like sticklebacks.'

As Hector's face relaxed in a grin at the picture, Lachlan's eye turned for a second to Farquhar Neas, waiting, ready, his narrow, pointed face as taut as Lachlan's own . . . But Lachlan shook his head and slapped the big man on the shoulder. 'Man, I never before saw myself as a fish!' His laugh bellowed. Farquhar's tension slackened immediately. 'As you say, Hector, it's no affair of mine if you let Ewan jest at you. It's just—it's not dignified.'

Hector snorted as he noticed the twist Lachlan had put on his words. 'Aye so? Well, Lachlan, let me worry about my dignity. Just you and your dallta deal between yourselves in your own way, and leave me and Ewan to deal in ours. Eachuinn Odhar would be less than pleased to hear of this.'

Lachlan's laugh was more genuine now. 'Aye, you're right there. Peace—my skinny wee nephew.' Both young men chuckled. 'But I still have the legs of you, spindleshanks! And there's the hill to prove it on!'

Hector was glad enough to shift the subject to a permissible rivalry. 'Aye, so? I'd back a deer running against a bear any day!' The men about grinned as Lachlan scratched his thick pelt and roared like a bear, pretending anger at the apt comparison. 'Is your running better than your shooting, then?'

'What's wrong with my archery? Could you have made that last shot?'

'I'd not have missed the first one. And I can beat you running as well. Would you care to lay a small wager on it?' Hector was already re-tying the leather thong that held back his long hair off his face.

'First cut at the roast this night?'

'Done! See you at home, Ewan!'

Leaving their ghillies to bring back the game and their bows, the young men swung away across the heather, their race-track the long sweep of rocky moorland up over the shoulder of Sgurr Dearg and down towards Duart Point, where the castle towered over the cliff like a broody eagle on its eyrie. Tall and whippy, Hector ran lightly, leaping the rocks and heather clumps, but the strength and bull power of Lachlan, thundering wide-chested and heavy-muscled behind him, reminded him he never had the race all to himself.

'Aye at it, eh? Dhia, will they never settle down?' Ewan Beg shook his head as the men laughed, and looked round at Farquhar. 'Let the dogs run with them, man?' he suggested. 'They've scarce had time to stretch their legs.'

Farqhuar nodded and released the great hounds' leashes. The long, narrow muzzles lifted as they leaped after their masters. 'Which will win, think you?'

Ewan chuckled, his massive belly quivering. 'Are you wanting a wager yourself? I'm your man for that. For a blow? My left hand against your right?'

Farquhar sneered, tossing his fair hair. 'A blow? I've a testoon to wager. Can you match it—or is your dallta less generous than mine?'

A ghillie to wager silver? The men were impressed. Ewan frowned. Farquhar was aye boasting about his dallta's wealth since the foreign wars. He didn't have even a groat to wager, but when it was put like that, for the sake of Hector's reputation he couldn't refuse. 'You're easy parted from your coin.'

Farquhar sneered again. 'Here's it. Match it?' He produced the silver and tossed it, and all eyes followed its twinkling lift and fall.

'Do I carry all my silver up on the hill?' Ewan snapped, hefted the deer on his shoulders again and turned smarting to the hillside. Sure and Hector would pay the wager if he lost—but he'd not lose!

Behind him Farquhar grinned sideways. 'All his silver!' he mouthed, rolled his eyes to make the others laugh at the boast, picked up Lachlan's bow and moved after the big lad. The ghillies lifted the stag's carcase and followed, excited by the big stake and by the by-play that they knew wasn't all play.

Neck and neck, as usual, the young men raced to turn the shoulder of the mountain and charge down the slope. The shaggy hounds loped along before them, enjoying the speed, flying ahead of the men with their ten-foot strides.

Near the bottom of the long slope the hounds swung apart for a moment. Hector glanced over and saw her quite by chance. A girl, lying face down, a brown bundle clasped under her green plaid. He shouted, and skidded to a halt.

For a second, Lachlan seemed to intend to go right on, but then he stopped too. 'What is it?' he called back. 'Do you yield the first cut, then?'

'Ach, never mind that now!'

Lachlan Cattanach's mouth stiffened, but then he too saw the girl as Hector knelt by her. 'Who is she?' He came back slowly, puffing only slightly.

'I don't know the sett of her plaid. She's hurt—see!' With one finger Hector lifted the edge of the scrap of cloth bound round her left arm. 'An arrow wound. A nasty gash. She's near dead of cold and loss of blood.' He sat back on his heels. 'We'll need to get her home to David Beaton.'

'But if she's not one of our folk? Or maybe not even a Maclean at all? One of the Allansons? A Campbell? What will father say?'

Hector glanced up at him in annoyance. 'She's a lassie and she's hurt! And who's to say who she is? If there's reivers about, and she gives word of it, grandfather'll welcome her even if she's a Mackinnon.' He lifted the girl in his arms as gently as he could. Then he stood quite still. 'Lachlan!' he said.

'Aye?' Lachlan was surprised at the strangeness of the tone.

'Look at the hounds.'

Lachlan looked round. The great dogs were gambolling down by the water's edge, chasing seagulls to pass the time. 'What's wrong with them?'

'Did you ever know them ignore a stranger before? Remember they killed the first man ashore from the shipwreck last year? But they ran right by her.'

Lachlan shrugged. 'They ran too fast to notice her. What does it matter?'

'Aye. I suppose so.' Hector didn't sound too sure.

Farquhar and a couple of the ghillies had run up to find out what was wrong. One of them offered to take the lass, but Hector Luath shook his head and got a good grip of her in his arms. 'Bring her bundle there, will you, Farquhar?' he said, and started off down the hill.

He turned back as Lachlan, in his turn, called him in a strained voice.

Farquhar was holding the bundle at arm's length. The folds of damp wool had fallen open, and its contents were flopping over his hands; a baby. Heavy and white and dead.

Duart

In the afternoon Luch was wakened gently. She was lying, warm and dry, on a pallet in David Beaton's little infirmary just outside the castle gate. Her arm had been properly bandaged, and Maclean of Duart himself was there, forcing a smile to his square, lined face to try to reassure her.

She paid no attention to him, silver belt and dirk-hilt, great plaid and all, nor to the other men clustered around her. She tossed aside the blanket, felt frantically round, gazed blindly past them all and started to scream. She screamed and fought, kicking and biting, struggling to rise, to escape, to find her baby. She screamed and screamed, wordless, chilling the heart.

They tried to calm her, to reason with her, to shout her down, to slap her quiet. Even when her shrieks faded she still would not, could not speak to them. Her eyes stared for her bundle. Her arms searched around her, or clung hopelessly round her chest as she curled in a tight ball. A constant whispered moan and a dreadful dry sobbing were all they could get from her.

The doctor finally chased the men out. A young man but sure of his skill and his position, he glared at his chief standing frustrated and annoyed in the doorway. 'You must just hold your patience, Duart! I can guess what's wrong, and what to do that the lassie'll be able to speak to you, but it will not be till the morrow's morn.

You'd best be sending runners all round the island to find out where there has been a raid, and leave her to me.'

He left Luch sobbing tearlessly in the arms of a lass with a broken leg, while he infused poppy and willow bark in a cup of boiling water from the pot on the brazier, with a spoonful of honey to smooth and sweeten it. Sip by sip he coaxed Luch to swallow. Sitting tense, sniffling on his bony knee, she slowly relaxed as the willow dulled the pain and the poppy brought sleep. He held her safe and secure. Her eyes blinked and closed despite all her efforts to watch, to seek her baby, till at last her head fell to his thin shoulder. With a sigh of pity and relief he laid her down.

Next dawn when she woke she reached out instantly, whimpering again for her lost baby, but he was ready. With one of the maids he had been at work half the night, making a gift for the child. 'Here, lass,' he murmured quietly, and set her groping hand on a new bundle, in her brown shawl carefully darned, washed and dried before the fire. Not her own baby, but a life-sized doll, with carved wooden head and straw-stuffed woollen body.

For a minute it was doubtful whether she would accept it. But something in her slow mind told her this was the best thing; the only thing; and she took the toy in her arms, at first with reluctance, then with joy, lovingly rocking the doll close to her heart, tears rolling down her cheeks. His mind's eye on a tiny body to be buried that day, the young doctor near wept with her.

When Duart came in to see her, she said little, but could nod and shake her head, or whisper a word to answer his almost-gentle questions. The story of the raid was told, but the reivers could not be identified. Iain Og? There were a dozen young Johns with their names to make.

But more than that she could not tell him. Where did she live? The clachan. Where was that? The shore. What shore? The loch. Which loch? She gazed blankly, clutching her baby. What was her name? Luch. Luch what? Was it Maclean? She gazed blankly. Who was the leader of her clachan? Iain Gorm. Iain Gorm what? What was her clan? Who was her chief? She gazed blankly.

He left her at peace eventually, and came back up to the hall to speak with his advisers, near a hundred of them, all agog to find out what was happening. There were the clan office-bearers: the dempster, the judge-arbitrator who held court in the Maclean's absence and knew the laws and customs of Clan Gillian even better than his lord; the sennachie or record-keeper; old Father Patrick the priest; the doctor, of the clan Beaton, the finest physicians in the land. Then the chief's own officers: Donald Crubach the bard; the master of his household, whitehaired Seamus Ban, and the grieve who ran his personal lands; his butler; his piper; the hereditary bearers of his purse, cup, standard, armour, sword and shield; the smith, master of the magic of iron. And crowding round, the fighting men: the castle guard, cousins and sons of cousins of the Maclean; the captains of the galleys, decked lymphads and half-decked birlinns, beached in the castle bay; tacksmen—tenants—of the Maclean lands; the fighting gentlemen, soldiers provided by the under-tenants as part of their rent, who crowded the castle yard in the day and the hall at night. Bristling like hedgehogs with dirk and sword, spear, axe, javelin and bow, eager to leap to battle at their chief's word, they had gathered to discuss the mystery of the lass found on the shore, to advise and support their chief in his decisions, as was their duty and their right.

But they found little to discuss.

'She's half-witted,' Lachlan suggested. His father grunted half-agreement.

Hector frowned at them both. 'You're less than generous, grandfather! You mind Annie, when her bairn was drowned, how she knew no-one, even her mother, for near a year? It will maybe come back to her in time.'

Master Beaton nodded. 'She's told you all she can for now, Duart.'

'It's not enough,' Eachuinn Odhar said gloomily. He looked little like the leader of one of the greatest clans in the west, a smallish man but wiry, his fine embroidered linen tunic aye stained and untidy despite his servants' efforts, his face lined, his nose three times broken, scratching irritably at the old scar that ran across his bald spot. 'We don't even know if this raid was on my land. I'll swear there's no Iain Gorm head of any clachan on Mull or Morvern. I'd look a wild fool to call out Clan Gillian over a raid on someone else, and against a man we didn't know! It's the laugh of the Isles I'd be.'

Most of the older men about him nodded in agreement, but Lachlan was angry. 'Father, there's one Ian Og we all know—John Campbell of Cawdor, third son to Argyll himself! And he's a greedy man, Archibald Campbell! You mind he and John kidnapped the Cawdor heiress, and John wed her. Clan Gillian and Clan Diarmaid are old foes. It's dishonour if we let them away with it!'

Some of the younger men cheered, but his father swung a forceful back-hand fist to his big son's chest that knocked him off his feet. 'You would dare!' he snarled. 'Will my own son teach me about honour?' Lachlan, coughing as he sprawled against Farquhar's knees, stared up in furious astonishment, for it was seldom his father was moved to let loose his temper. He scrambled up, struggling to hold in his rage, rubbing his breast-bone.

Eachuinn Odhar's frustration was relieved by the blow, and he felt a small flare of pride; he had shown his clan, and his son, that he could still floor a man forty years younger and six inches taller. His red glare softened and he tried to explain. 'Am I to be starting a war, then, for your entertainment? Look, son. We helped King James put down the Lord of the Isles—that arrogant fool Angus Og—so we're in his favour. For the moment. But if we stir up trouble just now, the king could turn against us just as easy. And wouldn't Archie Campbell like that fine!'

He scratched at his scar again in annoyance. 'We can't just take to the water in force against whoever we may think has wronged us. Not any more. It's a new world you're coming into, Hector, laddie, God help you, not like the good old days. A world where a man can't do as he must for the clan! Everything down on paper to keep the lawyers at work, the word of a gentleman not good enough any more! Argyll and his like should do well in it—he's a Scot himself, no Islesman. But you're right enough, Lachlan, that if the raiding's not stopped now, we're like to have little peace.'

'Peace?' Lachlan snorted sarcastically. 'Who wants peace but old women? That's not what I meant! Let Duart set his galleys to the water and find out who's at the reiving, and then be raiding back, I say. That's what a true man wants, the thrill of battle, not

18

peace!' The younger men cheered him again, and the piper, at the back of the crowd, loosed a drone or two to stir them.

'And God help the widows and fatherless children of Clan Gillian.' In the silence after Hector's interruption, the older men grunted approval, but the young men shared sneering glances. 'A clan chief is father to every one of his people. Must he not consider all of them, not just the warriors?' Hector's voice held a defiant challenge. They did not meet his eye, but he failed to convince them, and their minds were for Lachlan.

Eachuinn Odhar looked quizzically over at his grandson. 'That's a fair alteration from what you were saying last summer, my lad? It was the war songs you were singing then! What changed your mind?'

Lachlan, aware of his supporters, snorted in scorn. 'Changed his mind? Hector wanted to fight? And him so great at his harping and his reading and writing, God save us, half-way to a priest. Ach, I was forgetting—he's good at the running, too. Aye. A fine, manly pursuit.' His tone hinted 'cowardly'. 'Or maybe he's fallen in love with a Campbell lass, and that's why he'll be so peaceable towards them!'

Hector's fists clenched, but he held his temper. 'Man, it's an idea, but where would I be meeting a Campbell lassie? It's yourself is the great one with the lasses. Have you maybe been slipping away over to Lorn these long nights, to meet some lass? Or would Marion be after you with a stick? Maybe that's why you're so keen to get away to war!'

Lachlan turned red as his hair, his fury burning deep as the men chuckled and opinion swung to back Hector. He whirled away out to the courtyard, mouth and fists tight, Farquhar Neas at his heel as always, and a sharp yelp showed where one of the dogs had got in his way. Eye to eye, whisper to whisper, the word was already passing that he would be a good man to avoid for a while.

Duart, watching them, approved of both, one for spirit, the other for self-control and forethought. Aye, his grandson would be a good chief when his time came. And though Lachlan might not admit it, Hector was as brave, as keen to defend his people as anyone. The ill-feeling between them was bad, though. Lachlan was a fighting man. He'd be better away, winning lands for himself, than frowsting here at home, where his envy was fed every day. But now he was wed he'd maybe settle. Eachuinn Odhar tugged at his beard in satisfaction. Well, he'd just keep a firm eye on them. Fine men both, these two tall lads of his! But what was that had been said—something worth considering..?

Next morning, while the tables were being set up for the noon meal, the doctor brought Luch through the courtyard and up the tight spiral stair into the Great Hall. He sent a message up to the bower, to the lady of the castle, and stood watching Luch in some amusement as she gazed round her, her doll baby tight in one hand and his cassock creasing in the other. The sooty beams away above their heads echoed to clatter and chatter, for Seumas Ban the steward had left the serving men and lasses to their tasks while he spoke severely to the butler about the latest brewing of ale, and old Lady Bridhe, Duart's sister, was still in her bed with a bad cold. The lad blowing up the fire in the huge fireplace made a face at Luch, and as she ignored him he shrugged sneeringly to his friends.

The riot hushed as Lady Marion came down the corner stair and paused on the bottom step, her maids behind her, to enjoy the admiring murmur that met her always. She nodded to the lads to go on with the tables. Then, her skirt trailing on the rushes, she came over to David Beaton and Luch.

Marion Maclean of Treshnish was the hand-fast wife of Lachlan Cattanach. Aluinn, she was called; Lovely. Her glowing chestnut hair aye seemed to escape from the veil that draped her hennin, to spring in lively curls down to her slender, supple waist. She was not tall, but not too small neither; just as high as a man's heart. The olive skin that in Luch was dull and lifeless glowed richly warm on her high cheekbones. Her deep hazel-green eyes glanced large and slanting behind the dark silken fringes of her lashes, her lips smiled full, gleaming and red, her nose was a touch long, but shapely. She wore brilliant gowns of ruby and sapphire and the fairy emerald, high-waisted and long-trained as Lachlan liked them, that somehow were always fresh and clean, and clung to her figure to put a lift in a man's mind. Even now when she was seven months heavy with child, few men and no stranger passed her without a look and a long breath that she noted and relished;

discreetly, as the men eyed her; for Lachlan was a jealous husband. She was eighteen years old.

Now she sauntered disdainfully over to where Luch cowered, eyes downcast under the curious gaze all round her. One hand, soft and short of finger, sharp and long of nail, lifted the smaller girl's face, and she smiled sweetly down on her. 'What's this, then? A chicken plucked for the pot?'

Her voice was the least beautiful thing about her, thin and weak. She knew it and tried always to speak in a low, husky whisper to disguise it, but sometimes she would forget, if she found a victim for her malicious humour, and her tone rose to scratch at the ear. As now; and she heard it through the giggles of her admirers, and was angered at Luch as the cause of it.

Master Beaton frowned. 'A poor lass, Lady Marion, in need of your Christian charity.' He had little hope of a kind answer, for Lachlan Cattanach and his lady were well matched, but she would be enraged if he tried to avoid her. Later he'd speak to Seamus Ban about a simple task for the lass.

'Aye. Well, Master David, I'll need to consider this. I thank you for bringing her to me.' She nodded thoughtfully, gave him a dazzling smile, and raised an eyebrow. 'You'll be having other folk to attend to, will you not?'

He sighed slightly at the quick dismissal, and detached Luch's hand from his gown. 'I leave her in your kindly hands, then, lady.' It was the best he could do for the moment. Reluctantly, he left the hall.

'Well, now. What shall we do with you, eh? You're never a Maclean, surely, so thin and weakly!' At the light, sneering tone the older folk turned to their own work, lips tight in distaste; but a dozen or so of the younger ones gathered round the newcomer. The stranger. The outsider.

Luch said nothing. Silence and stillness were her only defences. She seemed to shrink within herself as they pressed round her.

'Turn round.' Her hair was tugged. 'Dhia, did you ever see such stuff—except in a dung-heap? And her plaid! I've seen better scouring cloths!' Marion's voice was honey trickling over a grater. Her audience sniggered. 'Now, what can we do with her, eh? Feed her to the hens?' The toadies giggled again.

The teasing grew from mild to spiteful to vicious. The young ones, encouraged by Lady Marion's smile, insulted Luch, pinched and poked her, spat on her, tossed dog's dirt and rubbish from the floor rushes into her plaid and hair. She was pushed right into the edge of the fire, till her feet were burned and her skirt smouldered. Some of them stopped, for shame or sympathy, but others took her silence as a challenge and doubled their attack, all in a strange, grinning soundlessness under Lady Marion's breathy laughter. Their eyes glittered, their breath came gasping with fascinated, guilty excitement.

In only a few minutes Luch lost all sense of time and place. In her mind she was again back by the gate, her foes all round her.

Then Marion noticed the bundle Luch gripped so tight in her left arm. 'What's this, then?' she smirked, and reached to tug at it, but stopped, half-frightened by the sudden rage in the wee lass's face.

Pulling herself together, she was about to punish the insolence when the men of the castle began to troop in from sword practice, a noisy, arguing crowd, rubbing off the sweat with their plaids as they came leaping up the steps and striding to the long trestle tables for their morning meal, laughing and keen-set with exercise. The castle dogs careered in with them, barking and excited, to hunt mice and scraps in the rushes; the smaller ones keeping well clear of the four great deerhounds stalking, lean and dangerous, round their master, disdaining the rabble, to fold limb by rangy limb before the fire.

Luch's tormenters scattered to fill the wooden trenchers and bowls to feed the men. Marion turned away to greet her husband, and Luch seized her chance. She ran for the only way out; the stair in the corner, up to the bower, down to the yard. In her panic she fell over the deerhounds, but she darted away as they tossed their heads and heaved to their feet.

As Luch started off, Marion saw her. In annoyance, she yelped. A couple of maids stopped on the upper stair, staring at Luch, arms raised in surprise. The child swung away down the spiral, slipping among the legs of the men thronging up it like a needle darning a sock, to dart out through the door to the courtyard at the foot.

As Marion cried out, she pointed and took a step or two after the little girl. Her admirers looked round, followed the direction of her eye and finger, started to follow her. 'Stop her!' 'Stop who?' 'A thief?' 'Thief?' 'Stop thief!' 'Thief!' One step, one shout, one body moving copied and encouraged another, till all the youngsters and many of the older folk found themselves in the hunt, racing yelling and laughing, cheering on the dogs that ran barking with them. The confusion as they jammed in the narrow stair gave Luch a good start.

In the hall, Eachuinn Odhar Maclean stared after his vanishing clan, a spoonful of porridge half-raised to his mouth. 'What the devil . . . Hold fast, there! Stop them! Hector! What's happened, lad?'

Hector was gone. He had just glimpsed the wee lass at the first of it, and was already away down the stair and across the courtyard after the yelling mob, out the gate, down the path towards the castle clachan. He wasn't called Luath for nothing; he was speedily past the rear runners and up with the middle ones, only a few yards behind the lass racing in terror.

Someone stretched out a hand to snatch her flying hair. Hector, now among the leaders, shoved him aside and called to Luch to stop. Instead she doubled back round the stables and smithy, and ducked in through a narrow gateway in a four-foot high wall beside the road. As he tried to stop and turn, the crowd just behind him jostled him on away from the gate and blocked his way back, cheering lustily, happy and yet frustrated.

It was a small grassy enclosure not far from the castle. It sloped to the south and east, sheltered by high walls, warm and sunny, and would have been a favourite place for lovers but for one thing; or rather, a lot of things. On knee-high rocks all over the grass stood over three dozen beehives. Luch was crouched at the foot of the far wall, too high for her to climb. She was trapped, and yet safe; right between two bee-skeps, her hand resting on one.

Her pursuers stayed back, clear of the skeps and their circling occupants, out of a due respect for their skins. But there they couldn't reach the wee lass. Well, not in person . . . Hector was forcing his way to the front of the crowd, yelling to them to stop, as the stones and clods began to fly, thudding and clattering heavily down round Luch. Naturally, some hit the hives, still light this early in the year. One of the straw cones tottered, balanced a moment, and fell, bumping another down in a cloud of outraged bees.

There was an enthusiastic, mindless cheer. More stones were aimed at the skeps deliberately. Many were hit; five tumbled and rolled, knocking down more. Within thirty seconds of Luch's arrival the bees were a violent grey thunderstorm roaring up round her out of toppled skeps all across the grass.

The front ranks stopped laughing and started to draw back, suddenly aware of their own danger, their unthinking blood-lust vanishing. The rear ranks, still shoving in, unaware of what was happening, pushed them forward again. More skeps fell. The crush held fast for a moment; then all turned as one and fought yelling and screeching back out of the narrow gate or over the wall, the bees following the movement, behind and above and among them.

As the first hives fell, Hector hesitated for a long second. Wonder flicked through his mind that the child wasn't screaming. Then he was driving himself forward, hoping that he could get in to rescue her and out without a death-load of stings, praying hard, mouth tight shut, eyes half closed to try to protect his sight, loosening his plaid and flinging it up over his head to scoop in the lass quickly, wrap her up and run for both their lives.

It was the bravest thing he had ever done; perhaps that he would ever do.

Even Lachlan, forcing his way in just as Duart bellowed, 'No! Stop, Hector!' - even he had to admit to himself, reluctantly, through the hot satisfaction of seeing his nephew heading for disaster, that he wished—almost—that Hector could succeed and escape unharmed.

The tall lad skidded to a stop beside Luch, felt the first sting on his arm, snatched her up, turned, and slipped on a broken honeycomb. He crashed down, displacing two more hives, cracking his head, all the breath knocked out of him by the fall and the lass's weight thumping onto his chest. Half a dozen stings stabbed up into his back from bees trapped beneath him.

Through the singing in his ears and the raging of the bees he vaguely heard the mob screaming. It grew louder, then fainter.

He lay still, gasping, blinking, trying to start moving again, his skin crawling, waiting for the pain to repeat, spread in agony all over his body.

It didn't.

Gradually his breathing recovered. Was he dead? He must be, surely. But his back hurt, and his head, and there was another sharp burning in one ankle, above the leather of his brogans. But then there were no more. Even the noise of the bees seemed less. He started to move, to sit up.

A little hand held him down, and a whisper by his ear hushed him. Dazed, he felt Luch moving off his chest. Her weight vanished, and then he felt the end of his plaid being pulled gently down and wrapped round his feet.

Amazed, he listened to her moving round him. She grunted a little as she slowly heaved up the straw skeps, lighter than they had been but still weighty and trickling with honey. She couldn't lift them onto their bases, but at least she set them upright. He waited for her to cry out at a sting, but she didn't. She sat down by him. He steadied himself to lift his plaid, heavy with bees, for her to slip in beside him, but she just patted it down again.

After a long, long time, the roar of the bees had almost died down to the normal busy hum. He even had peace for the fear to fade, though not the wonder; peace in his cocoon to feel almost bored.

In that, he was alone.

The castle folk raced for the doors to hall, guardroom, kitchen, jamming through desperately, and scattering in a wild rush to stop all gaps with cloaks, blankets, furs, straw mattresses. Big Ewan, who had been in the storerooms restacking barrels of salt meat, was weeping and cursing, but Duart, cursing too, would not allow him out of the kitchen. 'No, man! It's too late! Whatever has happened has happened!' In anguish for his heir, he turned on the folk there. 'What the devil were you at? Throwing stones at the bees—chasing that wee lass—in God's name, why?' No-one could answer him.

The main host of the bees roared round the castle. Alert

black-banded patrols lay in ambush at every arrow-slit, every window, every garde-robe hole, hovered in a throbbing fountain in the courtyard. The trapdoor to the battlements was hauled open for half a yelling second to let in the watchman. No-one would blame him for deserting his post that day. An eager brigade swooped in with him, and screams and curses lasted four swiping, panicking minutes. Outside each window there was a threatening, deep drumming. Every forgotten crack was a pathway in for their scouts and spies and columns. And regiments, armies of them still boiled round the overset hives.

A whisper passed among the young ones, that the bees were avenging the attack on Luch, for bees were beloved of God. Eyes turned on Lady Marion. She clung to a corner of the table, wide and wild of eye, a hand protectively on the swell of her stomach, praying with the rest for silence to return.

Outside, a battalion of bees invaded the stables. The grooms flung open the doors and leaped to their terrified beasts' backs to gallop them to safety. The smith and his sister abandoned in the heart of the dying furnace the shears they'd been mending. The sick in the infirmary huddled praying under their blankets, feeling the tiny insect feet crawling over them.

Clusters of bees hung shimmering and dripping like their own combs on every jut of stone, every gutter, every stem of heather thatch. Enthusiastic troops swung hopefully along the walls, quartering their battleground in search of any movement, any enemy.

The dark cloud of the war spread, like ink in water. The folk of the clachan down the track shut their doors, set their children to pack the cracks with heather, jammed their chaff beds up into their smoke-holes, and coughed and choked in a black swelter, safe if they didn't smother.

A man racing for his home took a moment to batter at the door of the bee-ward. 'Hey, Ruaridh, man! The bees are out at the castle!'

The old man heaved himself from his bed, his grandson's hand helping him rise, and peered out of his doorway at the glinting mist swirling round the battlements. 'Aye, so they are, then!' he shouted after the fleeing man. 'And what should I do, eh? Wave them goodbye?' He spat in disgust. 'Ach, what have they been doing to us, then, saints preserve us all?' he mourned, and stalked back in to make his home bee-proof; not for himself, for he was hardened to stings, but for the sake of his pig. And his daughter, of course.

Milk cows nearby threw up their heads at the flying torment, bellowed in pain, and lumbered madly across the pasture. Hens and geese on the shore squawked and flew off on clumsy, unaccustomed wings. A couple of lads dived into the sea, and spent a woeful hour wishing they could breathe underwater.

Slowly, slowly, with many false retirals and sudden sallies, the siege was lifted, as the bees retired in exhaustion, hunger, boredom, triumph, to repair and renew their precious combs. The noise faded, died. A tiny crack was warily opened; was safe. Another, a bigger, a high window, and at last the door.

Duart was the first man out and cautiously down the path to the bee-field gate, dreading what he would find. Ewan Beg was urgent to rush ahead, but a terrible delicacy held him from pushing in before his foster-brother's grandfather. Behind him walked Lachlan, unsure of his feelings.

Hector had been nearly asleep, in the stillness after the excitement, when he heard weeping, and his grandfather's voice calling hopelessly. A hand touched his shoulder and softly tugged at him to rise.

Slowly, smoothly, he rose, the hum alert round him, little hands guiding him and controlling the plaid so that it didn't flap. He opened a crack before his eyes to find his way to the gate, and saw his grandfather and foster-brother there, gaping in astonishment as he hobbled slowly towards them. Big Ewan broke from the men and ran forward, yelping suddenly as he was stung. But Hector, urged on gently by the hand at his side, kept moving discreetly and it was only a moment till they were all outside the bee-field again and walking swiftly up the path among an incredulous throng.

Eachuinn Odhar was frankly gaping. Ewan Beg kept patting Lachlan to see if he was alive, tears rolling down his plump cheeks, muttering curses that he'd not been there to go in among the bees instead, he couldn't run fast enough, he was useless, would

Hector ever forgive him . . . Lachlan shook his head admiringly and wished, both aloud and silently, that he had his nephew's luck.

Luch stopped by the gate and watched as they all trooped back towards the castle. Nobody noticed her, of course.

The Beeman

At dinner that night all the talk was naturally on the one subject. David Beaton was busy, and not just with stings. There was a broken wrist, a sprained ankle, a cracked skull from falling down the stair. Outside, several horses had been stung, one had broken a leg in its mad career to escape, and a cow and many hens were missing. Eachuinn Odhar was fair raging, and had ordered a dozen whippings. The culprits were easy to identify; those who had chased Luch hardest had suffered worst from the rage of the bees, and there were many swollen faces and sore backs getting little sympathy that night. No one accused Lady Marion, elegantly seated by her husband at the high table, who had done nothing—except start everything. No-one ever did.

But the main point of discussion was how Luch had remained untouched. The bees had stung nearly everyone else. Duart himself had three lumps on one ear that soothed his temper no whit. They had all seen the child surrounded by a black mist of bees. How did she escape?

The castle bard, Lame Donald, playing for their entertainment during the meal, silenced his clarsach. He had spent a satisfying afternoon condoling in a most unconsoling way with all those worst stung. A fully-trained poet, he'd have had a harper and singer of his own to play his compositions if he'd not enjoyed making music himself, and he had already half composed a neat, cutting little ballad about the morning's events. His words could sting as hard as the bees, and not a few had pled sickness and stayed away from the board rather than face his corrosive comments on their courage and kindness.

He leaned forward to catch their eyes. 'Aha, but that is not all, Maclean!' he called. 'There was something I noticed when the lass ran out, that maybe the rest of you did not, being otherwise occupied at your exercise.' Several eyes dropped away from his smile. 'You see the hounds there? You'll mind on how Borb alone near took the arm off Douglas Dhu MacNeill when he bumped into her last month. Well, the child fell right over them all there before the fire, and they leaped up, but not one of them bared tooth at her. Not a raised lip nor the whisper of a snarl.' He ran his fingers in an eerie ripple over his harp strings to raise a shiver of wonder and astonishment.

All eyes turned from the great deerhounds, shaggy bone-ricks sprawled dozing before the fire, to the wee lass crouched by the doctor's stool, holding the edge of his plaid for comfort, her baby safe in her arm.

'Is that true, Donald Crubach? How can this be?' Lady Marion's voice was sharp. 'Is she a witch? Or a fairy child? Oh, Lachlan!' At her charming alarm, Lachlan laughed, and slung a protective arm round her shoulders. She melted back gratefully and gracefully into it.

Old Lady Bridhe peered down from her seat beside Hector. 'A witch? I think not. But could she be a changeling? Donald Crubach? Father Patrick?'

They all studied the child, looking for signs of the supernatural, as she trembled before them. At length the bard, sighing, shook his head. 'How can we tell? She does not have the air of the fairy folk, but who can be knowing?'

The priest considered carefully before he spoke. 'I sense no evil in her. Though the Devil works stealthily, she seems too simple to be his servant.'

Hector, at his grandfather's right hand, agreed. 'How can she be a witch? At her age? And if she was a changeling it's ugly and wizened she'd be, and she may be no beauty, but that she's not.

30

But she has strange powers, that is sure. It was the same thing on the beach—the dogs simply didn't see her.'

Lachlan was less easily impressed. 'Powers, has she so? Let's try her.' His father frowned, but nodded; whether or not it was true, they should know it. The young man picked up a rib bone from the trencher before him on the table. There was meat on it, and as it rose soggily from the heavy oatcake under it, all the house dogs lifted head hopefully.

'Here, Breac! Grinn! Borb! Glic!' The deerhounds woke, their pointed grey muzzles coming up. Borb, the youngest and, fitting her name, the fiercest, rose eagerly, stretching her full eight-foot length of matted hair, skinny sinew and tough bone, long claws working like a cat's in her great paws. The others, older and wiser, lay still but alert. 'Here, then!' The bone thudded directly among the hounds. The lesser dogs tensed, and one yipped, but they made no move to get the bone; they knew better than to rob one of the great hounds. There was a moment's pause and poise of tension, and a lazy snarl; it was Borb who eventually lifted the bone delicately in her bright teeth, lay down a little apart and started to gnaw it, while the others watched quietly, knowing their own meat would not be long delayed. Lachlan nodded, smiling. 'Now, lassie! Use these powers of yours. Take that bone from the hound there!'

'Borb'll tear the hand off her!' Hector cried, but his father waved him to silence. They all stared at Luch, who crouched motionless.

'Ach, she was lucky with the bees. She just sat still till they flew round her. And she's too small for the hounds to bother with chasing her. Throw her out.' Lachlan's rich laugh echoed round the hall, and many joined him in relief; for the thought of a witch remembering how they had treated her was uneasy.

At that, though, the Maclean struck the board with his fist. 'No! Whatever she is, that we will not do! After she showed the courage of my grandson for all to see? She is a poor lass, needing help. Our guest, and welcome here! Remember it!' His eye and voice had risen grimly, to be noted along the tables, but fell again as he spoke privately to his son. 'That was unworthy of you—of the clan, Lachlan.'

31

After a jaw-clenched moment Lachlan nodded. 'As you say, father.' His fury at the rebuke was nearly hidden. But his eyes glowed as hot as those of his wife and his foster-brother Farquhar were cold.

'What's to become of her, then?' The harper's voice was soft. 'She must have her place. Is she to be a field or kitchen lass, or a bower maid?'

Lady Marion answered, her voice carefully controlled. 'Donald Crubach, the lass has chosen for herself where her place will be. I'll not have her in the bower.' At Eachuinn Odhar's raised eyebrow she smiled sweetly. 'Her mind is clearly touched, about babes, at least. There's aye the risk she might harm one of the babies here. Catriona's, maybe. Or mine and my lord's when he is born in July.' They all glanced at the swell of her stomach which she was smoothing proudly and possessively, and even Bridhe nodded approval of her foresight. 'She can go out to help old Ruari Beeman. He has been complaining it is too much for him and that lad of his, and his back so stiff in the wet weather. He needs a helper, and you'll agree, Eachuinn Odhar, that she seems well fitted for it!'

Duart nodded consideringly. To Marion's satisfaction a general murmur of assent and relief arose. It was a perfect arrangement.

Smiling with pleasure, Lady Marion was rising from the board with her maidens to leave the men to their drinking when there was a touch at Lachlan's sleeve. He jumped. His wife, always aware of him, glanced to see what brought the shock and disbelief to his face, and the gasp along the tables.

Beside him stood Luch, quietly holding out the half-chewed bone.

Next morning Hector took the trouble to escort Luch down from the castle to Ruari the beeman's tiny hut. The old man's grandson had seen them coming between the huts of the clachan that trailed along the shore of Duart Bay, unfenced and scattered so near the shelter of the castle, and Ruari was at his door waiting for them, his faded blue eyes watering in the wind. His skin might be dry and wrinkled like an autumn leaf, and he might carry a staff to help feet growing unsteady, but his voice was sharp and vigorous.

'Dhia, Hector Luath, what's this Marion Aluinn, saints sweeten her temper, has wished on me now? And me with three score hives to move up to the heather bloom, and my back near broken already with the work that's in it, saints pity me, and Ranald Gorach here more trouble than aid to me? And you needn't look at me in that tone of voice, my young gallant! Your uncle's wife, saints bless her, should have more sense than send me a weak little scrap like this, that'll scream if a bee comes near her, when what I'm needing is a couple of great strong lads like yourself and your dallta Ewan. Is it out of her mind she is, now, with looking in her unchancy mirror? Fine looks, saints preserve them, bring in no honey, and it's herself will have my head for a footstool if autumn comes and me with no sweetening for her bacon, or wax for her candles.'

'Wheesht, Ruari! You'll have the lassie scared from her wits!' Hector was laughing. 'She's not that weak. And she wasn't scared of the bees yesterday.'

Ruari's white brows bristled even more. 'Aye, the half of our skeps wasted entirely, and my poor children put off our work for a month, devil take the rascals! Not her fault, they say. Liars they are, so. The truth isn't in them.'

'It's true,' said Hector firmly. He smiled down at Luch. 'Never fear him, Luch, lass. His snarl's worse than his snap. And that lad there at the door's his grandson Ranald. The daftest lad in the whole of Mull, that! No wonder they call him Ranald Gorach, eh, lad?' The lad half-hidden in the doorway grinned a wide, gap-toothed gape. 'The tricks he's aye at—mind you and don't get caught up in them!' He beckoned to the lad behind the doorpost. 'Well, Ranald? Will you not say a word to your new assistant here?'

Grinning back at him, Ranald lurched out from the darkness of the hut. About fourteen, he was already nearly as tall as Hector Luath, and as skinny as his grandfather. His wide-flung ears and teeth seemed to flap in the breeze, like his elbows and wild, fair hair.

As he jolted forward, Ruari sighed. 'Aye, that's Ranald. The only lad ever known that borrowed his teeth from a hay-rake and his limbs from a daddy-long-legs, saints save him from breaking any of them this day for once! Make your courtesy to the chief's grandson, then!'

Still grinning wide as any bull-frog, the lad bobbed his head on his long, thin neck. His adam's apple bobbed too, as he swallowed. 'Aye, sir!' he said, his voice newly gruff, and turned to Luch. She was staring at him, but instantly dropped her eyes. He'd been looking for a lad, to play jokes on, and with. This wee lass was a disappointment, an insult to his grandfather and the bees, and he was all ready to be as rude as he dared. But somehow, when he saw the lass so scared, he couldn't. He reached out a long, gangly finger at the end of a long, gangly arm and poked her shoulder gently. 'Luch, is it? Aye, well, Luch, it's myself that's glad to see you.' She nodded, but made no reply. Ranald looked up at his grandfather and shrugged. He'd tried.

The old man grunted in annoyance. 'Has she no manners, then, or is it a dumb lass you've brought me?'

'Come away, Ruari, man, give her a chance. It's the Lady Marion's wish, and you know what she's like. So you might as well get used to the idea.'

'Aye, saints bless her, it's hard it is for your aunt-by-marriage to change her mind, and her so young and beautiful, and lucky for some, and long may it last to her. But let a notion no matter how foolish enter her mind and hell can freeze over before she'll alter.' Ruari glowered down from his immense height at the tiny lass before him. She glanced warily up, and then her dark eyes fell again to study her feet. He sighed over-loudly. 'Aye, well, Hector Luath, away and tell your uncle's wife, saints guard her, that I'll try the lass. But if she's not strong enough, I'll be right back up to the castle again for a strong lad, you're hearing me?'

'I'll tell her.' Hector smiled again at Luch and loosened the clutch she had taken on the end of his plaid. 'You stay here, then, Luch, and mind what he says. I'd wait a while, but Lame Donald's waiting for me.'

'Aye, aye!' Ruari approved him. 'You're a fine hand at the reading and writing, and the Latin, Father Patrick says, and you're setting up for a bard as well as a clerk, then? Learning the

34

dan direach and the covardadh slan, and all the tricksy verse forms, eh? And the great lays? When will you be singing us the Death of Finn, then? Or the Fall of Troy? It's myself fair enjoys that one, the seldom while that Donald Crubach rouses himself to sing it.'

'No, no, man!' Hector was nearly blushing. 'I'll never be a great harper, or singer either, but he's kind and generous with his time and praise.'

Ruari snorted. 'Donald Crubach kind? Were you the Lord of the Isles, or the Good Lord himself, God bless him, and you played badly, it's Donald would refuse you the good word.'

Hector grinned. 'My thanks for the back-handed compliment, Ruari!'

The old man stared in puzzlement; then scowled. 'Off you go, then, or he'll not have a word at all for you.'

Hector patted Luch on the shoulder encouragingly, turned and trotted off up the hill again. He missed her terrified gaze, before she again looked down.

Ruari had seen it, though, and his mouth tightened in annoyance. It was only wee lasses like this were afraid of him nowadays. 'You needn't fear I'll eat you!' he snapped. 'It's twice your size you'd need to be before I'd think on cluttering my six teeth with you, saints preserve them a while yet!' As she cowered, he beckoned briefly with his head. 'Ranald! Come along!' He swung round and stalked off towards the bee field, not turning to watch the lad and Luch behind him.

Trotting to keep up, tripping over the ends of her new old plaid that Lady Bridhe's maids had given her, the wee lass glanced up once or twice to the tall, lanky lad who stilted along beside her. Once he caught her glance and winked expansively. She looked away hurriedly, but a small warmth crept into her mind.

At the entrance to the bee field Ruari stopped. She halted just out of his reach, an untidy bundle of grey-green cloth, sniffing, hitching the over-large plaid awkwardly round her thin shoulders. As Ruari gazed at her in irritation, something lost and frail about her, gawky and unlovely like a pigeon chick, but appealing in its small helplessness, softened the edge of his temper. He snorted in resignation. 'Ach, I suppose we must just make the best

35

of you. Ranald, will you be sorting that plaid for her before she breaks her neck!'

With his huge, palm-leaf hands, the lad reorganised the plaid. Luch's brown-shawled bundle slipped as he lifted her arm to tuck in the ample folds, and he caught it. 'What's this, then, lass?' he asked. He was taken aback by the fierceness of her snatch. The doll was ripped from his hand and clutched tight to her heart, and she glared at them over it.

The old man tutted to himself as he recalled the story they'd been told. 'Saints pity you, lassie! You needn't look at us like a wren at a weasel. It's your baby? It's never myself would be wanting it, nor Ranald neither!' He turned in the gate, still annoyed that this was the feeble help he had been sent; but annoyed too at her for her fear of him, and at Ranald for tactlessness. The three annoyances together made his voice sharper than ever as he stopped among the higgledy skeps.

'Here, then, lass. Come you near, or as near as you dare, anyway.' He turned. She was right at his heels. 'Aye, aye, then! It is true, so; you've no fear of the bees?' For the first time there was more than irritation in his voice. 'Glory be to God and all the saints! You'll be maybe better than the heroes of the clachan, then, that daren't look a bee in the bite from nearer than twenty feet.' He shook his head in some wonder at her. 'Come you, then. I'm not wanting to disturb my children again so soon after our great upset. And don't think I believe a word of what they're telling me about you, you're hearing me? But the skeps have need to be lifted out of a mouse's reach, and set level, or the combs will never hang straight and we'll have to destroy the hives entirely, saints preserve them, to get the honey out.'

For all his sharpness to people, Ruari was a marvel with the bees, and carefully Luch matched his movements. Tucking her doll firmly into her plaid, working slowly, smoothly, gently among the flightpaths, she puffed smoke into the hives at Ruari's direction while he and Ranald lifted the skeps onto their heavy baseboards and set them back on their rocks. All the spilled honey from the day before had already been recovered by the bees, leaving only a sweet slipperiness on the grass to set Ranald sliding and Ruari tut-tutting.

Once among the busy insects, the old man's voice, his whole manner, changed. He murmured away in a soothing monotone, like a bee's hum, sometimes to Luch or Ranald, sometimes to the bees, sometimes to himself. 'Never move fast about bees. Will you stop flapping your elbows, then! Ach, a sore time of it we had that sad day, my children. And a sore time they had too, the villains, saints mend their manners for them!' He spoke sometimes as if he was a bee himself. 'If we're frightened you'll harm us or our hive, we'll sting, but we know we'll die for it, and we don't want to do that for nothing, like the good Christian souls we are, eh, my children? Every hive is blessed by Father Patrick, saints preserve the good man. Will you listen to the singing in this hive, eh? Deep and heavy. We can't be seeing into the hives, so we have to listen and smell. Hear it? And this one? We're ready to swarm, so.'

At last he stopped, beckoned the young folk with his head to the gate and looked down at Luch. 'Aye. That's it. Humph!' He grunted and sniffed. 'Well, I've seen worse, I suppose. I'm away for a bite to eat.'

As his grandfather strode away down the track, Ranald, released from the necessity of control, chortled and flung his arms wide-angled against the sky. 'Man, you'd never credit it! A lassie working with the bees, and granda pleased with her!' Luch cast a dubious eye up at him. 'Aye, he's pleased, lassie! Ach, he never says a good word to anybody, the old moaner! But if he wasn't, you'd have heard all about it by now. Come on and we'll get a bite ourselves.'

Luch shrank away from his grin, his happy exuberance, his high spirits. The lad's grin faded. 'What's wrong, then? Ach, you're a right wee mouse, are you not? Well, lassie, I'm no fox. Come on, my mother'll have something for us.'

In the tiny hut his mother, a short, skinny scrap of worry half his size, glared at Luch. 'Will she be living here, then? As if that gannet there wasn't more than enough to feed!' Ranald paid no attention, but lifted two oatcakes and filled a wooden bowl with ewe's milk. He handed Luch her oatcake where she stood hesitating at the door, and urged her out into the fresh, bright air. Mhairi's whine followed them clearly. 'Why could they not be giving her her bite up at the castle, father? Is she to sleep and eat here, then? Well, just you be telling the steward if he's wanting me to feed three of you to see to the bees, I'll be wanting my rent cut —four eggs in the month, instead of six. And just the one bag of oats at Michaelmas, or else three hens, not five. Tell him, mind! Or he'll get the lass back in the castle to feed whether the Lady Marian likes it or not. See her at the milk, so! Dhia, like a sow in farrow.'

Luch was scarlet. Ranald was embarrassed; a guest should be offered the best. 'It's just her way, lass. Aye, she's sharp of the tongue. But never heed her.' At last Luch realised he was as red as she was, with shame for his mother. It gave her courage to look up at him and smile shyly. 'Aye, that's better!' His wide mouth spread even wider as he grinned. Then he winked again and tempted the big black and red cock into his reach with crumbs of oatcake. Trapping the flapping wings down and holding its beak shut to keep it from crowing, he slipped in with it behind his mother's back, to lift the lid of the big meal-chest, silently drop the bird inside and close the lid unseen.

At last Ruari in annoyance interrupted Mairi's complaints. 'God and all his saints bless you for your generous heart, then, Mairi Ban! Come away, the two of you.' The mean whine followed them up the path. 'Aye, aye. The bees are kindlier,' he sighed 'But she's a good provider, is Mairi, in the hard times.' His tone apologised for her; it was warmer than before.

As they went, there was a sudden shriek behind them, a triumphant trumpeting from the released, well-fed cock, and Mairi's voice cursing wildly after them. Ruari looked suspiciously at his grandson, but Ranald's face showed only innocent surprise. The old man snorted, knowing that look too well, and clipped the lad on the ear.

'What was that for, granda?' Ranald protested indignantly.

'For that back at home, whatever it was. And if it wasn't your doing, well, it's one I've caught up on you.' Ruari sniffed and snorted, and Ranald, pretending hurt, winked again to Luch. She couldn't help smiling.

At the bee-field, the old man turned to his grandson. 'Ranald, run to the byre, fetch me a couple of the new skeps from the far end of the hay-loft. And straight back, mind!' As the lad ran off, elbows and knees flailing, Ruari explained to Luch, 'The feeling is in me there will be a swarm or two soon, lass. You heard it in the ones I told you to listen to right close? Aye. It's the young princes calling on their men to rise up and go with them to build a new castle for themselves. We've had sixteen already this year, so. We'll just put a couple of skeps out here beside the others, ready for ourselves. For when we lift from the old hive, you must find us quickly. We usually settle in a tree—often that old elder over there, you see it?—and hang on a high branch while our scouts find a new home for us. That's the time you can catch up with us, and get us into the new skep—I'll show you how. Never fear swarming bees. We're aye too busy to sting. Not like yesterday at all.'

As Ranald came in the gate his mind was all on the skeps that he had balanced wobbling on his head. He tripped and tumbled heels over head to his grandfather's feet, bouncing up with a skep in each hand and a toothy grin of relief when he saw they were unharmed. The old man was so used to it he just sighed, shook his head, and started without a word to set up the new hives.

Three rocks were pushed into a triangle and a wide, flat slab of wood levelled on top, as a base for each hive. Ruari carefully thrust three straight sticks through the top of each skep, 'For us to hang our combs on, that it'll be easier to get them out later if God wills.' Then he took out a lump of wax from a pouch at his belt, and rubbed it over the inside of the straw cones, and along the sticks. 'It has flower petals in it. That gives them the right smell. Now, a big stone on top to hold it in a wind. And if we should swarm when I'm not here, we'll maybe even go right into one. I've seen it happen.'

When they were done, he stretched. 'Aye, well. Ach, my back's that sore, saints mend it! I'm for my bed till the gloaming. We'll be busy these nights, for I can carry but two skeps at a time, and you'll manage just the one each, and they've all to be lifted four-five miles to the moor this next month. You heard me speak on it to young Hector? Aye. So we'll be back here at dusk again with smoke to stun the bees and some thick cloth to wrap the hives.'

Ranald nodded, but Luch just gazed. He shook his head at

39

her, scolding, 'Dhia, how much are you taking in? Am I wasting my breath, just?'

Ranald defended her. 'She's quiet as a wee mouse there, granda, but I'm thinking if she was called on, she could repeat every word.'

'Huh!' Ruari snorted. 'I'm pleased she has your approval, my lord!' Ranald shrugged, grinning, and the old man grinned back, sourly, before turning again to Luch. 'Aye. Maybe he's right for once. We may deal together better than I'd have believed. The lady, saints guard her, she maybe meant malice, for she's got a tricksy temper, but she might have done the right thing by chance, eh? But maybe not. Ranald, you stay here and if we swarm, come call me. I'll see you at dusk, then.' He turned down the path for home.

A minute later a yell made him swing round and hurry back. He had been right about the hives being ready to swarm. Two of them had started to vibrate, deep and steady, and bees were seeping out of the entrances and crawling like spilled treacle over the skeps, tight masses of glistening wings growing larger every second, starting to rise and hover.

Ranald was safely distant from the hives, but Luch was near them, watching entranced. 'Come back here, lass, and leave them alone!' Ruari called. But it was too late.

From one hive, the bees suddenly rose in a dense swirl and headed south. Ruari thought for a happy moment they were going to settle and cling in the elder tree, but they flew past it. He grunted irritation and turned to watch them. But then Ranald cried, 'Watch out, Luch!' and he glanced back.

Luch was standing right in the centre of the other swarm. The bees were starting to land on her. Her eyes were fixed on Ruari for help.

There was nothing he could do. He stood rooted, staring for a second; then stepped as close as he could to her, just outside the cloud of insects. 'Put your hand to cover your mouth and nose, lassie, that you'll can breathe! Never move, now! Mind I said swarming bees will never sting!' He didn't sound as sure of himself as he had done, but Luch's stiffness relaxed a touch.

'Can we not get them off her?' Ranald was white with fear for the lass.

'No, we cannot! Just leave her be! Thank God she's keeping still! She'll be fine as long as she doesn't panic, and start screaming and flapping. Dhia, there's not a man I know would be so brave. Maybe not even me!'

Three or four times the bees started to take flight, but each time they circled and returned to settle heavily on Luch's plaid. The grey-green cloth was gleaming with wings and bright black and yellow bodies, crawling over each other and over her. 'They think she's a tree!' gasped Ranald.

Luch, standing absolutely still, looked rather surprised. Ruari saw she had known this all along, and was only astonished it had taken them so long to realise it. It looked as if she'd be good with them after all . . . Luckily they weren't running over her face—not too many of them. But they would run up to the highest point . . . 'Luch, lass! Look here now, here's my staff. Take it in your free hand, gently now, gently, clench your fist. Now lift that arm up to the side, a bit above your head, and rest on the staff. Slow now, slow, don't startle us! And bend down, away to the side, away from the staff!'

Slowly she raised her right hand, her arm straight, and let the staff slip through her fist till she could grip it to support the weight of her arm and the bees clinging to it. Slowly, the bees started to flow up off her chest and head towards her hand, as if they could hear the old man's urgent thoughts and his grandson's prayers.

At length the whole swarm was hanging in a dark mass on Luch's right fist and forearm, shimmering and simmering. Ruari beckoned her over to where he knelt beside a new skep. He had a board leaning against it, from the grass up to the hive, and he drew a line of wax up the centre of the board right to the entrance. 'Over here, lass. Gently, now. Stop. Now, leave the tip of the staff back there, and kneel down slowly—keep your arm out and up. We're heavy, eh? Aye, but just for a wee minute more. Here, I'll help hold the staff still. Now bend down, and lower your elbow down, so that the swarm is over the board. Down yet. Down till we touch. Now, gently, gently, lower. Let us have time to get off the swarm, don't press us down. We could just knock us off, but this

41

is safer. That's it, lass, finely done!'

As the lowest bees touched the board, they dropped off the swarm onto the wood. Scenting the wax, they started to follow it up, and into the hive. Luch's arm was trembling with strain, but she still moved slowly and steadily, trusting the old man's advice. 'Aye, that's it. The scouts have found the skep.'

Ranald whispered, 'There—I see the king now. He's running up with the rest into the skep, granda!'

'Aye, so. We'll all follow him in. Lassie, lassie—you've done it!'

It took ten long minutes for the last bees to leave Luch's hand. At last she could sit back, sighing, ease and rub her aching, itching arm, and smile waveringly at her master.

He smiled as admiringly back, sitting back on his heels beside her. 'Well, lass! I'd never have credited it if I'd not seen it with my own eyes! There's no doubt we'll work well together! Well done!'

There was a mutter of agreement and applause from behind him. He turned to see Ranald holding back a dozen of the castle servants, and Father Patrick. 'The child's a miracle, Ruari!' the old priest cried, crossing the grass towards them. 'God must greatly love you, my child!' He smiled down at Luch.

She smiled back, but rather doubtfully, and edged in beside Ranald's worn leather tunic. He put a supporting arm round her shoulders, and the two of them, united in satisfaction, grinned up at Ruari and the elderly priest.

'Well, Father, it's not me will argue with you over her, saints bless the lass!' Ruari chuckled, and groaned as Father Patrick hauled him to his feet. 'O-oh! Ach, I'm too old for this! But now at last I can get away to my bed!' He scowled down at her. She shook her head. 'Why not? What is it?'

The wee lass ran to pick up the second new skep.

'There's another swarm to get, mind, granda!' Ranald grinned.

Ruari looked at the priest and sighed loudly. 'Aye, aye. Maybe I was wrong about working well with her. Well, lass, on you go, you and Ranald, since you're still keen, and come for me when you find them. No, leave the skep for now.'

He rolled his eyes at Father Patrick as the two youngsters ran out. The priest was laughing. 'She'll be a hard, hard taskmaster on you, Ruari!'

The Betrothal

Three times in the next ten days the beacons passed news from point to point—from Rubha Nan Gall across the Sound of Mull to Castle Nan Con, back to Aros, across to Ardtornish and back again to Duart—that the threat that had first been hinted in Luch's arrival had taken solid shape. The raiders slipped in past the Macleans' patrolling galleys, and killed and kidnapped, destroyed and looted, slaughtering or crippling what livestock they could not carry off and leaving the survivors to starve.

Eachuin Odhar was beside himself with fury. 'God damn them! Who are they? That's another runner with news, Hector! Tiree this time! Fourteen folk dead and the houses and boats burned. There's not six men left, and all the cattle are away, for they weren't out at the sheilings yet. When I catch them, may God pity them, for I'll not!' His face was puce with rage and frustration, but beating a fist on the battlements where they stood looking out over the Sound, he brought himself back to calm by sheer willpower. 'Well. I've landless men to send over to take the places of the dead, and fowls and beasts to get them started again. But that's not enough.'

'No,' said Hector. 'We must avenge our dead. It's our duty to protect the clan.'

'Duty!' Lachlan sneered. 'Aye, that. And pleasure!' His eyes were bright.

Hector's lips tightened. He relished the thought of fighting and slaughter less than Lachlan did. 'But grandfather, who the devil do we fight?'

'That's it!' snarled his grandfather. 'They're hiding somewhere close, but whoever it is is keeping the secret. I'd not have thought it possible. Let a wee thought just peep in a man's mind at dawn on the Mull of Oa and it's all the gossip at the Butt of Lewis by noon. But not this time. God set this Iain Og on the hot hob of hell for a thousand years—but not before I catch him!'

All this time, Luch was happy with Ruari of the bees. At least, if she was unhappy, or fretted for her family, she didn't say so. The folk of the castle clachan accepted her as an oddity, the way their eyes slipped over her, but harmless. Mostly harmless; remember how the bees avenged her?

Every night she and Ranald helped the old man move four hives up the four miles of rough track to the heather moor. The youngsters each could carry one end of a staff with two hives swinging in thick bags in the centre, while Ruari carried a second pole with a skep slung at each end. She scarcely needed to stun the bees with smoke from smouldering moss or puffballs, to wrap and lift the skeps unstung. The bees just crawled over her, paying no more heed to her than if she had been a treestump. Unfortunately, as Ranald discovered, her immunity didn't extend to the others.

Ruari slept late. Luch bedded on a bag of bracken in a corner, but she and Ranald woke earlier than the old man. Mairi Ban would grudge them a bowl of oatmeal sowens, and then tell Ranald to see to the pig, and the sheep up on the grazing land. Luch would be set to turn the quern to grind the oatmeal, and then she'd be sent to fetch hay, peats, water. She often brought in mussels, gritty with tiny pearls, for the evening meal, or sometimes nesting birds, or a hare that ignored her approach to its form till she had her hand on it. They ate well, but she got little thanks for it from the mistress of the hut.

Water was carried in leather buckets from the spring along by the castle, a quarter of a mile down the track. Mairi was furious when after a while Luch started to take long to return with the

44

bucket, but it did her no good; the wee lass often vanished for hours at a time, in spite of the scoldings she got when she returned late. She always did bring the water eventually, and to her cronies Mairi sometimes admitted she was glad to see the back of her for a few hours; but that never weakened her tongue.

If she had realised how Luch spent her time, the abuse might have been less. Or worse, maybe. For the wee lass started leaving her bucket by the spring, hidden under a briar, and slipping into the castle. She drifted, quietly invisible, among the clansfolk going in and out the great gate, past the sentries, across the courtyard to the door in the far corner. She would crouch by the steps, ignored, till there was no-one on the narrow spiral stair, glide like a slim shadow up to the hall, and when the next stair was free, on up to the bower, where Catriona, wife of the Maclean's piper, had a baby.

Luch would pause in the corridor, her own doll baby clutched tight to her side. When everyone was occupied she would waft into the room and over to the cradle, to peer quietly into it and then, satisfied that the baby was safe and well, to slip in behind the door. There was a hanging there of two people in a garden, with very few clothes on. At the foot of it there was a kind of dent in the stonework where she could crouch in behind the cloth, almost hidden.

If the women had been less busy she might have been seen while she was exploring, but with Lady Marion's own baby due soon they had plenty of fine weaving and sewing to occupy their eyes. Luch found her hidden niche before anyone noticed her. She would stay there until Marion and her attendants left for the evening meal in the hall, then come out of her corner, stretch to ease the cramp in her legs, and check the baby again before slipping away out.

She was once found, quite by chance. Old Lady Bridhe, widowed sister to Eachuinn Odhar and mistress of Duart Castle till Marion arrived, was late going down to the hall. The babe was fretful with teething, but as she came along the corridor she heard a gentle humming above the baby's wails. She looked in quietly. Luch had laid her own doll down on a stool, lifted the child from the cot, and was cuddling him softly, singing in a tiny, sweet voice to him till he quietened. Bridhe stood still, afraid to move, half-certain that the girl was about to harm the baby; but when she saw Luch lay the little boy back in his cradle and tuck the coverlet round him, rock him for a moment, and then turn lovingly to pick up her own child again, the old lady felt tears come to her eyes. She stepped aside into the doorway of the next room while Luch drifted out and down the stair. The baby was sound asleep.

Two or three times a week after that Bridhe, now alert for her, would notice Luch, or at least the slight bulge in the tapestry where she hid. But in dislike of the young usurper who had taken her place, memory of the nastiness in the hall, and pity for the wee lass, Bridhe kept her secret.

The visits helped Luch in her work, in a strange way.

The first night's long walk up to the moor with the hives, Ruari glanced back at the wee lass trotting along behind Ranald's lurch, gamely holding up her end of the staff. It sloped down like the side of Sgurr Dearg, he thought to himself, and grinned. 'Here we are, then. Let them down gently. Aye, we'll just have a wee few minutes before we set them up.' He eased his own burden down. 'Dhia, it's a new shoulder I'll need soon, never say a new assistant.' He was wearier than he'd admit, and glad to sit and rest.

'Ach away, granda,' Ranald said, stretching his angular arms into the blue of the sky as if reaching for a star. 'You're that tough, you'll outlive us all.'

'I'll outlive you, anyway, saints preserve you,' the old man nipped in smartly. 'If Lachlan Cattanach ever learns it was you cut half through his bow-tip he'll have the hide off you for brogans. They tell me he near strangled himself with the bowstring when the stave snapped on him this afternoon.'

'Heh-heh!' Ranald wasn't sorry. 'Serve him right. He shouldn't leave it lying about. He near killed Patrick Glas two days past on the big birlinn at the far side of the bay, him and his dallta, for slipping and falling in front of his lordship when he was in a hurry. Kicked him aside, so he did, and then Farquhar Neas threw the lad right off the side of the ship. Patrick landed across a rock, and lucky for him the tide was in to break his fall or it's crippled he'd be this minute. As it is he'll limp for a month.'

'That may be,' his grandfather warned him, 'but it's no part of your task in this world to avenge Patrick Glas, saints cure him. That's for his father to do. You just keep yourself out of mischief, saints help you. And specially out of Lachlan Cattanach's way. He's not a safe man to tease.' He scowled at Ranald. 'Or do I have to take my belt to your back?'

He never did, of course, and never would, but the fact that the threat had been made showed how strongly he felt on it. Ranald shrugged his shoulders up to his ears, and rolled his eyes at Luch. 'Do we tell the bees, granda?'

'Surely.' The old man saw Luch's puzzled face. 'Aye, we must be told the news. Birth, death, everything of importance. It's our due, for we're part of the household. All the gossip it is we must be hearing, or we'll just up and away, saints guide us. Seumas Ban the steward whiles comes down special to give me the word, so that I can tell the bees.'

Glad of the excuse to rest a minute longer, he frowned at Luch. 'You'll mind to tell us whatever gossip you have, eh? But you'll have to be speaking up!' Luch nodded solemnly. He suddenly laughed wheezily, his few teeth gleaming blue in the moonlight. 'Aye, maybe you'll be telling me too, then!' He heaved to his feet. 'Come away, the pair of you, this'll not get the work done. Ranald, do you find a rock the size of these two, and we'll use them as a base for the first skep. Try not to crush your toes, saints pity you!'

Luch never actually gave him any news, but hidden in the bower she heard all the gossip of the maids, and Lady Marion's occasional rages, and learned a great deal of the events in the castle. Seumas Ban brought the news that the Maclean wanted the bees to hear; Luch knew more. She often went to sit quietly beside the hives, in the bee-field or on the moor. No-one ever heard what, if anything, she told them; but the hives grew amazingly heavy.

There was a grand bit of news for the bees at the end of the month. Eachuinn Odhar had been busy with Father Patrick, dictating letters to all parts; the Abbot of Iona; the king's court in Edinburgh; even Archibald Campbell, Earl of Argyll, at Inveraray; messages had been going and coming in almost daily by boat and weary runner. But though everyone was near dead of curiosity, he had kept it a secret what he was planning.

At last, at dinner one evening, the conversations and laughter died away raggedly as Duart stood up at the high table and raised his hand. But though silence fell speedily, Eachuinn Odhar took his time in getting to the point. 'Listen you all to me, now, for this is a matter of importance.'

The last of the noise died. Even the dogs seemed to hush in expectation.

'This past month we've suffered eleven raids, and still no man can say for sure who the reivers are. The folk at Fanmore gave them a good fight last week, and drove them off with five men dead, and they've not been seen since. But they'll be back, when they've gathered more men, if we don't do something about it.' There was an eager murmur, for something in his voice promised the action they all longed for. 'Aye, well. Lachlan, I'm thinking you were in the right of it; there's no proof, but from the description, this Iain Og is most likely John Campbell of Cawdor, Argyll's lad.'

'I knew it!' Lachlan's face filled with delight, and his teeth grinned white in his great red beard. 'The Campbells! Give me two days to raise the clan, and oh-ho for Inveraray Castle in a blaze! Let Clan Diarmaid rue the day they ever raised hand against Clan Gillian!'

'Ach, be quiet!' His father was scratching at his scar. 'There's more to it than that! Listen to me, now, all of you! King James is sore vexed by the lawlessness in the Isles. With all Scotland quiet as a flat calm under his hand, he wants us to be quiet too, and let be the Mackinnons and the Maclaines of Lochbuie for a year or three.' There was a laugh. 'Besides, he's wanting to take an army to England, to overthrow Henry Tudor and set the Duke of York on his rightful throne. So who's the King's new Lieutenant in the Isles, with commission to uphold the King's Justice and keep the peace? And take for his reward the lands of the folk he decides have broken the law? Archie Campbell, the bold man. Aye. Argyll himself. The very man whose son is raiding our coasts. What justice will we get with him as a judge, eh?'

Against the roar of rage he waved for silence. 'But if we move against him openly, and him the King's friend, the King may call out all the clans against us, with the promise of our land as prize for them when they've destroyed us; and we've unfriends enough would jump at the chance.'

Lachlan was on his feet, towering over Marion Aluinn biting her lip apprehensive between them. 'Well, Father? What now, eh, for the honour of the clan? Fight like men, or kiss the Campbells' feet as they trample our faces?'

Eachuinn Odhar thundered on the board with his silver-mounted drinking horn for the tumult to be still, and waved violently at his son to be seated again; but it was long before there was hush enough for even his bellow to make itself heard. 'Ach, have sense, man! And the rest of you! Sit down and stop your noise! You aye think the only way out of trouble is by the sword!' Gradually the din faded. 'You should know by your age, Lachlan, there's more ways of getting to the other side of a mountain than by chewing through it. There was a time Clan Gillian could put two hundred galleys to the water, but that time is past, and it may be long till it comes again. And the Campbells are powerful, and growing more so. The last time we fought them, five thousand Macleans died. I'd not have it happen again if it can be avoided in honour.'

'None of us would, surely, grandfather,' said Hector. Lachlan stirred, but settled again at his father's glare.

'And I'm not getting any younger,' Eachuinn Odhar continued, his eye hard on his son. 'Not that I'm fair done yet, mind, but I'd like to see the matter of the chieftainship of the clan settled soon. Hector is twenty. Old enough to wed, and have a child to secure the line. But wed who, that's the question, eh?'

Lachlan's hand clenched. There was a breathless hush. They could all see what was coming. Who did the Maclean have in mind for Hector, then?

'Lachlan,' his father announced, 'a while back you said Hector wedding a Campbell lass would stop the raiding.' Lachlan's jaw was clenched tight as his hand. 'Well, Argyll has a daughter. Elizabeth. She's sixteen, and not ill-favoured—I'd not wish that on you, Hector, whatever. I've sounded out Archie Campbell; he's willing to take Hector as a husband for her, and the Father Abbot of Iona will wed you. There, now. What have you to say to that?'

There was a silence; then a growing murmur, that grew rapidly to a hubbub of comment and argument around Eachuinn Odhar, while he had his horn refilled to ease his throat and sat back, ears alert for the tone of the reaction.

Marion's urgent hand on his arm cooled Lachlan from explosive down to merely seething. 'Dhia!' He drained his own cup. The ale could have been sea water for all he tasted. 'Damn the pair of them! Hector wed! That settles it. I'm back for Ireland. Or Spain, to fight the Moors. I don't care, as long as there's fighting!' Farquhar grinned in satisfaction behind him.

Marion was furious too. 'And what of me, then?' she hissed. 'Must I bide here, under another woman? Hear her criticise and change my ordering? Say aye, lady and no, lady, and do her bidding obediently? And Bridhe grinning at me?'

Unused to thinking of anyone else, Lachlan frowned. 'Well, come with me! As soon as you've birthed your child—'

'Our child!' She was trembling with anger.

'Our child, then, you can leave it safe with a foster-mother here, and be free to join me.'

'Traipse at your cart-tail? What reputation does a camp-follower have?'

'My wife!' he protested. But as he spoke, he was wondering . . . She was demanding company; did he really want her with him? Or would his freedom be more agreeable? They were only hand-fasted, and the year the contract lasted nearly up . . . He could set her aside . . .

Marion saw the thought, and could not keep her tongue still. 'Aye, and do you truly want me, then? I know your roving eye, gallant man. It's wandered to every lass in Mull and Morvern while I've been carrying this babe for you!' In her rage and fear, the good meat she had eaten rose sour to the back of her throat. She stood suddenly, hand to her mouth, and ran out, her maids flurrying after her, careless of the gossip she would cause.

Old Lady Bridhe smiled slightly. That bitch's turn now to be superseded!

Hector himself, the most concerned, was least concerned. He had to wed somebody. He trusted his grandfather—most of the time, anyway—to do his best for him. And if it stopped the raiding, and put the Macleans firmly on the side of the Campbells and the king—yes, the advantages were there.

He glanced aside at his grandfather, to see the old man's eye on him. They grinned together. 'That's shocked them, eh!' muttered Eachuinn Odhar. 'Another woman to queen it over Marion Aluinn! And friendship with Clan Diarmaid, that we've been fighting off and on for five generations! Listen to them, they're coming round to it, like Archie Campbell did. We're still a powerful clan, and it's a good match for the Campbells. What do you say, lad?'

Hector shrugged. 'I'm trying to recall if I've ever set eyes on her; I've a vague memory of a plump wee lass at a cousin's wedding three or four years back. Cuddly. Passable teeth—'

'She's better than that! I'll not say there's songs written about her, but I'm told she's fair enough. Gentle. Interested in ballads and songs, they say—you'll have that to talk about. If you want to talk to her. A bit advice, lad; best give a wife a clachan of bairns, and leave her alone to rear them.'

'Is the lassie happy about it?' asked Hector.

'The lassie? What's it got to do with her? She'll do as she's bid, and be grateful you're young and whole.' His grandfather was quite shocked.

It was as well he couldn't see the scene at Inveraray castle that same minute. Lady Elizabeth Campbell, sixteen, gentle, interested in poetry, cuddly, was discussing the matter of her marriage, which had just been broken to her at dinner by her father, Archibald Campbell, Earl of Argyll, King James the Fourth's Lieutenant of the Isles, chief of Clan Diarmaid; and her teeth, which were indeed passable, were much in evidence.

'A barefoot, barelegged, bare-arsed Islesman? Never!' She was throwing a fit of screaming hysterics and every plate, cup, stool, cushion and knife she could set hand to. Her aim was excellent. Her mother was furious. Her brothers and sisters, sisters-in-law, all the clan dodged the ricocheting missiles, clustered in the corners, watched with appalled glee. 'I'll wed none but Hugh Despoins! A Maclean? Never! Murdering redshanks!' A fine pewter plate glanced off her father into the fire and melted. Her mother swore. 'Filthy, flea-bitten reivers! I am a lady of the Campbells!

I spit on the Macleans!' She did.

Scarlet with fury and exertion, she heaved one of the heavy tables right off its trestles, driving her mother back. She snatched up one of the spears racked handy beside the hearth, and her father ducked fast as it slashed just over his head into a tapestry hanging above the fire, cut a two-foot gash in Saint Peter's side and raised a shower of sparks. She threw the spear at him, but missed. One of the maids yelped as it pinned her skirt to a cupboard.

Argyll leapt over the clattering boards and rolling stools. He grabbed his daughter's long sleeve, but she jerked away, ripping the flower-embroidered linen, towards the other table. A leg of lamb bounced off her mother's head; wooden platters clattered on the walls. 'Vile, traitorous reivers! You'd wed your daughter to a stinking Viking! Traitor yourself! Tyrant!' A silver cup whizzed an inch wide of her father's ear; her eldest brother caught it just before it sailed out of an arrow-slit window.

At last her mother distracted Elizabeth, and her father got a firm grip on her waist. Skidding on a gravy-greased platter as she tried to kick, she lost her balance, and her mother slapped her face hard. She screamed, more in rage than pain, but she was tiring, and her father managed to control her struggles. 'God damn you, you bitch, would you defy me?' he snarled.

'Aye would I!' she shrieked. 'Curse you! I'll never wed Hector Maclean! I'm not Muriella Cawdor, easy bribed with a kind word an' a sweetie!' In her corner of the hall, John's wife Muriella lost some of her grin. 'Nor you'll not beat me into it neither!'

'We'll see about that, my bonny bird! John! Bring me up my whip!'

The audience flowed in behind as Argyll and his tall, raw-boned wife dragged Elizabeth, screaming, swearing, fighting every step, out of the hall and up the stair to the empty guest room next to his own. They hauled her in. John ran up with his father's riding whip, and the door was slammed on him and the rest. But at the sounds that penetrated the heavy wood, the excited grins slowly faded, to be replaced by worried frowns.

'I've never seen father as angry. A-ach! I can feel the blows myself!'

'Well, can you blame him? With a spear thrown at him?'

'No—but . . . For him to break it to her like that, in public!'

'With no warning, and he knows she's in love with the English lad!'

'He said only last week he'd no objection!'

'They're still at it. Listen to mother shouting!'

'Why does she not cry out? Maybe they've gagged her—or killed her!'

'She's had beatings before—'

'No wonder, the temper she has—'

'But nothing ever like this! Sh! Hear that! Oh, poor lass!'

At last Argyll came out, panting slightly, but white, not red, of face. Great clawmarks down one cheek had just missed his eye. He stood aside for his wife to leave, a bite-mark showing through a rip in her bloodstained sleeve. The watchers caught a glimpse of a huddle of torn, stained pink cloth before the door was locked, and the key thrust into the chief's pouch.

He stared grimly round at the crowd of silent watchers. 'Let no man nor woman enter this door. My daughter dares defy me. My own flesh and blood stands against my will. Well, she'll repent of it and agree to all I say before one crumb, or one drop of water, crosses her lips. You hear me?' As no-one spoke, his voice fell to a harsh whisper. 'Are you hearing me?'

Among a general nodding and murmur of assent only Morag, their eldest daughter there, dared object. 'But father—mother— she's needing care.'

'Care? When she cares for me, then I'll care for her.' His hand touched the scratches on his face.

Morag nerved herself to go on. 'But she may die, father.'

'Then let her!' At her expression, his face hardened even further.

Suddenly the whip that his wife held slashed across Morag's cheek. 'Will you also defy your father? By God, you'll join her! Well?'

Morag's hand rose to the crimson weal. Her eyes sank. Her father, under a soft, plump, vague appearance, was rock-hard. He usually persuaded rather than forced, and her mother simply battered down any opposition with her tongue; but they could do

53

it, and in their present temper they would. 'We'll do as you command, father. Of course.'

Much later, Elizabeth stirred, and moaned in pain. She was hanging from her hands tied to the post of the bed above her head with her own belt. She couldn't move. She ached all over, from the whip, from kicks and blows, from the bonds that tied her cramp-tight. Father said she'd not eat or drink till she gave in? Well, she'd starve, then! She wept with rage as well as pain.

But deep inside her, she knew she wouldn't. She'd agree. And live.

And make him regret it—him and this Maclean!

It was a long, long night.

Next day when the lock rattled she stiffened in fear and defiance, but it was neither of her parents. It was her third eldest brother John of Cawdor who entered. She almost cried out to him to free her. But she still had—just—too much pride to beg. And besides, he had fetched the whip.

He carefully locked the door behind him, shutting out the world again. She turned her head away in disdain. With his dirk he cut her free. As the last linen strands parted, she toppled, hissing with pain. He eased her to the floor and squatted beside her, rubbing her shoulders to help her arms relax.

'Sister mine, dear, dear sister,' he said comfortingly, 'that was a damn-fool thing to do. I thought you had more self-control. Flying out like that! 'A lady of the Campbells', indeed! The Campbells would disown you if they could, you vixen! For no Campbell lady would act so badly. Or so stupidly!'

He turned her outraged face to him, bruised from the beating, and to her fury a tear trickled out of one purple, puffy eye. But she still refused to make a sound. From the pouch hanging at his belt he brought out a leather flask. 'Here. It's water, with a little wine. Come, drink it, you must be dry. Rinse your mouth at least, and let me see did he shift any of your teeth.'

'No,' she husked at him, 'it was mother did that! And you helping them!' But her eye was drawn to the flask. She was indeed dry. She rubbed her wrists.

'Well, what did you expect me to do? Refuse? Encourage you to defy him? Don't be a fool, Elizabeth. You never have been before. What came over you? If you'd planned to set his mind like glue on wedding you to this Islesman, you couldn't have done better. And of course mother supports him.' As he spoke, he took a kerchief from his pouch, dampened it from the flask and started gently to wipe her face. The wine's sharp sting on the grazes made her wince. He put the flask on her lap to free both his hands for the cleaning, and before she knew it, she had raised the bottle to her lips and taken a sip. And another. And a swallow. She looked up, to see him smiling at her.

'Ach, you, John Campbell!' In spite of her split, swollen lips, loose teeth, and the pain of the cloth dab-dabbing, she couldn't help smiling back. 'Charm a bird off a tree, so you would, let alone your poor sister.' Slowly, painfully, she stretched. 'A-agh! Damn father! And damn this man he wants to wed me to!'

'This man he will wed you to, sister!' John warned her. 'Face it. It's his pride that's involved now. You've made it impossible for him to change his mind, with your carry-on in public. How can he give in to you after that? Ach, Elizabeth, what a witless way to behave!'

Reluctantly, she nodded. She'd been thinking just that for most of the long, aching, sleepless night. She sniffed dolefully, and drank again. 'How did you get this in past father?'

'I didn't tell him. I just said I'd try to talk you into accepting what he's decreed. Mind you, I'll not swear he didn't guess I had it. No man's fool, Argyll. This way you get your drink, and he doesn't know about it—officially. But if I go back out without you, and you agreeing . . .'

'What else can I do? I'll not die for him, or his Maclean friends.' Her voice was tired and bitter, and she slumped against the side of the bed.

'And there's no reason for you to.' He nodded at her. 'No, sister mine. If you're clever—cleverer than you were last night— you can do as father says and have your English love. Later. He's not the man to rescue you—'

'No, he's not,' she agreed with a sigh. You had to face facts. Romantic, rich and handsome Hugh was; determined, bold and practical he wasn't.

John grinned. 'But there's nothing says your life in Duart will be too bad. I'm told the heir's not an ill-looking lad. And it needn't last for ever. The redshanks go fighting at the change of the wind. Or murdering each other.' There was a peculiar significance in his tone. 'Once you've produced an heir, you'll be the mother of the next chief. A position of some influence, even if you were to become a widow. A rich widow. Sooner than anyone might expect.'

As their eyes met she straightened suddenly, ignoring the stabbing pains. 'You think so? Would you . . .' She changed her mind. 'No. I'll not say it.'

He smiled, helping her to her feet. 'Wise, wise, little sister.'

'But if I should ask you for—say, a cordial, to relieve my troubles . . .'

'I'm sure I'll be able to find something to help you.'

They smiled, in perfect accord.

'And as a widow, I can choose for myself who I'll wed next! Well. I'll see how I can help you in the meantime. News of their opinions? Or a word in my husband's ear to make him agree with whatever you're wanting?'

'Carefully, though; he'll maybe not be ruled as easy as Hugh Despoins.' She nodded. 'Now that's my sensible sister again. Come then, my dear. Here, I brought you a cloak. Muriella has warm water and bandages waiting, and ointments, and a fresh gown. Oh, and you'd better apologise to her, as well as to father, for insulting her. And me.'

'What? Oh, that.' She actually laughed, wincing. 'As if you needed sweeties to charm any girl. Aye, I'll apologise. And to father, of course. And mother. May God curse them! No, you needn't fret. I'll be all sweet penitence and grief that I've dared set my will against his. And if they guess my true feelings—'

'They'll say nothing. Not in public, at least, if you make a thorough job of your repentance. And you will, dearest sister Elizabeth, won't you?'

'Of course, dearest brother John. What else?'

Plans and Plots

After Elizabeth's charming, tearful apologies for her ungodly
want of duty and respect, and for throwing a spear at her father,
affairs moved swiftly. The wedding was set for October, and
Elizabeth was offered a reward, for which she was sweetly grateful; the Maclean was invited to bring his heir to Inveraray for the
betrothal. They could get to know each other before they were
wed.

Lachlan was being left in charge of the castle, and Lady Marion
could not go to the ceremony, for the baby was near its time.
Bitterly resigned to the betrothal, she took a fiendish revenge. She
made sure that Duart and his heir would be magnificently turned
out for this visit to a foreign clan. She knew better than to urge
them to dress in the fashions Lachlan had learned abroad; but all
the maids were driven frantic sewing silk and linen, gold thread,
fur and leather. Eachuin Odhar and his grandson spent much
effort on dodging her, for whenever she set eyes on them she tried
new tunics on them.

But the worst was the day she ambushed them as they rose.
'Would you meet Argyll like a rat-chewed, three-year-old hearth-
rug, Duart?' She sniffed. 'He'd sneer at you, him and his daughter,
and at me for letting you go out so, and that I'll not have! I have
sweet soap here and hot water, and either you wash yourself, all

over, or I call in the women to hold you down and scrub you myself. They'd laugh at you from here to Bergen. And you needn't hide, Hector Luath. I see you. Shut your mouth, so, and see how speedy Ewan can be at getting that fuzz scraped off your face. Beard, indeed! I've seen thicker mould on a cheese. I'll return in an hour to shear you.' She whisked out, chuckling.

'It makes a fair difference,' Hector had to admit later, admiring his shining shoulder-length locks in Marion's tiny mirror.

'Huh!' Eachuinn Odhar muttered, scratching itchily and irritably at the newly pink scalp gleaming through his newly white hair, 'different isn't aye better!' And checked hastily to see that Marion couldn't hear him.

A hundred ghillies were burnishing silver and steel to an equally mirror finish; renewing silk braid and red sharkskin on belts, scabbards, quivers and the shoulder-slings of the ceremonial claymores; re-fletching arrows with peacock feathers. The two silver-collared hounds that were gifts for Argyll were groomed to a silken sheen, and their teeth and nails polished like ivory. The captains of the galleys chosen for the voyage drove their men to work, repainting the dragon-heads, stitching new sails and pennons. Luch and Ruari had to supply ten pounds of wax, to polish the bulwarks.

Every clansman was determined to outdo the Campbells in display, and looked to his finery. Each had a feather-plumed bonnet and the filabeg, the small plaid, heavy wool an arm's length wide and four arm-spans long, pleated and belted at the waist, the free end swung up and pinned over the shoulder of his saffron-dyed shirt. Officers strutted in their brightest breacan-feiles; the same length of a finer cloth, four and a half feet wide, held at the waist by a silver-buckled belt to fall double thickness, and the outside layer at the back drawn up over the left shoulder and pinned with a great silver brooch.

The rest of the Macleans' costume was made up of weapons—dirk and sword, spear and tall Lochaber axe, javelin and bow, and even a couple of new-fangled handguns. Scarcely needed, of course, for one Maclean was naturally worth any four Campbells.

They knew better than to insult their hosts by open mention

of this superiority; such bad manners would disgrace the clan. Eachuinn Odhar would deal with any offender. Personally.

The Campbell clansmen wore the filabeg also, but the castle folk of Inveraray wore the modern court fashion; knee-length gown of fine wool, linen damask or velvet, the sleeves trailing nearly to the ground, all braided, slashed, looped, laced, furred and embroidered for the occasion; bone-white shirt, long hose and long-toed shoes. Their townsfolk sneered at the Maclean chiefs' rawhide brogans and bare knees, kilted tartans and dyed linens. They hid their laughter, naturally, for their wild guests were touchy and sensitive. It would be ill-mannered to make open mention of Campbell superiority. Argyll would deal—impersonally, as was his way—with any offender.

So for the time of the visit there was a truce.

Elizabeth walked with Hector, taking care to turn away from him the last yellow stains round her left eye, and smiled sweetly to hide the deadly steel of her thoughts. She was childishly round, of face, eye, mouth, cheek; and of figure, plump and short. An unfortunate liking for pink satin didn't help her pink complexion. He gave her a delicate necklace of amethysts and pearls set in Scottish gold. Cheap, but quite pretty, she thought, thanking him charmingly for his delighful gift. She chatted in a superior way of painting, spices, jewellery, fashions, medicines, saints' shrines, and was pleasantly surprised by his education. She had to admit he had his good points. He was handsome, for a savage. His legs would look quite good in hose. Best of all, he was tongue-tied in admiration of her. Yes, he could be civilised. Though he wasn't, of course, as attractive as the man she truly loved, Hugh Despoins.

She had no idea that knowing Marion Aluinn, Hector didn't think her very pretty. He was silent only because he couldn't think what to say to her. He walked with her, looked polite, and noted that her teeth and her temper seemed fair, and she was fine and broad across the hips for child-bearing. She'd do.

He escaped as soon as he could to the company of her brothers. They tested each other in hunting, drinking, fencing and wrestling. They talked of interesting things; ship-building, the invasion of England, cannon, the path newly discovered west to the Indies, chess, dogs, the king's mistress. The Campbells found Hector hardy, which they had expected, and intelligent, which they hadn't; while he found the same thing about them, in reverse; and they were each surprised to find that they liked the others well enough, in spite of their ridiculous clothes. Pity they were probably enemies, marriage or not.

On the whole, considering the close contact of a hundred Macleans and three hundred Campbells each itching to do down the others, politely of course, the week's visit went off quietly. There were only four fights, proper fights, that is, one house burned—and that was an accident that Ewan apologised for most handsomely next day—nobody killed, and just six men what you might call damaged. Rather dull, in fact.

The Macleans' three galleys took the two-day trip back gently, rather hung-over after the farewell feasting. But Duart Bay was empty. They woke up smartly. Eachuinn Odhar strode splashing up out of the water to meet Lady Marion. 'Where are they, Marion? Lachlan? The other galleys? Don't tell me—'

'Aye, Duart. A raid. Noon yesterday, at Arinagour on Coll. But there was a man captured, and Lachlan got it out of him who was behind it all.'

Hector waded ashore. 'Well, it wasn't John Campbell,' he said. 'He was as drunk as us two nights back. I couldn't have run a raid yesterday, and I'm certain sure he couldn't. Who is it, then—Mackinnons?'

'No, Hector Luath. 'Iain Og' is the second son of MacIan of Ardnamurchan. He and his friends—David MacRuari of Moydart, Angusson of Keppoch, and Donald Dhu, Allanson of Locheil's son. Those four. That's who it's been.'

Eachuinn Odhar growled deep in his throat. 'Dhia! What have we been doing this past week at Inveraray, eh? Just wasting our time! Well, we can think about that later. Do I need to ask where Lachlan is? Ardnamurchan, eh?'

'Kentra Bay. He said he must go at once, Duart, for the honour of the clan.' She spoke proudly, tossing her head at Hector.

Eachuinn Odhar snorted. 'I'm glad he thought of that.' He rubbed his scar.

'Kentra Bay, grandfather?' asked Hector, grinning. 'Lachlan'll never let us hear the end of it if he clears them all out and us not with him—and we've a week's good behaviour to work off!'

There was a joyous roar as the old warrior, pretending reluctance, nodded. 'Aye, well. Why should Lachlan have all the fun? Kentra Bay!'

Ranald tried to slip away to join the warriors, but Ruari grabbed him. 'What are you thinking of, eh? What would you do there, saints save you? Fall over your feet?' Ranald was disappointed, but Luch smiled in relief.

Cheering, in wild enthusiasm and their best clothes still, the clansmen swung back aboard their galleys, and heaved them round and away again, a sight happier than when they'd gone to Inveraray. The lads on the shore cheered and waved and the wives, mothers, daughters, and Ranald, sighed in resignation.

Marion Aluinn, smiling, turned to go back up the beach, caught her foot and staggered. She suddenly gasped and laid a hand to her stomach.

'What is it, Marion?' asked Bridhe.

'A pain. Low down—like a belly-ache. It's gone now.'

Bridhe looked at her shrewdly, and glanced at the other women. Eyebrows raised, they nodded to one another. As the lady walked back to the castle on Bridhe's arm, Catriona ran ahead to ready the bedroom. It didn't matter that David Beaton was away with the ships; this was women's business.

It was a first baby, and Marion Aluinn was narrower in the hip than the Campbell lass; it was a long, hard labour in spite of the raspberry-leaf tea Lady Bridhe had brewed. But by the time Eachuinn Odhar's great lymphad led the other galleys sweeping back in triumph along the Sound of Mull, Ruari and Luch had told the bees that Lachlan Cattanach had a fine bull-voiced boy, named Alan.

This time the waiting women got their men back—most of them. The reivers had been burned out, they boasted. Lachlan was a right wild fighter, and Hector fought well too, in a quiet but effective way, all credit to the lad. And did you see Ewan Beg take off the two heads at one stroke? Man, what a man, eh? Singing and limping and shouting memories and boasts, they staggered off home, supported by their women, loaded with recaptured loot.

Lachlan walked slowly up to his room and stared down at his wife lying smiling at him; and at the red, crumpled face and red, crumpled hair of his son, yelling just like his father in a temper; and back to Marion again.

Her eyes were bright, her hair brushed shining, her cheeks beautifully flushed with satisfaction. This day she need fear no rival! 'Mind you,' she whispered in his ear as he collapsed to his knees by the bed and clasped her in his arms, 'I can't promise you a son every time you're away!' And gasped in pain and content at the strength of his hug.

Next day Eachuinn Odhar stormed into the hall. 'Hector! Do you still want this marriage? Now we know it wasn't John Campbell was at the reiving?'

Hector was at his breakfast, sharing a cold leg of mutton with the hounds. 'Why not, grandfather? They'll keep us in good standing with the king still. And more especially now that we've started raiding back against the MacIans and their friends. You will be going after the MacRuaris and the rest, I suppose? Well then, you'll maybe be needing the Campbells' good word.'

'Hah, good lad. I was afraid you might want out. It would be a right insult to them to back off, and as you say, their goodwill could be handy. She's not a bad lass, is she?'

Hector shrugged. 'I couldn't understand half what she was on about, but either I'll be learning or she'll be giving up on me. Or I'll go deaf. Her brothers had a grand idea, though. If we get two serpentines and set them—'

'Ach, we can see about cannon later. We've a campaign to plan, before the king hears of it and puts a stop to it! Aye, Lachlan! Get a bit meat and look here. Oh—how's the baby? And Marion? Fine, fine. Now what we'll do . . .'

They leaned over the map, arguing, the castle fighting men all ears round them. Loch Eil this time—leave Moydart and Keppoch for next trip? Lachlan slapped the table, his booming laugh echoing in the rafters. 'Aye, let's not be greedy!' Six ships—sixty men each—just carry oatmeal—Cameron cattle are aye fat . . . In half an hour it was all planned.

Next day they were off again, leaving the wounded and rejected to make life a misery for their womenfolk. For nearly two months they raided all over Keppoch, Moydart, Ardnamurchan, up into Cameron country. Usually they were successful, occasionally they were driven off; but the bees could be told that the Maclean dead were amply revenged.

In the castle, while baby Alan grew out of his six-week colic, there was an added sharpness to Marion Aluinn's tongue, for she realised she had a more serious rival than any lass; Lachlan's rediscovered love of fighting.

Then, towards the end of August, Eachuinn Odhar got the message he'd not expected for another month. The king called Maclean of Duart to Edinburgh, to explain just what he thought he was at, creating havoc all over the west coast.

'He's fast off the mark, eh? Ach well, we've had a good run,' he grinned.

Lachlan, a bandage round his left thigh which had been axed open to the bone, growled from his stool, but Hector nodded. 'Aye, grandfather. We've aye missed their galleys, somehow, but we've cleared our name in the Isles.'

His grandfather stretched. 'Aye, it's been a good summer. Well-a-well, I'd best go and see what's wanted of me—an oath, most like, to keep the peace.'

'Will you take it, father?' Lachlan asked.

'Well, of course, son. Am I not a peace-loving man?' Grinning, he gently rubbed his swollen nose, newly broken a fourth time. 'But they'll have to take it too. We can get a bit rest in the winter, before somebody breaks their word in the spring again. Not us, of course.' He grinned again.

Lachlan snorted. 'Oh, never us, father! Never us!' He started to bellow with mirth. 'We'd never dream of it, eh? Man, this could be a right handy wee pastime for the summers. I might just stay!'

They laughed together as Marion danced in. 'That messenger can pour back the ale near as fast as yourself, Lachlan,' she laughed. 'Well? When will we be setting out, Duart? I've aye fancied seeing Edinburgh.'

Lachlan stretched on his stool. 'I'll stay here, Duart,' he said. 'I'd not manage the ride with this leg.' That wasn't true, and he and they all knew it. 'And besides,' he said ruefully to their raised eyebrows, 'I'm too short in the temper. I'm like you, father—I

63

can't abide Scotsmen. I'd put a dirk in one of them, and then where would you be, and you trying to convince the king of your peaceable nature?' It was sensible, if a trifle unexpected from the man himself. 'But take Hector, and Marion. She'll enjoy it. Look at her!'

Eachuinn Odhar seemed about to agree when his smile died a fraction. 'Er—no, I think not. I'll not take any of you. Marion, if you've things you're wanting, give Andrew a note of it. Spices or whatever. But this is like to be a boring trip, see you—business, just. And then, I've little silver to spend.'

Lady Marion smiled teasingly at him. 'Come now, Duart, you've tenants from Jura to Loch Sunart! Silver? Aye, and gold, enough for both of us!'

He was sheepish. 'Ach, Marion, you're aye too sharp for me! Well, I'll tell you. I've never been to Edinburgh before, myself. I'd prefer to be alone while I'm finding my way about. And that's the truth of it. No.' And in spite of her charms, pleas and tears, to her incredulous annoyance he stayed firm.

Hector said nothing. When she finally sulked out, Lachlan limping after her, he looked over expectantly. 'Well, grandfather? What's the real reason?'

Eachuinn Odhar nodded in satisfaction. 'Good lad! It's not that I don't want your company. I'd be glad of it. These Scotsmen fairly make my flesh creep, with their laws and papers and fancy airs and lying words. But if you're that clever, then, Master Fox, you tell me why I'll not take you.'

'Well.' Hector considered. 'It was when Lachlan said he'd not come that your face changed. You're not happy about that.'

'Good again! He did the same as me; gave a poor reason and then a good one that was embarrassing, to stop us seeking further. But tell me why, now?'

'H'm. Why should he really want to stay? Ah! You fear he's wild enough to make one last raid just while you're away promising to stop raiding. And—' suddenly his voice turned grim instead of gleeful—'you want me to stop him.'

'Aye.' Eachuinn Odhar was grim too. 'For if he did so he'd be proving my word worthless. Shaming me, and the clan. Before the king himself.'

64

'Order him not to, then.'

'And insult him, if it's not in his mind? I can't do that. I've been at him too much about the clan's honour. No, lad. I'll hint—strongly. But that's as far as I can go. And if I insisted he came with me, he'd likely cause trouble, just as he said. So I must leave him here, and you to keep an eye on him. Don't let him take out the men. It's you are my heir, not him. I'll hold you responsible for the clan while I'm away.'

'I thank you for the honour, Duart,' Hector said formally. Control Lachlan Cattanach? Hold a bear by the tail. Well, he had to start sometime.

Marion Aluinn moved quietly away from behind the doorpost. She had returned to try one more plea, but had stopped to listen. Hector to hold back her Lachlan? A mouse to stop a lion. How could this be turned to advantage?

Lachlan was leaning on the battlements, watching the boats in the Sound. She checked that the sentry was out of earshot, and told him what she had heard. Then she had to hold him back from charging down to challenge Hector's fledgeling authority at once. 'No, my lord. Wait you till your father's well away. Then we'll see can we not set you next in line for chief of Clan Gillian.'

'What?' He was taken aback.

'I've been your wife for a year, Lachlan Cattanach. What kind of fool do you think me, not to know what's closest to your heart?' She nestled close in by his side. 'And we'll make it happen yet, my man. When Eachuinn Odhar goes to his just reward in heaven or hell, it's yourself will be Maclean of Duart, not young Hector Luath.' And that, she thought in satisfaction, would surely bind him to her forever.

'A child born out of wedlock can't be chief.' He was testing her.

'It has been known. If there's no-one else.' He glanced sideways at her, and she smiled. 'As you know well. It's been in your mind.' Reluctantly, he nodded. 'Hector could die. I know you can't simply kill him, even with a seeming accident, or you and Farquhar would have done it long since.' She wasn't at all shocked at the thought. 'We'll think of something.'

Lachlan scratched his healing leg. 'You know why I'm against him, Marion? He's just not the man to be chief of the Macleans.

He's clever enough, and brave in spite of all I've said—in that last raid he took on four men to save Ewan Beg's life. He's a good lad. Too damned good!' There was frustration in his voice. 'Maclean of Duart needs to be more than good and honest! We're rogues, Marion. And our chief must be a bigger rogue than us all—and ruthless with it, when need calls. And the plain fact is that Hector isn't.'

She smiled up at his frown. 'But you are, my love, you are!' They laughed together. She wondered just how much of that rubbish was true. Ach well, it didn't matter, anyway.

He slipped a powerful arm round her and held her tight in to his side, where she purred, rubbing against him like a cat. 'Aye. Marion, there's not a lass to match you in Mull. Not in all Clan Gillian—Scotland—the whole world!' His face was already full of triumph. So was hers.

The guard carefully out of earshot at the far end of the battlements smiled to see Lachlan and his lady so close. All the talk about the Cattanach losing interest in her was clearly false. Then he sighed. It was a pity, in a way; they could do with a kinder mistress in the house. But then, they'd be getting one soon. And Marion Aluinn would find her long nose out of joint . . .

Eachuinn Odhar had a good week in Edinburgh, in spite of the crowds and the stink. He visited Falkland Palace, and made his duty to King James. The Earl of Argyll, Archibald Campbell, introduced him to many of the Scottish nobles, and he found some of them less objectionable than he'd expected. With the fathers of the lads who had been raiding him, he swore solemnly before the earl and the other Lords of Council to abstain from mutual injuries and molestation, under a penalty of £500. The five of them eyed each other stiff-faced and stiff-necked, drank a glass of wine together with the earl to seal their new friendship, and parted in complete mutual understanding and distrust.

He'd meant to stay longer, but a wee niggle in his mind made him return early. It was justified. As his lymphad turned into Duart Bay not long after noon, the bay was empty. His gnarled hands throttled the bulwarks.

His oarsmen held his great galley back off the beach, ready to leave again at a word as Eachuinn Odhar leaped thigh-deep to surge ashore, energetic and agile almost as in his youth, and much more dangerous. They were ranked to meet him in the misty rain, every soul from castle and clachan, fidgeting and nervous, and in front of them all Marion Aluinn, eager to break the tense silence, lovely in her excitement. 'Duart, thank God you're back!'

'Aye?' His tone wasn't encouraging, his eyes suspiciously narrow.

She could weep beautifully, whenever she wished. She did so now. 'I have bad news.' She sobbed, but with a gallant effort controlled her tears. 'Word came that the reivers had hidden their galleys in the sea lochan at Arivegaig.' That was true, at least. 'And Hector Luath dared Lachlan to destroy them before you got back. He said you'd enjoy the joke on the king! Lachlan said no, it would damage your honour. Hector said they both knew you were going to break the truce yourself in the spring anyway. But Lachlan still refused, though it hurt him to miss a fight. You know what he's like. And Hector sneered at him for a coward! And laughed!' The old man's face was unreadable. She sobbed again. 'Lachlan was furious, but he wouldn't do it! But last night a boat brought news of a raid on Coll, and it was more than he could bear!'

'Lachlan went out to avenge them, and Hector after him?'

She was surprised by his ready understanding. 'Aye, my lord!'

His icy hot gaze moved to Seumas Ban, uneasy beside her. 'True it is, Duart, some nights back they were laughing like donkeys about who would first break the truce.' At the fury on Eachuinn Odhar's face he swallowed before going on with considerable courage. 'A boat did arrive last night, after Hector Luath had gone to his bed. I did not hear the sailor's words, but Lachlan forbade me to waken Hector, he said the morning would do for the news. And before dawn Lachlan left with three galleys, and Hector went after him at mid-morning with two, saying he must prevent Lachlan harming the honour of the clan. And no-one can tell you a word more than that.'

'I can tell you every word they said!' Marion stormed at him. She swung in anguished sympathy to Eachuinn Odhar. 'I know you love Hector, my lord, but I have to say it, if you kill me for it.

It was a deliberate insult. A challenge. And you know Lachlan. When he heard the word about Coll—I tried to stop him. I knew you'd be angry. I told him.' She sank to her knees on the damp sand at his feet, wringing her hands.

'I have no doubt you told him.' The words fell heavy as an axe into a rotten tree-stump. 'So. You tell me Lachlan has gone out against my wish, on a challenge from Hector, who planned to disgrace him in my eyes. This is a vile, evil thing. Angry? Aye.' She was weeping, her face hidden in her hands, her heart singing. His voice did not change. 'And I know who to blame.'

It took her a moment to recognise the accusation. She froze, shocked; what about her fine acting? She looked up at him; really looked, to see him, not the picture of him in her mind. This was not the simple old man she knew well, sometimes annoyingly obstinate, but usually easy to coax or control with a smile. This was Maclean of Duart, Chief of Clan Gillian, unchallenged lord of life and death; her life and death; and her scalp rose at the dread of him.

'You are lying, woman.' His voice was cold and deadly. 'I know my heir. And I know Lachlan. And you, with your smiles hiding your lies. Am I to credit that Hector would plot against Lachlan? Why should he?'

She didn't understand. Her Lachlan hated Hector; so automatically Hector must be Lachlan's foe in return.

'No. It is Lachlan, eaten up by jealousy, who is plotting against my heir. I have closed my eyes far too long, in hope . . .' Eachuinn Odhar stood absolutely still for a long, long breath. 'My son. And I loved him! I loved him too much.' The pain, the tight-held rage at Lachlan, and at himself, grated in his voice. 'But he knew I was pledging my honour to the king's peace. The clan honour! At that very moment! God damn his soul! And to try to set the blame on Hector!'

Suddenly he reached down and grasped Marion's wrist cruelly. 'But it's you are the crafty one, Marion Aluinn! You planned this. You lied to me for him!'

Her tears and her throat had dried in terror. Deny it? No use. He had somehow seen the truth. Who would have thought the old man could be so clever? Dhia, he meant to kill her! How to save herself? Act fear? Regret? Ach, to hell with him! That was her best chance, too . . . But not the whole truth . . .

She faced his dirk bravely. 'Aye, Duart. I lied to you.' He hesitated, impressed by her defiance as she had hoped. 'But I did only as Lachlan ordered me. As any wife would. What else should I do?' she challenged him.

'He planned it? If I find out different, I'll kill you, as I will kill him!'

'No!' she cried. 'You can't mean that! He's your son!'

His voice was ice. 'Aye, I mean it. He is no son of mine. No true Maclean would do what he has done—may still do. For I have no doubt of the welcome he is preparing for Hector when they meet. I will destroy him. And you.'

Lady Marion tugged at her wrist, still held in his fierce grasp, and then flung her free hand dramatically up towards the castle folk, and Alan in his nurse's arms. The thought flashed—with Lachlan and Hector dead—he was next heir . . . 'And what of my son? Your other grandson? Will you destroy him too?'

For a moment's shudder she thought he would, there and then. But he paused, and nodded slowly. 'Aye. If Hector dies through your treachery, I will. You and him both.' He threw her aside. 'Get you from my sight, woman!' he snarled, turning back to his ship.

Her heart beat violently, shaking her. She was free for the moment, but still terrified, for she knew Farquhar was awaiting Hector at Arivegaig . . . Only one thing might save her—and her baby, of course.

'Duart!' Her voice was as hard as his own, and he swung round. 'I am daughter to Maclean of Treshnish. I am not wed to your son by church law. After a year and a day a hand-fast marriage can be broken, by the man or by the woman. As is my right, I break it now. He forced me into an action which has disgraced me and my son as he has disgraced you and the clan. I will no longer be his wife! I am again Marion Maclean of Treshnish.'

He eyed her for a moment, spat in disgust, and ignoring her, turned to his men crowding the galley's side. 'You have heard, men of the Macleans! We go to Arivegaig! For the honour of Clan Gillian!'

Within two minutes the great galley, packed with every fighting man left in Duart, was heading out of the bay.

Crouched on the shore, Marion was aware that she was defeated. She was at least alive. There was a space and a silence all round her.

She slowly gathered her wits, and looked round. The whole clan was standing watching, motionless. She stirred, trying to gather her strength, to rise. Her damp dress dragged on her. 'Catriona!' she called. 'Come help me! Peigi!' She pushed herself to her feet angrily, then stared, bewildered, frightened again. Every soul there was turning away, ignoring her completely.

Seumas Ban beside her was turning too. She grabbed his sleeve. He looked at her coldly, but at least he admitted she was there. 'Seumas Ban! What is it? I am mistress . . .' She remembered. Her voice trailed away.

He shook his head. 'No, Marion Maclean of Treshnish. You are mistress here no longer. You have broken with Lachlan Cattanach.' He coldly removed her hand from his arm and moved to join the women on the path.

'But—what shall I do?' This was something Marion had not foreseen.

'Duart never turned any beggar from his kitchen door.'

'Beggar?' It took her breath away like a blow. She was suddenly furious. 'What of my clothes? My jewels? Will you steal them from me? What of my son?'

At that they turned, insulted. 'There are no thieves here, Marion Maclean. Your property will be kept safe.' Lady Bridhe spoke sternly. 'And for Eachuinn Odhar's own sake we will see to his grandson.'

'My jewels will pay me a passage home to my father!' she shouted at them. 'Someone will help me! I'll take my son away! My son!'

Eachuinn Odhar's sister shook her head, scarcely hiding her satisfaction. 'You will not be allowed in the bower, Marion Maclean. Nor in the hall.'

'And no-one will help you leave. Duart will wish to see you when he returns.' Seumas Ban's tone was final, and the folk listening nodded approval.

Losing all control, she raced screaming towards them. 'My baby! Give me my baby! Alan!' He was something to bargain with, maybe; all she had. And her love would impress them . . . But two women leaped forward and held her, though she shrieked and struggled, till the nurse had disappeared into the castle.

Desperately, hands outstretched, Marion screamed after them. 'Stop! Stop!' Not a head turned. A lad lifted a stone to throw. It was firmly slapped from his hand by his mother, and abashed by her glare he turned away with the rest, to leave the accursed woman alone, abandoned, shunned like a leper.

Marion's legs collapsed under her; she sank down on a rock, and wept. 'My man! Oh, Dhia, Lachlan, how did it all go wrong? Lachlan! Oh, Alan! My baby!' She sobbed on and on, no longer beautifully. 'My baby! Oh, my baby!'

A hand touched her shoulder. She looked up slowly, dully, to find a tiny lass standing by her, silently beckoning.

The Honour of the Clan

As the great Maclean lymphad rounded Ardnamurchan Point to ship oars and sail eastward towards Arivegaig, the men rested in their places, sharpening their weapons, muttering uneasily to each other. Eachuinn Odhar was standing alone in the bows, one hand on the high dragonhead that was no more rigid than himself, staring forward after the grey veils of rain that swept past and away ahead. The back flap of his breacan-feile was drawn up as a hood over his head against the weather.

At last Donald Crubach approached his chief. 'Duart?' The old man did not move. Donald, in some desperation, tried again. 'What are you planning, Duart? To take your sword to your son?' There was still no reply. 'Will you call on your clansmen to fight him and his men, and they Macleans too?' Still no answer, no movement. 'Dhia, Eachuinn Odhar, answer me!' The bard leaned forward to peer into his chief's face. The water drops lying in the deep creases below Eachuinn Odhar's eyes could have been rain.

Without another word Donald Crubach bowed, and returned to the stern of the galley. Grimly he started to sing an old war-song, to lift the weight that lay on them all. Understanding, the clansmen joined grimly in the chorus.

At last Eachuinn Odhar stirred. Grey-faced, he walked the heaving deck towards them as if it was a firm path, and the singing hushed at his coming. As he climbed up from the rowing-deck onto the poop, he tossed back the great plaid and turned a bleak gaze on his clansmen. 'My children, I am at fault. I have drawn you in, and involved you in my own anger at my son's disobedience.'

Donald Crubach spoke for all the men, to give the required answer. 'Duart, Clan Gillian is one family. What affects us affects you; what harms you harms us all, for you are our leader, father of our clan. We are one with you. You insult us to suggest anything other. If your heart is troubled, ours are troubled with you, for our name also is Maclean.'

Eachuinn Odhar bowed his head in acknowledgement of the murmur of assent that rose all round him.

Donald was not finished yet, though. 'We cannot direct you, Eachuinn Odhar. But we can ask you, for your own sake and ours; consider carefully. Lachlan Cattanach is a wild man, impetuous and hardy. He takes much of this from you, for you also were wild in your youth—and you're not changed that much in your maturity!' Another murmur of approval as the bard softened his plea with a delicate touch of humour. 'Now we cannot and would not ask you to forget the clan's honour, or your own. If this is indeed a trap for Hector Luath, it is a terrible thing; but you —we—may be wrong to suspect it. Could there not have been a misunderstanding? And is a father killing his son not an act against nature, unholy and loathesome, and maybe even worse for the clan?'

Eachuinn Odhar nodded stiffly. 'I hear you, Donald Crubach. I have been considering this.' He paused. 'What I will do when I meet Lachlan I do not know. It must depend on what we find at Arivegaig. Let us wait till then.'

No-one looked happy; but the worst of the depression had perhaps lifted.

Hector had hoped to catch Lachlan before he attacked Arivegaig, but the packings at the base of his galley's mast started to shift. If they rowed all the way they'd arrive exhausted. He kept his temper and signalled the other galley to turn to the shore at Drimnin, to do the repairs. It took them four fuming hours. It would all be over by the time he got there!

73

As it happened, it wasn't. Lachlan, racing out to set up an ambush for his nephew, insisted against his shipmaster's warning on taking a corner just too neat, and stranded his birlinn just off the Rubha Aird Druimnich. And then, raging at himself for his mistake, he would not give the ship up. He kept the other galleys heaving and hauling at it till the tide rose and they could pull it off the rocks. It was, to his delight, leaking but still seaworthy; but an interested crowd of MacIans had gathered on the shore, and even Lachlan could see that to row up Kentra Bay to attack Arivegaig, with an audience eagerly running ahead to arrange a warm welcome for him, was scarcely sensible.

He mastered his fury. 'Duncan Rua, steer away towards Eigg,' he told his shipmaster jovially. 'We'll try a wee trick.'

He called his officers to come aboard his ship. 'Listen to me, now. They're expecting us. My fault, I admit it. Anybody who likes can take a thump at me!' Nobody accepted the offer. He grinned at them, scratching his aching leg. 'But the way we're heading, they'll think we plan to rest this night on Eigg, and raid at first light, as usual. So they'll send to Castle Tioram for men to meet us at dawn. But when we're out of sight, we'll turn east again, and sneak round the back of the islands and down the far side of the bay tonight, in the gloaming! We'll burn the galleys and the whole place and get away while the MacIans are running to put the fires out. In and out in an hour, a bit healthy exercise, and the folk of Coll avenged!' They considered; and one by one, laughed with him.

As the officers leaped back to the other ships to spread the plan, Farquhar whispered privately to him, 'But if the fighting men are there—'

'Ach, don't be a fool, Farquhar!' Lachlan muttered. 'Why should they be, and the oaths fairly flying at Edinburgh? They're safe at home with their wives! There's been no raid on Coll! That's just the story I told the clan!'

'Aye, I'd forgotten. You're that convincing!' Farquhar grinned sideways. 'But what about Hector, then? Maybe he'll get to Arivegaig ahead of us.'

'Dhia knows.' Lachlan suddenly bellowed with laughter. 'If he does, they'll think he's the raider! And we can go in and rescue

74

him! Father'd like that, eh?' He grabbed a leather bottle that was being passed along, and started a song.

Some hours later, under a dull red sunset, they were creeping up Kentra Bay in the shadow of Beinn Bhreac, past the bay where they'd stopped too short the first raid, through the narrow channel to the sheltered pool behind. 'There are the galleys!' whispered Lachlan, pointing bright-eyed to the five long ships beached safe from any storm. Every man nodded, grim or excited. Laughter and song drifted over the water from the clachan. 'They'll sing a different tune in a minute, eh? Now!' His long arm waved the ships on. The clansmen, grinning with him, pulled hard, driving the packed ships up onto the gravelly beach, pealing the slogan. 'Bas no Beatha! Death or Life!' They leaped down and charged up the shore, yelling triumphantly. 'Bas no Beatha!' Screeching MacIans ran for the woods. Easy, exciting, satisfying, fun. Just what they expected.

A horn blew. The Macleans, confident and happy, paid little heed.

Suddenly from every house, from the beached ships, from every garden wall MacIans were leaping out. Four hundred well-armed, rested, enthusiastic fighting men. At the edge of the woods the crofters snatched up waiting spears and ready-strung bows to drive the Macleans back to the huts and the eager blades.

In the first minute, twenty-two Macleans died.

The MacIans had meant their oaths no more than the Macleans. They had been preparing for a raid themselves the next day; a big raid; five galleys of men, gathered in Arivegaig ready to board the ships in the dawn. When word came to them of the Macleans' three galleys off the Rubha Aird Druimnich, they just sat and waited quietly for their enemies to arrive. And though, as Lachlan had planned, they had expected the attack in the morning, they were quite happy when their lookouts reported the Macleans' approach in the early evening. They just warned the clachan folk what to do, waited till the Macleans were well in among the huts, and then leaped out, cheering, to slaughter them.

As he saw the first men fall in the ambush, Lachlan's shipmaster yelled for his men to fall back. 'It's a trap!' An arrow thudded on his helmet. Half-stunned, he struggled back aboard, to defend his ship like a fortress. A great wedge of MacIans had driven in to cut off the Macleans' attacking force; the few men left fighting by the ships had neither time nor numbers to relaunch them. A blazing torch landed beside him, and desperately he tossed it away to sizzle out in the water. Where in God's name was Lachlan when he was needed?

Suddenly behind him, out on the pool, another horn blared. He turned, his jaw dropping for a second, before his attention was recalled to more immediate matters. He stabbed a man scrambling up the bulwarks beside him, and cheered as Hector's galleys swept up to the shore and another horde of Macleans poured from them to the rescue of their clansmen. The Macleans on the beach took fresh heart; they were still outnumbered, but at least they had a chance.

Hector waved to the shipmaster. 'Get the ships off, Duncan!' he shouted. 'We'll keep them off you! Where's Lachlan?'

'Up there somewhere!' Duncan Rua gestured towards the clachan.

Hector and Ewan set off together. They forged up through the clachan, stabbing and striking up the crowded lane. Ewan Beg swung a huge claymore's massive blade like a willow wand in sweeping figures-of-eight to clear a twelve-foot-wide arc. Hector trusted him to guard his back, and concentrated on the men poking spears at him from the front and sides. He preferred a modern single-handed sword; it was lighter for fast work. A head flew off at a sideways flick of Ewan's sword. 'Good work, man!' Hector called. He dived into a hut, found four men, kicked the embers of the fire into the heather bedpile to distract them, knocked aside a spear with his targe, and the spearsman was within reach of his blade. Shoving the body backwards onto his friends, he swung out of the hut again. 'Ewan!' he yelled. 'Have you spotted Lachlan?'

'Up ahead there! Dhia! He's berserk! He'll not move. Never listen to sense, Hector. Kill anyone comes in his reach, anyone at all!'

A red man alone in the midst of his enemies, helmetless, red hair flying over his red plaid, mouth red as if from drinking the blood that flowed from wounds on his cheek, his hip and his right elbow, airy as a dancer, careless and crazy with excitement, yelling, singing, laughing and cheering, Lachlan was fighting six men together and winning. His double-headed axe flickered in his powerful hands, light as a birch twig. He had no shield, nor needed one, for till the fit wore off a berserker would notice no wound lesser than beheading.

Hector paused, gathering his breath, trying to decide what to do. Farquhar? Couldn't see him. Maybe dead. Lachlan didn't need him just now, anyway. But how to make him attend and retire with them? A berserker was a fine thing if you just wanted to kill the enemy; but if you wanted to manoeuvre, he was harder to handle than a charging bull. 'Stun him?' he panted over his shoulder, parrying a sword-thrust. It was hard to think in a fight, and harder still to speak. He'd like just to leave Lachlan, but he was a Maclean, in spite of all. Oh, damn him!

'Not a chance, man!' grunted Ewan, heaving a spearsman left-handed over a wall. 'Never get near enough!' True.

Above all the din of the battle Lachlan's voice rose triumphantly. 'Hear now the axe sing—Axe of Gillian—Gillian made me —Shaped me for slaying!' The song was bellowing out over the din of the battle.

'Dhia, would you listen to him! I've heard sweeter dogs howling!' Hector panted, grinning. 'I wonder . . . Get the clan back to the ships. Now!' He danced about in front of Lachlan, shouting and waving. 'Lachlan Maclean, you bellowing bull!' he yelled. 'Come away and learn to sing!'

'Hector! Are you daft?' Ewan was horrified. A black dot was flying towards them. 'Ware archers!' He pushed his dallta aside, and the arrow pierced deep into his right shoulder. 'Ach, to the devil with all MacIans!' he grunted in pain and satisfaction, tugging it out and knocking aside a spear left-handed. 'Get you away from my Hector! Macleans! Back! Back to the ships!'

The fire Hector had started was spreading, and smoke was drifting all across the clachan. Lachlan sneezed, and suddenly his crazy eyes came to a focus. 'Hector Maclean! The minstrel! The half-priest thinks he can fight, eh? The great chieftain! Come here till I show you a real fighting man!' Laughing still, he swept two men aside like straw wisps, took a gash in his left arm without noticing it, and sprang straight at Hector, axe raised to strike.

Hector turned and ran. Down the clachan street he ducked and dodged through the retiring clansmen, half-hidden by the smoke, Lachlan yelling after him, till suddenly they were clear of the huts and into the fight round the ships. Right into the thick of the MacIans he raced, screaming the Maclean slogan. His speed and Lachlan's bull charge through the fight, drawing their own men after him in the vacuum of his passage, ran him and them down into the water as well.

Thigh-deep in the loch, Hector swung round. His uncle's axe was striking at his head. He deflected the blow, and the razor edge cut deep into the gunwale of the ship. Before Lachlan could free it Hector had tripped him and soused him, for the cold water to bring him to his senses.

As he rose from the loch, spitting salt, the wild delight in Lachlan's face was gone. His eyes turned up, quite white, for five full seconds. Slowly, blinking, he came back to the present. His eyes focussed on Hector. Hector fending off a MacIan sword from him. He blinked again, and shook his head. Then he glanced aside, and yelled, 'Watch out!' as he tugged his axe free.

At the warning Hector swung round. 'Farquhar!' he gasped, and was borne off his feet and down into the water by the force of the attack.

Ten feet away, Ewan saw him vanish, and with a yell left his own foe and surged forward, his huge sword swinging at Farquhar. Lachlan's axe clashed with it in mid-sweep. The blades caught, sparked wildly and crashed down on a head just showing through the welter of foam round their legs, knocking it under again. Ewan's former opponent, freed for a second, thrust forward with his spear. Lachlan killed him almost absent-mindedly.

At that instant the Maclean slogan rose again round the ships. 'Bas no Beatha! Death or Life!' Eachuinn Odhar's galley, guided through the gathering dark by the beacon of the blazing huts, had arrived. There was a huge swirl in the water and the crowd as it swept right into the centre of the fighting men, crushing more than one under its keel. In the screaming, struggling melee, a knife blade in the wrong place was never noticed.

The fresh men piled out into the fight, driving the MacIans away from the ships for long enough to grab every Maclean they could find and heave him aboard. One of the groaning bodies took four men to lift; 'Hector! Hector!' he was crying as he was dragged up and set to an oar. Burning brands from the huts and from two galleys the MacIans had fired were seized and thrown into the MacIans' own ships, to draw some of them away to put out the fires. Slowly, as fast as they could, the Macleans shoved off for home.

They had to leave the two burning galleys, and a third, Lachlan's damaged one, was sinking under them; they transferred the men from it to the others just in time. Six ships they had had; and they left with only three. The nearest friendly land was Coll, thirty miles to row against a strong, cold wind. But they made it, and beached the ships, made fires and tended the wounded. A hundred and twenty-eight men were dead or missing, out of three hundred and seventy; and as many badly hurt.

They found Ewan Beg lying in a corner of the deck, and thought him unconscious, but he wasn't. He had rowed, uncomplaining, till they were safe; bleeding silently to death from a deep stab wound in his back.

Farquhar, unhurt apart from a huge lump on his head, bandaged Lachlan's wounds quickly before joining him at the oars. None were too serious, though he had lost much blood.

In the last moments of the retreat, Eachuin Odhar had taken an arrow deep in the side of his neck, and though he could move about and gesture to organise their camp, he couldn't speak.

But David Beaton's greatest worry was for Hector. There was a great gash across his face, a heavy blow from a sword or axe that had smashed his nose and cheekbone, and slashed right across his eyes. Even if he lived, he would never see again.

The year before, Ruari had built himself a wee turf hut among the skeps on the moor to keep an eye on them, but Mairi complained about having to bring his food so far, and he'd given up using it. That was where Luch silently led Marion Maclean, slowly recovering from her shock during the four-mile walk.

'Dhia!' Marion exclaimed in disgust as she stooped through

the door. 'The roof's fallen there, and the place is full of sheep droppings. Here, lass! Clear this—Where are you?' The child had disappeared. Marion ducked back out, surprised and annoyed, but there was no sign of her. Damn her!

She looked again at the tiny hut. Her lip curled, and she nearly turned to leave, but where else could she go? The clachan? The women would drive her out. Beg at Duart gate to be let in, where she had ruled till two hours ago? With the sentries jeering and the kitchen girls free to throw dirt, glad to see her fallen? Never! Better here, in spite of all. For a while at least.

A runlet of water trickled past the end of the hut. She stooped down to drink where a stone had been set for a firm landing beside a foot-wide pool. Her reflection looked up at her from the dark water. Her eyes were swollen—she shouldn't have wept like that, genuinely. Automatically, she tossed back her hair and smiled. That was better. She scooped water to rinse and cool her face. This wouldn't last. When Lachlan returned . . .

She had repudiated him. The worst insult of all.

She'd had to save her life, and their baby. Yes, that was the right thing to plead. His baby. She almost smiled as she imagined the touching scene.

She bit her lip. He wasn't famous for understanding and sympathy.

She loved him, didn't she? She'd done it for him. If it had worked . . .

It had failed.

Lachlan could never resist her for long. When he returned, she would weep, beautifully, and he would forgive her. She would go back, under the Campbell woman for the moment . . . And the maids who had scorned her would regret it!

He might not come back. For the first time, the thought entered her mind. He might be killed in the fight; or his father might . . . She shuddered.

A tiny glow of comfort; she'd be safe from Lachlan's anger then, anyway. But if Hector was dead, the old man had promised . . . And Farquhar was waiting . . .

Maybe Duart himself would be killed. And Hector. And

Lachlan, She'd be mother to the heir! Or would the clan choose someone else, since Alan was only a baby? And then what of her?

She didn't know what to wish for.

Ach, well. It seemed she'd have to stay here for a while. She could do without food for a day or two, or maybe the wee lass would bring her something. Who was she, anyway? There were aye shellfish on the shore. She'd need a fire. Could she mend the roof? No, not alone. But she could cut heather for a bed. Make it thick and it would be soft enough, and warm enough.

No more weeping! She set aside her cloak, kilted up her long red skirts and drew her eating knife decisively.

In the clachan Mairi Ban, predictably, was furious at what Luch had done, but Ruari for once stopped her. 'Enough, now! Saints soften your heart, woman! It was a kind thought of the lass, and there'll be no more said about it!'

'It's easy seen you've not a son or a husband risking his life for that one and her scheming!' Her tone was vicious.

'Neither have you, mother!' Ranald grinned. He aye enjoyed a row, if he wasn't involved. It didn't happen often.

'Or have you no thought of Hector Luath, and him maybe murdered dead?' She glared at them, and at Luch silent in the corner. 'Well, I'll not feed the evil bitch! She can go up to the castle to beg her food. Or must I wait about while the brat traipses away up there with meat for her, eh?'

'Why, mother!' Ranald interrupted ironically. 'Luch never lifts a finger here, sure!' He snorted. 'It's yourself grinds the meal and fetches the water and guts the fish and digs the garden and scours the pot—'

'And you be silent also!' Ruari snapped. 'Don't take it on you to use that tone to your mother! The lassie works hard enough, saints help her, that you've no call to scold, Mairi Ban. See you, you've made me right angry, the pair of you! I'll hear no more about this. No more, now!'

He might not, but Luch did. Not that it stopped her.

All the hives were up on the moor, and there was little to do except check that no fieldmice were getting into them, sniff them to detect foul brood, listen for late swarms, and cut out a comb from any that weighed too full. Ruari and Ranald normally lazed about, cut peat, or borrowed a boat and rowed out to do a bit fishing to stock up for the winter, while Luch did her usual tasks and her usual check on the baby—the babies, now—in the bower.

But next day she dared to go into the kitchen, under the fearsome eye and flying spoons of Iain Reamhar; Fat Iain; the only man of the clan bigger than Ewan Beg. He sat beside the wide fires all day, overflowing his stool like a walrus on a rock, half a dozen wooden spoons ready at hand. 'Tog ort!' he would screech in his high-pitched voice. 'Rouse yourself, you lazy rascal! If that roast burns there because you've not basted it, I'll spit you in its place the morrow's morn! And will you be turning the spit, Donal? Or do you expect the poor beast to get off and skip round on its own for you?' And a spoon would whirl across the kitchen to rap the skull of the offending scullion.

Through the gate and into this hot, noisy, bustling cavern Luch drifted in her usual invisible way. Iain didn't notice her for a while, but eventually it dawned on him that the blur in the corner of his eye wasn't just a blob of grease on his eyelash. He turned to look carefully, and saw her.

'Dhia!' he squeaked. 'Who's this, then? Ruari Beeman's lass, is it?' His small, red mouth grinned. 'Luch the mouse, eh? Did you not hear, lass, that I chase mice out of my kitchen?' All the kitchen lads and lasses laughed. 'And have none of you any work to do, then?' They scattered to their tasks. He sniffed. 'Gavin! Mind that stew, it's burning!' A spoon flew, Gavin ducked; it hit the lad behind him, who hadn't kept his eyes and ears open, and splashed into the soup pot. 'Bring it back!' Gavin fished the spoon out, wiped it on his shirt, and gingerly offered it to his master, who gripped his wrist, jerked him forward and clattered his ears for him before letting him go. 'Take care next time!' he snapped, and turned again to Luch. 'Well, lass? What do you want?'

Wordlessly she held out a bowl.

'What's this for, then? Soup, or stew? For yourself?'

An old woman gutting hens told him, 'That's the lass took Marion Aluinn, bad cess to her, up off the shore yesterday! It's maybe for her.'

Iain Reamhar pursed his mouth. 'Seumas Ban said she was to be fed.'

82

'She was to be fed in the kitchen!' the old wife protested. 'Let the vixen come and face us, and beg from us here!' She was gloating.

'Dhia, Mor, you women won't let her off easy, will you!'

'Would you expect it, Iain Reamhar?' The woman's voice was sharp. 'Ach, men will forgive anything to a pretty face!'

Iain frowned, and a spoon twitched. Sulkily, she turned back to her work, slashing into the hens as if into Marion Aluinn's throat. The cook looked down at Luch. 'You're wanting stew for her?' Luch nodded. 'Aye, well, then. Gavin, put a good ladleful in the bowl.' Gavin, with an innocent air, carefully scraped up the worst of the burned shell from the stewpot, but then saw Luch watching; somehow he found himself dropping the charred scraps into the fire, and ladling out some better meat. Iain scratched his head. 'Wasn't it you she was teasing that time, when the bees came out? Aye? Well, why are you doing this for her?' Luch stood silent. 'Can you not speak? Ach, well, off you go, lass.'

Put to it, Luch could have spoken, but she couldn't have told him why. It was something about losing a baby . . .

Ranald went up with her to the sheiling, carrying a pot with charcoal burning in it. Not that he liked Marion; he was curious.

She was sitting by the sheiling door as they approached. 'What's that, then, lass? Stew? Well, well.' She sighed. She was cold, tired and aching; her bed hadn't been thick enough, and she'd been wakened several times by sheep trying to share it, or eat it.

Ranald grinned. 'Better than an empty belly.'

She was affronted by his familiarity; but she mustn't snap at her only helpers. 'Aye. Thanks, lassie!' Her smile was sweet, and Luch smiled shyly back.

'And no need for you to eat it cold, neither.' Ranald knelt to pull the hearth stones into place and build her a fire of peat from the fallen roof.

'I thank you also for your kindness, gallant hero!' Marion's charm for any man was automatic, and rather in spite of himself Ranald softened towards her, though he snorted in mockery of the title. 'No, sir,' she insisted. 'A lad who'll brave the anger of all the clachan for a wretched outcast like myself is a true son of Gillian.' Her eyes and smile gleamed in admiration.

'Ach away, mistress.' Ranald was scarlet, but Luch could see he was pleased. 'It's but a bit fire. To put you by till—'

'Till my husband returns, and rescues me from this misery!' But that was too much, and his mobile eyebrows flew up. She immediately laughed. 'No, no, laddie, I am well served, I that thought just to serve my man! But it is hard to be parted from my child.' She sighed, and noted his sympathy. Men were aye fools over bairns, as if there wasn't aye another one about! She let the tears well into her huge eyes, but bravely wiped them away. 'No, lad!' she whispered huskily. 'You must not stay. They'll be angry, sure. Away you go—I'll do fine.'

She suddenly remembered the stew, and the lass—there she was! How did she aye seem to slip from sight? 'Thank you, my dear.' She gracefully drew Luch close and kissed her cheek. The child gazed up, fascinated by the beauty so slender and warm and bright above her. She touched her cheek wonderingly, cupping her hand over the kiss. Marion smiled down at her. 'Aye. On you go, now, and my heart's blessing go with you always. I'll see to the roof when I've eaten.' She drooped in pretty weariness.

Ranald offered awkwardly, 'No, mistress, I'll—we'll give you a hand!'

'Oh, I thank you, sir! But you'll not get into trouble? You're sure? Well then . . .' She smiled and let him have his way. How easy it was! Watching Ranald drop a rafter on his head, Marion sneered at herself that these children, this filthy hovel were all that was left to her. But it would change . . . She went over to help lift the beams, and then hand new turfs and heather up to Luch, who was light enough to clamber over the roof to mend it without breaking it.

Once Marion nearly stood on the doll baby, set carefully in a soft, sheltered hollow. She was about to kick it aside, but luckily glanced up to see Luch's watchful eye on her. There was something dark and threatening in the look—Ach, she was imagining it! But she smiled and stepped round the doll.

At last Ranald wiped his forehead with a peaty hand, leaving another long dark trail across his forehead. 'There, then, that'll be better . . .' He stopped, mouth agape, gazing down across the Sound where Luch up on the roof was pointing. Marion turned to look herself.

Galleys were rowing in. Three, when six had set out. Only half manned; oars missing unevenly; like crippled beetles crawling painfully against the current. One was Eachuin Odhar's great lymphad; but Lachlan's galley wasn't there.

The two youngsters gazed; and turned to Marion. White as any linen, she had sunk down on a rock. She looked up at them. 'Go! Go—and bring me word what's happened!' Her tone was shrill. She didn't dare go down herself, but she must know. The best—or the worst—whatever it was!

The Moid

Ranald and Luch reached the shore as the galleys beached. They watched among the crowd as Eachuinn Odhar was lifted ashore unconscious, and Hector, under David Beaton's supervision; and over a hundred others, to be carried or helped by their keening womenfolk up to castle or clachan. Then Ewan's body, and two score more. The others had been left to the MacIans. Dead or alive.

Grim-faced, grim-voiced, Lachlan ordered it all, Farquhar Neas guarding his back closely. The men were sullen and never met his eye; but someone had to organise them, and no-one cared to oppose him. Not yet, not till they were less tired. Till they saw whether Hector died. And their chief. He felt their resentful eyes burning the nape of his neck. His own temper rose, but he held it in check. He was in charge, while his father was injured. He gathered his great strength, remembered the lessons he had learned abroad, and drove himself and the weary men on to do what must be done.

His father's men had told him of Marion Aluinn. He never mentioned her.

Iain Reamhar had food ready. Lachlan ordered it served out at once. He set sentries, to watch in case of any raid, and the clachan was warned to be ready; the MacIans might just try it, though they were sore hurt themselves. Messengers ran out to call for help in men and gear and food. The smith and his sister, equally brawny, set their apprentice sweating at the bellows of the forge, to repair weapons, ship's fittings, armour.

The galleys were in bad shape. Two of the shipmasters were dead, and three wounded; but the last was by chance one of the few uninjured men, and could be left in charge of all for the moment. Carpenters, ropemakers, sailmakers—most were dead or hurt. The folk of the clachan turned their best hand to work. Ruari had the knack of plaiting leather ropes, and Ranald raised blisters on his hands cutting out long strips round and round cowhides.

Luch helped Mairi Ban for a while in the castle hall, carrying water and clearing away filthy bandages for washing. In a lull, she drifted up to see to the babies, but misjudged mounting the stair; Bridhe, desperate for more hands, was coming down and grabbed her. 'Luch! Dhia, you're just what I need! Go you to Duart's room, and watch him and Hector for me. Come and get me if there's need, mind! And tell Peigi she's to come and help in the hall. Run, now!'

Late that night Lachlan visited the wounded, smiling cheerfully, near dropping with exhaustion and loss of blood; kept going by the force of will. And at last all was seen to. He could relax for a while. Relax? His mind was roiling. Hector—his father—Marion — Farquhar—Hector again.

Wearily he mounted to his father's room. Not noticing Luch half-asleep in a corner, he stood over the bed. What if his father or Hector died while he was there? Who would believe he hadn't killed them? Or he could . . . He looked down at the men lying there, unconscious, breathing shallowly; and Luch jerked to wakefulness and tensed as his hand moved to his dirk . . . But he hurled himself out, across the corridor to his own room, to throw himself on his bed in rage and self-disgust.

Farquhar Neas, wordless, brought him a leather bottle of whisky. He poured a measure into a shallow quaich, but took thought; and held out to Lachlan the whole bottle. Lachlan lay still on his back, one arm over his face, ignoring him. When Farquhar nudged his hand with the bottle, he merely grunted and gripped it, rolling over to face away from his dallta as he drank.

Farquhar drew a deep breath. His face tightened. He drank the quaich, and tossed back his fair hair. 'Lachlan Cattanach, there is speaking to be done between us, and no-one by to hear.'

He waited. Lachlan lay unmoving. 'Is it blaming me you are, for doing as you ordered? Are you wishing it was I had rolled under in the waves, not your father's grandson, because he was hurt while saving your life? Or are you thinking it was maybe yourself struck the blow?' The wide shoulders winced. He nodded to himself. 'Think, Lachlan. How do you know what happened to Hector?'

There was a long pause. Suddenly, with a heave that shook the floor, Lachlan flung himself over and up on his feet. 'What are you saying? Farquhar? What are you saying?' His fingers were tight on Farquhar's shoulders.

Farquhar stood still under the pain and the pressure. 'I am saying, Lachlan Cattanach, that whoever hurt your father's heir it was not I. Nor you.'

Lachlan released him, and sank on the edge of the bed. 'No, Farquhar,' he said with a bitter chuckle. 'You'll not cozen me so. I told you to kill him—'

'Is he dead so? And have you ever known me to miss before? Or yourself? Look here! See you this lump on my head! Do you know what caused that? It was your axe, foster-son of my mother. That was you, trying to kill me.'

'No, no, man!' Lachlan protested. 'I was trying to save you! Ewan had seen you leap on Hector, and struck out at you—I tried to hold back his blow!'

'Aye, so, then. But it was your axe that hit me, borne down by his sword. Now think again of the wound on Hector's face—a heavy blow, a wide gash. No knife wound, that! So it was not my doing! And was it you, then? But your axe struck my head, not his. But where did Ewan Beg's blade go, when it glanced off your axe, and all his strength behind it? Tell me that, Lachlan?' Lachlan gazed at him in mingled disbelief and hope. 'Think! There was need on Ewan Beg to be silent and row till we were through the narrows, but he had time after that. Why did he not ask help, have

88

his wounds bandaged? What was in his mind—except that he had killed his dallta, and wished to die with him?'

'It wasn't you? You set no knife in him? You swear it? Nor in Ewan Beg?'

'It was a spear Ewan died from. A deep cut, but wider than any knife. Ask David Beaton. I never touched him—either of them. I swear it, on my mother's milk that we shared. On my hope of heaven. Nor did you. It was none of your doing that he was hurt. Nor your father.'

Absently, Lachlan lifted the bottle to his mouth and drank long and deep; then handed it absently to his dallta. 'Not my doing—after all. Not mine. Ewan Beg. Poor Ewan Beg. Hah! Thank you for that, Farquhar Neas.' He laughed longer; fell back on the bed, chuckling still, and started to snore.

Farquhar looked down on him, his twisted smile on his lips. 'I swore, Lachlan Cattanach!' he murmured, too softly to disturb the big man drifting in happy, relieved sleep. 'When you left my mother's house, and I behind you, I swore to her that whatever was your need, I would do it for you. And if I will kill for you, my dallta, will I not lie for you also, to make your heart clear again? My soul for you, my heart.' His fingers touched the dirk at his belt. 'Aye, a heavy blow, or a deep blow—but a long knife can make them that little heavier, or deeper, and never be noticed. True it is that Ewan Beg thought he had killed his dallta—for I told him so. Fool. Now Hector will die, sure, and you will be the next Maclean of Duart, Lachlan Cattanach. And I at your shoulder. And Marion Maclean of Treshnish just nowhere at all.' He gently lifted Lachlan's feet onto the bed and covered him with a plaid. Dhia! The door was a crack ajar! He hastily looked down the corridor, but no-one was there. He sighed with relief, and sat down by the bed to keep watch.

The next day, the bees heard a fine secret bit of news.

Eachuinn Odhar suffered a week of fever before he came to his senses. He was tough, though, and at last he opened his eyes and demanded some ale to wet his throat. Luch, who was still employed watching him, ran for Bridhe and David Beaton. As the old man reluctantly accepted a sip of water, he glanced over at the other bed. 'Hector? How is he?' he breathed.

'Fine, just fine, Maclean,' Master Beaton said reassuringly.

Too reassuringly. Eachuinn Odhar caught the professional smoothness, and grasped the doctor's hand fiercely. 'Don't lie to me, physician! Never lie to me! Tell me the truth!'

Master Beaton shrugged and nodded. 'Very well. He does ill, Duart, I fear. He has a fever. He drifts into and out of the world. And when he is conscious, he grows worse. It is only when he is out of his mind that he strengthens himself unwilling.'

The Maclean stared up at them. 'You cannot mean he wants to die?'

'That is what I mean, Duart.'

'But why? Why should he—'

Bridhe looked down at him with pity. 'Did you not know, brother? The wound in his face. He is blind. Forever. And in his waking times he knows it.'

'No!' The dry whisper could scarcely be heard. 'No! David Beaton, as you love God, say it's not true! He can be cured!' But the doctor could not answer.

Hearing of his father's recovery, Lachlan leapt up the stair to visit him, but was turned from his door. And the next day. And the next. The priest was aye in and out, running busily about sending letters, and calling in this one and that. Donald Crubach; the dempster; the sennachie; Seumas Ban. But it was three days before Lachlan received word that his father would see him.

All this time he had been working like a madman, limping about overseeing the repairs and helping in spite of his own wounds wherever his strength was needed. This was a new Lachlan for most of the men—quieter, grim but not violent; and his efficiency and drive won him more respect than ever his temper had done. He never discussed the failed raid; and no-one else dared to, either. There had been no retaliation by the MacIans, but they all knew they were ready for it if any had come, and who to thank for the readiness; and no-one mentioned who they had to thank for the threat. When the message came, he left the smithy and went quietly up to the castle.

An hour later he left his father's room and walked out, alone, along the shore path and up to the moor. Seeing his face, no-one approached him. Luch, returning from taking Marion some soup, drifted aside out of his way, and pattered back behind him to the shieling to find out what was happening.

Marion was sitting in the sun, her back to the hut that sheltered her from the cold wind. Hearing a footstep she looked up, smiling, thinking the lass had returned; and startled saw Lachlan studying her.

She was afraid, and nearly scrambled to her feet. Then, as he made no move to come any nearer, she sank back and lifted an eyebrow. 'Well, Lachlan Cattanach? Have you come to revenge yourself on me for failing you?' She leaned back, seductive, her colour returning, her smile challenging. Lachlan gazed, but didn't move. 'Speechless, Lachlan? I was told it was Duart was struck dumb. And Hector near death. Our trick has worked, after all.'

He drew a breath deep into his chest, as if it hurt him. 'Aye. It has worked, after a fashion. Hector is blind. And a blind man can never be accepted as chief of the Macleans. A moid of the whole clan is called in two weeks, at the start of October. I am to be legitimated, and made heir to Duart.'

At that she sprang gracefully to her feet to face him. 'So!' She tossed back her hair proudly. 'I told you it would happen, my man!'

He laughed abruptly. 'Your man no longer, Marion Maclean of Treshnish!'

'What would you have had me do, so?' She faced him, head up, colour high and glowing. 'Die? And your son die with me? That was what your father promised. What else could I do?' He gazed at her in silence that she took for acceptance. 'And it was my plan that has brought you to your heart's desire.' She reached out a hand to him, pleading, suddenly submissive. 'I know I should have been stronger, Lachlan. I should never have let your father drive me away from you. But I am weak, and I was afraid.' The tears welled, beautifully, in her eyes as she gazed up into his face, then down in sorrow. 'Forgive me, Lachlan. Tell me that you understand.'

He smiled sideways. 'Aye, Marion. I understand you.'

She sighed as if relieved of a huge weight and leaned against his chest, waiting for his arms to go round her, her heart singing as his heart thudded fast beside her cheek. 'Then—will you take me

91

back, Lachlan? Take me again, my hero! In church, this time. For Duart's heir should not be wed left-handed.' Her huge eyes, gleaming hazel, rose to his, triumph carefully hidden.

Oddly, he did not embrace her. He was still smiling, his eyes gleaming like her own. 'I agree with you, Marion. Duart's wife should be his in the sight of God and man.' He paused, and suddenly wary of something in his tone she drew away. Head on one side, he watched her as he spoke. 'That is why, next month, the Abbot of Iona will wed Eachuinn Odhar's heir, as agreed, to the Lady Elizabeth Campbell of Argyll.'

In the heather Luch crouched rigid, frozen by Marion's screams of rage and hatred, and Lachlan's laughter fading down the track.

The full moid was the most important clan gathering; greater even than the installation of a chief. That was a time for rejoicing and oaths of loyalty; but now every man was called on to help decide the future of the clan.

Every head of a house attended, sleeping in the castle rooms, corridors, stables and stores, in the clachan and on the moor. Though the clan was all one family, and every man had the right to address the chief as a cousin, yet the older and greater branches of the family had more influence than tacksmen or recently-adopted incomers. But all were called, and all came. Cattle and pigs, sheep and deer, fowl of all kinds both tame and wild were roasted by the dozen to feed them all with a generous hand, as Maclean honour required. Iain Reamhar wore out a dozen spoons. Wine and ale flowed free. Yet they were not there for celebration, and there was neither gluttony nor drunkenness.

Maclean of Treshnish arrived the day before the moid was formally opened. Standing at his father's shoulder, Lachlan noticed Farquhar's hand on the hilt of his knife, and gestured secretly to him to remove it. Treshnish ignored Lachlan, bowed to Eachuinn Odhar with respect and asked, 'Duart, will you tell me now where I may find my daughter, who handfasted with Lachlan Cattanach a year ago? I would be speaking with her.'

Eachuinn Odhar nodded gravely. 'In an hour, Treshnish, the wee lass who fetches your daughter her food will come for it. She will lead you.'

Marion had seen his pennon on the galley, and was waiting for him as he walked tall and dignified behind the little girl. She tried to gauge his mood. Always he made her uneasy, as if he could see right through to the deeps of her scheming soul. She braced herself to outface him.

Silently he looked round at the tumbledown hut amid the zooming bees.

Marion had to speak first. 'Well, father? Have you nothing to say to me, cast out here like a leper? No word of comfort? No greeting even?'

His face was withdrawn and severe. 'I have heard much of you this year past, Marion Maclean,' he said distantly. 'Your man, they tell me, adorned you with jewels and fine gowns. He did not beat you, and gave you a fine son. And yet this was not enough for you. No, do not interrupt me. You set your man to slay his chief's heir. And when your treachery to your clan was discovered, you tried to lay all the blame on your man, and left him, betraying him also.

She had never been able to stand against those pale, cold eyes, that flat, unimpassioned voice. She started to argue, stammered, bit her lip. 'Father!' she pleaded. 'I had to save my life! I did only what Lachlan wished! Oh, father, take me away with you! Back to Treshnish! Or to a nunnery on Iona. But help me away from here!'

As she flung herself down to clasp his knees he stood rigid. 'It is true, then. Stand up, Marion Maclean! Have I reared a coward as well as a traitor?' She shrank away from the icy condemnation. 'Tell me, then, what would my wife your mother do if I took you home with me? It's your lying tongue she would tear from your head. Aye, for so she told me. Or what nunnery would take you, in your dishonour? No. Bide you here, where you have a fitting home for yourself. As you have made your path in life, continue on it, so. Your jewels Eachuinn Odhar gave to me, to return to you or not as I judged you innocent or guilty. They would repay me for the dowry I wasted on you, but I have no wish to be reminded of you. Here.' He pulled a handful of gold and silver chains from his sporran, tossing them beside her where she crouched. 'Wear them, if you have the stomach. When you are returned in honour to your man's side, come you to my house again. Until then, you are no daughter of mine.'

He turned, ignoring her, and walked away. She pulled herself to her feet. 'And what of Lachlan, then?' she screamed after him. 'It was his plan too! Will you put as hard a blaming on him? Damn you and him both! Father!' But he neither turned head nor slackened speed.

Marion's curses stopped abruptly. She stared after him, malevolent fury filling her face with ugliness. 'Damn you both!' she whispered again. 'Aye. I'll wash my hands—up to the elbows, in Maclean blood! Some day!' She swung round. Luch was by the fire, fishing a heating stone out from the soup bowl. The little girl hesitantly offered the bowl to Marion, who for a moment looked as if she would snatch it and throw it at her. However, she controlled herself. She knelt down by Luch and started to drink the soup. 'Aye, lass!' she hissed. 'I'll take all I can get, from you or anyone else. And some day . . . Some day . . .'

She lifted the thin chains, set with amethyst and agate, pearls and one round, glowing ruby. 'If I have the stomach, he said.' She laughed abruptly, tossed them over her head, and smoothed them on the red dress. 'I have the stomach for anything, Treshnish! No, you did not rear a coward!'

Next day, the clan met out on the shore, where Eachuinn Odhar could stand up on the rocks among his officers, Donald Crubach at his side, and speak to all together. As he whispered, Donald's resonant, trained voice repeated each sentence after him so that all could hear, from the Macleans of Morvern and Coll and the seven other members of the Clan Council away past the tacksmen and subtenants to the farthest cottar on the damp sand.

He began by welcoming each man by name. He knew nearly every one, and where his memory faltered, his sennachie behind him knew them and could prompt him. Then he came straight to the cause of the conference. 'You have all heard of the tragedy that has struck my house.' There was a general murmur of assent. 'I thank you for your sympathy, my children. God bless you for it. But now, we must think of the clan. My son's son, Hector Mac Lachlan Mac Eachuinn, is a fine lad, strong and brave, learned and thoughtful beyond his years; he would be a great chief. But he has been blinded. Can the clan accept him?'

Maclean of Ardgour, the second branch of the clan, answered him. 'Our hearts are sore with yours this day, Duart. But no man who is crippled so can be acceptable. In war, how could he lead the clan? In peace, how could he judge us?' A murmur of reluctant agreement arose behind him.

Eachuinn Odhar nodded. 'I had expected no other reply. And —' grimly—'I have to agree with it.' He paused, strangely shrunken, while Donald repeated his words, to fly round the walls of the castle to the women watching from the cliffs and battlements, and to the window where Hector lay staring into multicoloured darkness, wishing the blade had struck harder.

'So now, my children, we must choose a new heir.' Heads nodded. This was what they were waiting for. 'I have few male relations left, and all too young or too old, or equally crippled with my grandson. These are changing times. We need a man, a strong man, now; for I am myself old and must soon die.' They murmured agreement again. In spite of the weight of his grief, he felt a twitch of annoyance. 'My children, there is only one man who can be considered; a proved man, a trained soldier, brave, strong, sharp of mind. Lachlan Mac Eachuinn Maclean, my son by Morag Maclean of Salen.' His voice was a breath; he did not look at Lachlan as he drew him forward beside him.

The tall man towered over his father, vigorous and proud. His red beard and hair were combed and trimmed, his silver belt-buckle and the huge silver clasp that held his red breacan-feile no brighter than his eyes. There wasn't a man watching, or a woman, who hadn't had an eye on him in admiration.

But there was no instant roar of approval. He knew why.

For three days the discussions and arguments went on. Every man had his say—some at extraordinary length. That, after all, was what they had come for. Lachlan heard rehearsed over and over his rages and violence. But against that stood the report of his excellent behaviour over the last month. He held his temper tight-reined, in face of all offence. If he let it loose here, his chance of becoming chief would vanish. His control was noted, and approved.

95

He was grimly prepared to face criticism of his trick on Hector, but Eachuinn Odhar was determined that Lachlan should be chosen. He kept a kind of official silence on it, though it was in all men's minds and considered quietly in private talk. They all condemned what had happened to Hector, but there grew a feeling that well, it was only natural for a strong young man to be ambitious . . . Young Hector was a bit soft, after all . . . Maybe the clan could do with a leader who wasn't afraid to risk everything, his honour as well as his life, for them . . . A man who knew all the tricks . . . And of course, it was that evil bitch Marion who had made the plan . . . They didn't notice the contradiction.

And so at last, though not happily nor of one mind, Lachlan was named as the legitimate heir of Duart. He, not Hector, was to wed Argyll's daughter, and be their next chief. Being no fools, the clan noticed that of all men there Duart himself seemed least joyful. Well, it was only natural. He loved young Hector. He'd just have to accept it too.

They didn't hear Lachlan stop his father, as the old man returned after seeing the last visiting galley off the shore. 'Duart!' he said steadily. 'I have to thank you. Without your support I'd never have been accepted.'

Eachuinn Odhar did not look up at his tall son. 'Never thank me,' he husked, for the three days had been hard on his injured throat. 'If there had been another—any other—I would have backed him, not you.' Now he looked up, and Lachlan was hard put to it to meet the bitter glare. 'I curse the day I got you. I curse myself for not strangling you in your cradle. And I set my curse on you if ever again you betray the clan. May God's punishment be a thousand times worse on you than the harm that you have done to Hector.'

Lachlan's hand fell from his father's arm. Fury at the rejection welled up in him, but he forced it down. The old man was upset, but he'd soon change when he saw how well his son behaved in future. Soon, he'd accept Lachlan as a better heir than Hector would have been, and all would be well again. But he wished his father had let Hector die . . .

At Eachuinn Odhar's order, David Beaton had kept the lad well dosed with poppy, till he slept himself all unwitting and unwilling back to health. Donald Crubach played to him by the hour. 'For you must have something to pass your time, Hector.' Expert in controlling his tone, he scarcely hesitated as he passed over the customary nickname, for Hector Luath would be swift no longer. 'You'll practise on your harp, and you'll soon be making your own songs again.'

'Never!' Hector whispered from the bed.

'Aye, surely!' Donald insisted. 'Maybe not soon, but some day. And the great lays—you can learn them, meantime. Come, now. Again. "Mac Mogachoirb."'

Hector, passive, repeated in a whisper the Lament of Maeve over her lover. '"Mocharb's son of fiercest fame, Known his name for bloody toil, To his gory grave is gone, He who shone o'er shouting Moyle."' As he sang, the tears flowed from the bandages, sliding slowly down his pale cheeks, till Donald, playing for him, wished he could play one-handed to wipe his own eyes.

Hector never asked what had happened at the moid. He knew.

Every day his grandfather came to sit with him. With him and Donald, David Beaton, Father Patrick, his aunt Bridhe and the other lasses, Hector had many folk to fill his day. None was as close as Ewan had been, but they did their best, bringing him the gossip, chattering, urging him to rise, to dress, to come out, come down and eat his dinner with the other folk. But he wouldn't. He felt the wreck of his face with delicate fingertips, and refused to leave the room. He couldn't face the world. Not yet. He sat dreaming, weeping, hating pity, driving away his well-wishers.

One day towards the end of October, a week before the wedding, Eachuinn Odhar surged in, Bridhe protesting behind him. 'Dhia, Hector, will you rise? It's not natural for a young man to be frowsting away indoors, in a fine crisp day like this! The sun's fairly scorching the bracken. Come out!'

'Why? Would you have me run a race against Lachlan? Or hunt? Or dress ready to greet my bride? Lachlan's bride!' Hector laughed, low and fierce, and turned to beat his fists on the wall.

'Aye! That's exactly what I'd have you do!' Eachuinn Odhar snapped. 'Will you rot in here till you die? Come! Now! Or do I drag you out?'

'Lay a finger on me and I'll—Let go!' Eachuinn Odhar had

gripped his arm, and started to tug at him. Hector struck out, and his blind fist hit his grandfather's throat. Not knowing what he had done, he yelled, 'I mean it, man! I'll come out when I'm ready, not before! Now leave me be!'

The old man, gasping, held his neck, where the blood was oozing again. He shook his head fiercely at Bridhe; in silence, lips tight, she helped him out.

Hector was lying back exhausted, the weak tears creeping shamefully from his ruined eyes, when he suddenly realised there was someone else in the room. It wasn't the first time he'd thought that, but this time he was sure. He cocked his head, trying to hear. 'Who's there? Who is it?' His voice, too, was weak. 'Speak up, then? Who is that? What do you want?' He stopped, and braced himself. 'Lachlan? Is that you, come to finish what you began?' He gave a snort of laughter. 'You can scarce know how little I care!'

Silence. Then the rushes on the floor rustled faintly, and a gentle drift of air raised the hairs on his bare arms with its chill. Something brushed his arm, without warning, and he leaped with shock. His yell was strong, this time, and Bridhe came running. 'What is it, then, Hector?'

He couldn't admit to being afraid of a breath of air. 'I didn't call, Bridhe. Maybe someone was shouting in the courtyard.'

She nodded, then bit her lip. 'Aye, that would be it, Hector. But is there anything I can be doing for you, my heart? Will I send for Donald Crubach?'

'No, no. Nothing.' Then his conscience bothered him. 'Bridhe —tell the lasses I'm sorry for aye shouting at them. It's just—'

'Ach, Hector Odhar, we know, so. Never let that rub at your heart, my dear. Dhia, have you never heard your grandfather, then? You shout at us as much as you like, if it eases you.' She patted his hair. He hated being touched unexpectedly, and winced; then sighed as she apologised and flustered out.

He waited, listening hard. Sure enough, in a moment the rushes whispered, and the tiny drift of air came again. It seemed to be heading from the far side of his grandfather's bed towards the door.

'Whoever you are—whatever you are—stop! Tell me—who are

you? Why are you here?' The thought chilled his mind—'Are you a ghost?' He waited, the hair crisping up the back of his head. 'Ewan? Is that you?'

Silence. The movement came closer to him. He tensed, waiting.

Something—someone—lifted the rumpled wolfskins over his feet and smoothed them gently. The movement came up towards him. Half-terrified, half-relieved, he reached out a hand. After a moment a tiny hand slipped into it. He gripped tight, and heard a slight hiss of pain; relaxed the tightness of his grip, and gently pulled the hand towards him. He felt up the arm, discovering the small person not quite dragging away from him, a tight bundle clutched in its left arm. 'Luch! It's you that's in it! Luch, the bee-lass! Dhia! What a fright you gave me!' In relief, he started to laugh, and she smiled with him.

She came in every day, after seeing to the babies, if there was no-one about. When he realised that if he had company already then, she'd stay away, Hector made sure that he was alone in the early afternoon. He didn't tell anyone about her visits; he had a kind of superstitious fear that if he spoke of her, she'd vanish like the fairy folk. Besides, she was his secret, something that he knew and nobody else did. Day by day, he grew more cheerful.

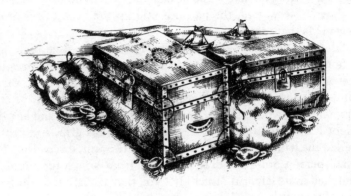

Return to Duart

The autumn was a busy time for Luch. Apart from her visits to Marion and Hector and the babies, she was busy at the hives, for it was the end of the season, and they had all the honey to draw and store. Dawn and evening the three, tall Ruari, gangly Ranald, tiny Luch, tramped in uneven procession up to the moor carrying a dozen bags of leather.

'Right, then,' Ruari would say. 'Luch, go you and get a spark from that woman's fire.' Though he'd not stop Luch helping Marion, he had no intention of speaking to her. Luch ran across to the little hearth and smiled at Marion, who smiled back, her eyes growing larger as her face thinned with every day that passed. Luch would light a length of heather stem, and carry it back carefully to Ruari, who touched the red tip to a handful of broken, dried puffball, and held it in a leather bellows bag in front of the busy entrance of one of the hives. He puffed softly, then strongly, to force the smoke from the smouldering fungus into the skep. Gradually, as the bees stifled, the buzzing faded. At last, listening to the sound, he nodded to Ranald. 'Now, lad!'

Carefully they cut round the base with a knife, to free any wax that was sealing it down, and eased the skep up off the base stone. They set it tilted for a moment, leaning one side on a stone that Luch slipped under for them, while Ruari listened and sniffed and weighed the hive in his hand. Then, usually, he set more puffball to smoke in underneath, to kill off all the bees, and they would move on to the next hive.

Often, though, he nodded approval. 'Aye, we've a fine strong hive here, saints bless us, my children,' he muttered. Then the bees were not killed off. Instead, after the buzzing was muted, they turned the hive on its side. 'Ranald, steady now, up with it. Careful, saints strengthen your foolish hands! Now, Luch, will you be puffing smoke in at us still!' As the half-stifled bees crawled drunkenly across the stone and straw, they swiftly cut most of the heavy slabs of honeycomb off the sticks and laid them in the leather sacks. 'Take care now that we don't take away the king, or we'll die on us!' The skep, with some comb still hanging to feed the bees through the cold times, was lifted onto a cloth, the spare bees scooped back into it, and it was wrapped to be carried back down to overwinter in the bee field.

The weaker hives had all their comb cut out and packed into leather sacks for easier carrying, and the skeps stacked by the old hut to collect later. Twenty pounds of honey each hive, they gathered, or more; sometimes twice that. Ruari was delighted. 'Man, Ranald, we've not had as good a season in years! Was I not right about the wee lass, saints preserve her! She's been a grand help!' And Ranald grinned and winked at Luch.

When they got it all home, the honeycombs were cut and drained through cloth into jars. The wax was put into a huge wooden bowl, warmed at the fire, and worked by hand to get the last honey out. Luch hated that task; Ranald loved it—he never seemed to get sick, though there was aye less came out of the bowl than went in. Then the wax and the brood combs, with all the pollen, dead bees and larvae, were dropped into a pot by the fire, and hot water poured in. The wax melted, and rose to the top. The rubbish stuck to the bottom of the wax, and could easily be scraped off to leave the scented fawny cake clean and pure. The sweet water was strained, and used to make mead.

The castle took most of the honey and wax, but Ruari and Mairi naturally made sure they kept a fair bit to barter with their crofting neighbours for oats. They had their own calf and two lambs to kill and salt down in November, and a pig to smoke, with a ham sent to the castle that had provided the piglet in the spring; they had dried and smoked fish. The hens that roosted on the rafters would scavenge as usual along the shore, and hunt for dropped oats in the straw and bracken Luch had been gathering from the moor all summer. The cow would be brought in to live in the far end of the hut when the weather finally broke; they'd all keep each other warm. Their hay would be fed as it had been cut, handful by handful, and should be enough with seaweed and oat straw to feed her till she was helped out in the spring.

As Luch hurried gently about her many tasks, she often wondered how Marion would manage with just her bowl of soup from the castle. She only had the one dress, and a cloak, both worn and thin. The hut roof was fairly whole now, and she had built a tiny hearth under the highest part of the roof where she might risk a fire. She had gathered plenty of heather and bracken for a warm bed; she had made a fishing line from the hem of her dress, and caught some codling from the rocks to dry and smoke; she had gathered mussels and cockles, and dried them by her fire. But it was not enough. There was little Luch could do, apart from laying aside a few blocks of honeycomb for her.

One cold, windy day Marion nerved herself to take it down to the clachan to barter for food and wool, and found herself still ignored. Wanting the honey she offered, the folk walked by her. They didn't even spit. At last she left, her head still high, her heart black with fury.

A few men were willing to forgive or at least forget; but the women hated her, for by deserting her man she had somehow disgraced every woman, and where the women were still united against her, what man dared help her openly? And she'd not deal with them in contemptible, contemptuous secret—Lachlan would never take her back then . . . Would he ever? She'd not think of that . . .

She would not give them the satisfaction of seeing her beg. She raked round their rubbish heaps at night; she stole from them—peats from the stacks outside their huts, oats gleaned at night from the fields where they drove her away by day, once a half-grown lamb with a broken leg, that she killed with her knife and carried furtively back to the hut, praying they'd think an eagle or fox had taken it. It gave her meat for now and to smoke for the winter, and a jacket, stinking but warm. But she'd not beg.

They saw her sometimes, watching them from the hillside as they carried peats or hay, wood or baskets of fish that they'd not sell her; and each one could feel the chill as she silently vowed vengeance on them all.

And on Lachlan Maclean and his new bride in particular.

The Earl of Argyll had made no protest about the change of bridegroom for his daughter. Indeed, when he read Father Patrick's carefully-penned letter he had seemed almost relieved. 'Eachuinn Odhar's own son, eh? Legitimated by the moid. Aye, well. He's a fine big man, they tell me, Lachlan Cattanach, and more fitted to control that hellcat down the stair there than young Hector. I agree.'

And Elizabeth could, like the Macleans, make the best she could of it.

As the day of the wedding drew closer, the young Campbell lass found herself caught up in the arrangements. Try as she might, memories of her true love faded before the fascination of satin and velvet, furs and pearls, braids and laces. Whenever she settled down, posed gracefully like a romantic heroine, Isolde or Deirdre, gazing wistfully out over the battlements south towards her beloved, her mother's sharp voice would echo up the stair. 'Lizzie! Is that you mooning about again? Come down here, and be brisk!' Poor dear Hugh's face was somehow much less vivid than the tall hennins a married lady could wear, that gave her extra height. She could wear longer trains on her high-waisted gowns, and longer toes on her shoes. She could even pluck her eyebrows!

She did wonder what her new bridegroom would be like. John told her what her father had said; 'He's not so Western as his nephew. He's been abroad, fighting. Knows the modern fashions of dress and behaviour.' It shouldn't be too bad at all, she said to her brother, if he was as charming as Hector had been, and more polished with it! And if John looked dubious, she didn't notice.

In fact, Lachlan was working very hard at being polished and charming. He was determined to let the clan see they'd made no mistake in choosing him, and was off on a round of visits to all the main families, to impress them with his strength and intelligence, good sense and good humour. He could please folk when he wanted to, and for the moment he did. Let his father see that he truly merited the chiefship, in spite of his wild past!

Farquhar, at his shoulder, turned a cynical eye on all this worthy, pious mildness, and wondered to himself how long it would last.

In October, three days before the wedding, Abbot Kenneth of Iona was the first to arrive, followed by ship after ship bearing not just the heads of the Maclean households from Colonsay to Loch Eil, but their wives and children, cousins and friends. This was a great chance to meet the family. And while one marriage was in the air, many others would likely be arranged.

The next day, when the galleys from Inveraray bore into Duart Bay Lady Elizabeth Campbell, her mother, her maid, her chests of clothes, her dowry, her brother John Campbell and his wife Muriella, they were met by Abbot Kenneth and Lady Bridhe. When the guests had been carried ashore Bridhe, smiling welcome, made Eachuinn Odhar's apologies; 'My brother is unwell from a recent wound. There are rooms awaiting you, my ladies, and you, my lord, and hot water being taken up to them this instant for you.'

In the middle of the crowded path, Lady Campbell stopped and reared her rawboned head like a balking horse, neighing, 'And the bridegroom? Lachlan Cattanach, we understand? Is he not here to greet us?' She sniffed, loudly.

'He is expected tomorrow.' Bridhe's smile tightened slightly.

Among the crowd helping unload the galleys behind her, Ranald grinned to his grandfather. 'Turned into a saint he has, they're saying!'

'Aye, for the last two months, saints preserve him!' Ruari nodded. 'But a wolf doesn't turn into a watchdog just by folk wishing it. Mind now—drop that bale and the captain'll have your ears for belt buckles! Dhia, what a great mountain of bundles! The men from the castle should be here to help, saints give them strength, instead of pouring ale into their gullets!'

'Ach away, grandfather! You had not a bad skinful yourself last night!'

His grandfather shook a fist at him and turned to take a chest from a Campbell sailor. They tramped with it across the mud to the grass. 'Whoo! Not as young as I used to be! Ranald, lad, I must sit for a while.'

As Ranald looked at him with some concern, the old man waved him off. 'On you go for another, then! Would you let the Campbells think we're feeble? I'll do fine!' But the lad slipped aside to find his mother. One good look at Ruari's strained face and Mairi Ban had him on his feet, his arms over their shoulders for them to help him home. 'There's not a thing that's wrong with me!' he was protesting, breathless, his hands and knees trembling. 'Saints have mercy, woman, I've drunk too much before this!'

'Aye, father, often,' Mairi agreed. 'Mind your head on the lintel, now. But you've been working too hard this past while. That lassie hasn't—'

He reared up suddenly, much like the countess. 'Now you be listening to me, Mairi Ban! I'll not have you blaming that lass! She's worked this summer like a lad three times her size! If we've done well this year, and we have, it's thanks to her—' Gasping, a hand pressed to his chest, he collapsed on his bed. When she spoke to him and tugged at his arm he just moaned, his face grey and twisted with pain. Mairi, as pale, sent Ranald racing for David Beaton.

A few minutes later Luch drifted in from the castle. Mairi turned on her, focussing her fear onto Luch in a flood of complaint, scolding and slapping. The lass cowered down by the bed until Mairi shoved her aside. 'Out of my way, you useless lump!' she snarled. 'Here, father! Warmed ale, to put heart into you!' The blue lips were slack under the horn cup. 'Dhia! He's gone! He's dead!'

A few of the women, coming back from the shore, were drawn in by Mairi's screaming. 'Dhia, Mairi! Is it dead he is, Ruari? Oh, the poor old man!'

'Aye, and it's this bitch that's to blame for it!' Mairi launched herself again at Luch, tearing at her hair and clothes, beating, kicking, punching her till Ranald, racing back, pulled her away from the child.

'What did she do, then, Mairi? Ach, here's David Beaton

running. It's too late you are, then, physician. The poor man's gone from us.'

Mairi was still shrieking and striking at Luch while Master Beaton bent over the bed. Trying to control his breathing, he laid his ear to Ruari's chest. The women were starting to wail, when he hissed at them to be quiet. 'He's not dead! Nor like to be, unless you drive him to it with your noise!'

There was a sudden hush. In surprise Ranald let go of Mairi, who had hit Luch another half dozen blows before the sense of what the doctor had said reached her. She stared at the doctor. 'Not dead? It's not dead he is? Oh!' She started to sob again.

'Are you not glad, then?' Master Beaton panted, pressing rhythmically at Ruari's chest. He beckoned Luch forward with his head. She had the start of a fine black eye, and her face was scratched and swelling. 'Luch, isn't it? Dhia, lassie, it's the hard finger she's put on you there! But nothing damaged, eh? Fine, then. I'll see to you in a minute.'

He returned to his rub-rubbing. Under the kneading fingers they could all see the fluttery movement of Ruari's thin, bony ribs, and the doctor timing his pressure to work with the breathing, not against it. 'Here, wife! You see what I'm doing? You do it now!' But she was wailing among her friends.

Ranald spoke up, an arm round Luch's shoulders. 'Let me, sir?' The doctor, knowing him, looked doubtful, but the lad's hands, strong from working the wax, settled smoothly into the rhythm.

'Fine that, lad!' Master Beaton turned to Luch. 'What did you do, then, lass, to make Mairi Ban so terrible angry at you?'

Luch shook her head. It was Ranald who explained, always keeping on at the massage. 'It's not her, sir. It's my mother. She's never taken to her. But she's never hurt her before, not like this.'

'H'm.' Master Beaton pondered. 'I thought she was going to kill the lass!'

'Luch can't stay here, sir.' Ranald was worried, but definite. 'Not now. My mother'll drive her out. Sooner or later. She'll not forgive her.'

Luch bit her lip. Where could she go, then?

'Could you not take her up to the castle, sir?' Ranald suggested.

'It was Marion Aluinn ordered her away, and she's gone herself now.'

David Beaton clapped him on the shoulder. 'That's it! This new lady may let the lassie stay. And I've got the very task for her!' He knelt, to gaze level into Luch's eyes. 'Lady Bridhe told me, lass, that you come to visit Hector every day, if there's no-one else about.' After a pause, she nodded. 'Aye, so. He seems to be at ease with you, more than with anyone else. Will you come look after him for us? And see can you get him back into the world?'

Luch considered.

She looked at Ranald, who grinned, toothy and encouraging. 'That's grand, sure! You can come down and see us whiles, lass!'

She looked at Mairi, who happened to glance over and catch her eye; and the woman howled and started to moan at the very sight of the wee lass.

She looked at Ruari. 'He'll be fine in a few days, my dear, with an infusion of clover and foxglove to steady his heart. Rest is all he's needing. And will he get that while you're here, and Mairi Ban shouting?'

At last she nodded again, almost reluctantly.

And so it was that Luch was taken up to the castle for the second time.

Ranald walked up with her, but at the gate he halted, shy, ready to turn and run back to his grandfather. David Beaton stopped him. 'Come in, lad, come in! You'll not be noticed in the crowd, and your mother will never forgive you if you don't stay to see the visitors, and tell her about them!' The doctor's elbows were awkward on the youngsters' shoulders, one high and jolting, one low and smooth. But somehow, he thought, the lanky, lively lad and the small, dull-looking lass fitted together in friendship.

In the bower, a rigid veneer of courtesy hid Lady Bridhe's mounting fury.

The Campbells' rooms had been given up by the officers of the household for the visitors. But Lady Campbell was less than happy. 'In Inveraray, the rooms are far grander. And better furnished. Elizabeth, my dear, we'll have to see to that at once.' Bridhe smiled, and seethed.

Iain Reamhar had been working his spoons to splinters, but

Lady Campbell still found fault. 'Cinnamon with the venison? Heavens! Elizabeth, dear, we'll have to see about training a new cook.' Bridhe seethed, and smiled.

Then the countess started on the family. 'I understand that Lachlan Cattanach is away. I trust he will return in time, eh, Elizabeth? Heh, heh. But is Duart himself absent? No? Then when may we see him? And Hector? Elizabeth does wish to express her condolences. They liked each other so well—what a pity! But she will do her duty—won't you, my dear?'

Bridhe, smiling, cast a desperate eye at Abbot Kenneth. He fended off the awkward questions diplomatically. 'Duart is forbidden visitors today, my lady, so that in two days he may be fit for the ceremony. We do not wish it to be postponed.' That stopped her. Abbot Kenneth went in to the attack. 'And will Argyll not attend his daughter's marriage? A pity, so.'

'He would have done so, Father Abbot, but he was called to attend King James. And as you must realise, that summons takes precedence over any other.' The lady smiled triumphantly, more like a mare than ever. 'Besides, with four sons and six daughters—' more than the Macleans could manage, her sneer said—'a wedding is no novelty. Our third son John here will represent him.'

Elizabeth, nibbling at her food in unaccustomed silence, glanced down the table at John. The reality of her marriage was coming frighteningly close. John winked. 'Not for ever.' That was a reassurance. She looked round the bower. Only one hanging, and that a tattered old thing of Adam and Eve! The whole place was darker and colder and more echoing and empty than Inveraray. Hugh Despoins' home had bright panelling and carpets on all the walls. Oh, Hugh!

Sensing the atmosphere, David Beaton led Luch and Ranald past the bower door, and on to Eachuinn Odhar's room. The old man, pretending an appetite over a roast leg of mutton, grinned greasily across at him. 'Seen the Campbell mare? No? I kept well clear. Good excuse, eh?' As he touched his neck his face almost brightened with glee, but his weak, hoarse voice grated on the doctor's ear. Something was far wrong there. And there was a new red stain seeping through the cloth. 'Put a huge bandage on it tomorrow, David. It'll get me away from them. Hellish woman.' His eyes sharpened. 'What's that behind you?'

Luch drifted shyly out into plain view. Hector, picking at his food, sat up suddenly as the rushes moved gently under her feet. 'Luch!' he exclaimed. 'Is that you?' She put a hand on his, in her usual way of announcing herself, and he covered it with his own. 'What are you doing here, lass?'

The doctor explained, signing to the old man to look at Hector's face. He ended casually, 'So till the beeman is well again, Duart, I thought she might return here. And I brought her friend Ranald along too, to—er—escort her.'

The wee lass had picked up a cloth and was wiping Hector's unshaven chin free of grease; then his hands, and the handle of his knife. When the other women had done so, Hector had flared out at them. Now he submitted, laughing. 'Are you done, so?' he demanded. 'Am I tidy enough for you now, my lady? Can I go on with my meal?' He drank a good draught of ale, and ate another slice of meat. 'Ranald? What mischief have you been at this last while, then?'

Ranald, his shyness fading, started on a long story of honey and ants and his mother's bed, that set Hector smiling, then chuckling, and at last rolling about with laughter. 'Dhia! In her hair, even! No wonder she was near demented!'

David Beaton caught Eachuinn Odhar's eye, frowned, set a finger to his lips and shook his head. Eachuinn nodded. 'Aye, well,' he said, pretending reluctance. 'We'll maybe find a use for the lass in the kitchen.'

'No. She can stay here, grandfather. She doesn't bother at me. And the lad, too. I can be doing with someone to run errands, now Ewan's gone.'

Satisfaction was broad on Eachuinn Odhar's face. 'Aye, well, so, a pallet for them will not take up that much room,' he grunted grudgingly, his heart leaping. Hector had never said Ewan's name so easily, nor shown such interest and determination in weeks. Maybe this would be the turn for him.

To their surprise, Ranald wanted to refuse the honour. 'My mother, my lord, she'll need me, and my grandfather ill!' But it was soon settled that he would stay at home only till Ruari was better. Bumping and alarmed shouts rose behind him as he ran out in ecstasy, tumbling heels over head down the last twists of the stair, to tell his mother he was a castle ghillie now!

Next afternoon, when Bridhe was just starting to panic, Lachlan's galley at last drove in from Glensanda, red and green pennants brave in the breeze. His father wasn't down at the beach to greet him. Nor at the gate. Nor in the hall. The Campbells were waiting to greet him in the hall, and Elizabeth saw him for the first time. Her heart suddenly thudded hard. He was the finest man she had ever seen! But he ignored them, leaping straight up the spiral to his father's room. John Campbell frowned at the rudeness; his mother was furious.

As Lachlan knocked, Luch opened the door and he strode past her unseeing. Huddled in his great chair beside the window slit, Eachuinn Odhar was coughing, a dry, hacking bark. Abbot Kenneth was holding a cup of medicine to the old man's lips, but Eachuinn Odhar pushed it away and turned, eyes hooded, to face his son. 'Well, Lachlan. You're in bare time for your wedding.'

'Duart,' Lachlan said respectfully. 'Father Abbot—you are welcome.' He knelt beside his father's chair, reaching to take the knotted hand that his father surrendered absently to him. 'Father —is it your neck again?'

'These two-three days, it has bothered at me,' Eachuinn Odhar admitted in a whisper. In spite of himself his expression softened at the sight of his fine son, till his eyes moved beyond the handsome face turned up to him. His lips tightened. 'But have you no word for Hector, then?'

Lachlan spun to his feet, and froze. Hector was behind the door, as if he'd been hiding there, painfully thin, still unshaven, a stained rag over his eyes. He was smiling, but not in welcome. 'Greetings, my uncle, returned to take my place, my bride, while I —no, I cannot watch, can I? I'll listen, then.'

It was the first time Lachlan had seen Hector awake since his blindness. Now, bearded to bandaged face, they stood in utter stillness. The watchers all waited tensely for the first word, the first greeting between the two.

At last, Lachlan moved. He stepped forward slowly, and set his hands on Hector's shoulders. He drew closer till at last his forehead was leaning forward, touching Hector's. He stood still again for a long moment; then lifted his head, sighing deeply. 'My heart, Hector. What can I say? I led you, from my pride and greed, into danger. Nobly, you saved my life, and were struck down in the doing of it. My grief for you, Hector. If I could have any day of my life over again, at the price of my right arm, it would be that day! But I cannot. All that I have now, I have only because of that blow which blinded you. And yet I cannot refuse it.' Utterly sincere, he was near weeping in repentance.

'For the good of the clan!' Hector mocked him bitterly. 'A thought of that two months back might have spared you this grief now. Have you not made confession, then? Abbot Kenneth here will hear it, and give you a sweet little penance, and then you may be easy again.'

The monk shook his head in frustration. 'Be at peace, Hector! You must turn your mind to forgiveness before the fires of hate consume you.'

Hector's head turned as if his eyes were seeking the abbot. 'Fires of hell, Father Kenneth. Say what you mean, in God's name. What fires could be worse than this? Death or life, eh? I have both, and neither!' He swung back to Lachlan. 'Or is it not Farquhar who should be seeking absolution? Was it not his knife that blinded me, at your order?'

'No!' Even Lachlan could feel his denial was scarcely convincing, but he had to try. 'I swear it to you. He did not do it! Nor did I!' He urgently gripped and shook Hector's shoulders, trying to make him believe.

'Then who did?' the younger man spat at him. 'Tell me that, Lachlan Cattanach? If it was not you or your dallta, who, then?'

Lachlan drew breath to name Ewan; but a rush of generosity stopped him. Why say it? He'd not be believed, and would just hurt the lad more. 'How should I know? But I swear to you, nor Farquhar nor I blinded you. On my hope of—'

Furious, disgusted, Hector interrupted him. 'Hope of what? Can you hope for Heaven, then?' At his tone, rising sharply, Luch lifted her head. Something was wrong . . . Worried, she moved gently towards him as his speech grew ever faster. 'Dhia, what more do you want of me, Lachlan Cattanach, that you take the trouble to lie to me so? My forgiveness, to ease your weeping heart? Then you must stay wanting it, I fear. For you'll never have it!'

He raised his left hand to touch and grasp Lachlan's plaid. The abbot started to cry out, far too late. Hector had judged his distance, drawn his knife and was striking like an adder at Lachlan's face—at his eyes.

But someone clutched desperately at his hand, dragging it down, tugging it with astonishing strength and speed away to the side, while Lachlan twisted himself free of Hector's grip and ducked away. The blind blade missed by a foot. Luch, swung off her feet by the force of Hector's thrust, let go. Hector stood poised for another blow, but there was no clue to tell him which way to strike. He slashed wildly, and heard a tiny gasp. 'Who's that? Luch? Is that you? Have I hurt you? Oh, God!' His knife clinked to the floor. He sank on his bed, shaking with great dry sobs.

Abbot Kenneth stepped between them. 'The child is not badly hurt, Hector. No thanks to you. She has a cut on her arm. Thank God she was here. For if not . . .' He turned to Lachlan. 'It will be best if you leave now, my son,' he said firmly. 'I beg you, say nothing of this to anyone.'

The big man's face was as bitter, as resentful, as Hector's had been. 'Protecting him again, Father Abbot? As my father aye did. Aye does.' He turned his back on Hector, and walked deliberately over to Eachuinn Odhar's side, waiting in vain for him to look up from his fingers, nervously rubbing at his fur coverlet, and meet his son's eye. 'The monk would warn me, father, but not you. That child would save me, but not you. Why? Did you want him to kill me, then? Or blind me? And who would you find to lead the clan then, Duart?'

Abbot Kenneth interrupted again. 'Enough, my son. Do you not see your father regrets what he did?'

'What he did not do, rather! All that holds him back from doing it himself is the desire for an heir to the clan—an heir of his own blood!'

The monk's face was stern. 'Go now, my son. Go in peace.'

'Peace?' Lachlan stared at him in amazement. 'Peace, after this?

Dhia, are all monks such fools?' He swung back to his father. 'This marriage—aye, I'll go on with it. For the honour of the clan! But when I have got you an heir, I'd best be careful, eh? There might well be a knife on a dark stair for me! Eh? Father?' He laughed again, his face twisted in disgust and grief, and a strange relief, and swept out, his plaid swinging. As he leaped down the stair he was shouting for Farquhar Neas, and whisky to take a foul taste from his mouth.

'God be with us all!' Abbot Kenneth prayed, his face stern and accusing. 'I was thinking that responsibility, and maybe guilt, had turned Lachlan Cattanach onto the straight road. He might well have settled to be a good chief for the clan that you say you're so concerned for, Eachuinn Maclean. If you have between you driven him back to his old ways, your souls will bear a heavy charge on the Day of Judgement!' He sighed. 'I will go and speak to him. Will you come with me? Either of you?' Neither of them moved. 'God pity you both, then. See to the lass.' He went out, leaving them in a bitter silence.

Down the stairs, in the hall, a noise of rough laughter and shouting arose, and grew. And grew, unchecked.

Soon the only sound came from the carousing in the hall below. At last the choruses dropped to a quartet, to a duet, and finally even Lachlan's fine solo baritone petered out. There was a crash as the big man stood up, tipping his chair over. Two sets of footsteps, one heavy and unsteady, and the light ones aye behind them, mounted the stairs and paused long at Eachuinn Odhar's door, before turning into the room opposite.

Elizabeth, awake and nervous beside her snoring mother, heard them. Eachuinn Odhar heard, lying still not to waken Hector. Hector, lying rigid not to waken his grandfather, heard as he stared into the great burning swirls of furnace-fire and blood that roared in front of his darkened eyes.

All three thought of their hopes, and dreams, and the changes and chances of fate.

Luch slept quietly on a pallet in the corner, her sore arm bandaged, her baby tucked safe beside her.

Mistress of Duart

Before first light the castle was bustling. Lads were hanging bright flags and cloths in the hall. Fresh barrels of ale and wine were rolled from the cellars. The scullions sweated and ducked at the spits and bake-ovens built around the exercise ground for the clan to feast.

Elizabeth's wedding dress was vivid rose-pink velvet, the sleeves braided in scarlet and lined with ermine, over a quilted silver brocade undergown. It made her look even plumper, and clashed vilely with her mother's regal crimson and gold. Her sister-in-law wore canary yellow trimmed with black marten fur. When John Campbell—who had refused to go bare-legged under his breacan-feile; there were limits!—saw them, he blinked at the dazzle of colours, the triple-layered jewels before controlling himself and advancing steadily. 'Well, John?' his mother said warningly. 'How does your sister look?'

He knew his duty as she did hers. 'Beautiful, mother. As are you all. The three finest flowers in Scotland!' His wife and mother beamed at him as he kissed them all in turn. Elizabeth clung to him, trembling, but their mother glared; not in front of the Islesmen! She stiffened her spine.

As they went down, the two married ladies were in high spirits. It was quite true; there wasn't another woman in the castle dressed as richly and fashionably, not even the Maclean's sister. They preened like popinjays.

Eachuinn Odhar was awaiting them among the crowd in the hall. Hector had refused to be present. The lad was better out of it anyway, his grandfather thought as he bowed, and wished he was away himself. And where the devil was Lachlan? The Campbell mare was sneering. He sighed grimly, and sent his own man Andrew to help Farquhar get his son down; if not sober, at least tidy.

There was hot, spiced wine to hearten the bride, who drank it gratefully. Maybe he'd refuse? What would happen? It would be an insult to her father. And herself, of course. Maybe there would be a feud over her! Exciting! At the second cup she warmed slightly, and her hands stopped trembling.

At last Lachlan descended the spiral and stopped on the final step. Aye, a fine man, Elizabeth thought admiringly. His red hair and black leather gleamed equally polished, his breacan-feile was bright and full, the silver on his belt, brooch, sword-hilt and knife glittered in the morning sunlight. The tall eagle feathers on his bonnet cocked proudly over his head.

Behind him, Farquhar propped him up unobtrusively as he swayed slightly, his glazed expression half-hidden by his neatly-brushed beard. With the wild night, after two months' sobriety, he had a hangover would stiffen an eel.

He opened his eyes, blinked, and saw the bowl of mulled wine. In three seconds he was tilting it down his throat, ignoring the cups. He sighed with relief, wiped his beard and looked round more clearly. As his bloodshot eye fell on the brilliance of the three Campbell ladies, he winced. John Campbell felt a sudden amused sympathy for him, but couldn't show it, of course.

Lachlan looked the women over. 'Dhia!' he muttered, not quite under his breath, and visibly braced himself. 'Well, which of you is it?'

It could have been a compliment; it wasn't. Elizabeth's jaw sagged; John's clenched rigid. His wife's mouth, under less control, was twitching, and they carefully avoided each other's eyes. Lady Campbell, crimson with rage to match her gown, indicated her daughter. 'This lady is Elizabeth Campbell, your bride.'

Lachlan stared at the dumpy, over-dressed little figure gaping and gasping in shocked astonishment. Dhia! He recalled Marion, slender and exciting. He sighed deeply—Elizabeth's fury joined her mother's—and turned to his father glowering beside them. 'Well, let's get it over, then.'

Such enthusiasm, John Campbell thought wryly, taking his sister's hand to lead her towards Abbot Kenneth standing waiting at the head of the hall. But it couldn't be avoided, not now.

As the happy couple took their places there was a stir and a rising babble behind them. Eachuinn Odhar turned to glare; then, his face changing to incredulous welcome, abruptly pushed back through the crowd towards a young man at the foot of the stair, newly washed and shaved, tall and striking in his best breacan-feile, a clean white cloth over his eyes; led by a little girl. 'Hector, my heart! Come in! I thought—'

'I decided to come, grandfather.' Hector's voice was quiet, almost lost in the buzz of welcome around him. He smiled and nodded to the words of greeting from the crowd, and his blind face searched for someone. 'Lachlan? Elizabeth?' Eachuinn Odhar led him forward. 'Lachlan?' Hector reached out his hands to find his uncle. 'I pray you forgive me for what happened yesterday. I was wild—not myself. Forgive me as freely as I forgive you.' Looks of surprise were exchanged all round them as he set an arm round Lachlan's shoulders that stiffened and then relaxed; and then the cheering erupted. Under it, Hector turned his head to the bride. 'Elizabeth, I wish you every happiness that my uncle here can bring you. He is a far finer figure than I am—as fine a man as you are a woman! You'll make a well-matched pair.'

John Campbell caught the double meanings, and lifted an amused eyebrow. Aye, the lad was clever. He said nothing, though. The assembled crowd rejoiced at this unexpected joy, and Luch stood quietly unnoticed by the steps as they all turned away to where Abbot Kenneth stood in a perfect haze of delight.

The feasting lasted the whole day. The bard was fair, but she must teach them some court dances, Elizabeth thought. And at last the roystering procession when the castle ladies escorted her to her room. Giggling—even her mother!—they undressed her to her shift and set her in the bed, uncomfortably decorated with fruit and sheaves of barley, to await her husband. He in his turn was carried in by the men. Shouting rude jokes, they dumped him in beside her, drank a toast of long life and many babes to the happy pair, blew out the candle and reeled out to continue their feasting in the hall.

She sat stiff with apprehension and excitement. At last, as nothing happened, she grew puzzled. 'Lachlan?' she said. There was no reply. She tried again. She reached out a tentative hand to the heavy body beside her. 'Husband?' This time she was answered; Lachlan grunted, rolled over slowly as she tensed, settled comfortably on the pillow and started to snore.

Well! What an insult! A relief, too. Between a snoring mother and a snoring husband, what difference? Oh, Hugh! Sniffing, she fell asleep herself.

Next morning, she yawned, wakened, saw his beard, and yelped in alarm before she remembered where she was. He opened a bleary eye and growled, 'Who the hell are you?' Then he remembered too, and started to laugh. After a shocked second, she joined him. Poor Hugh never came to her mind at all.

When her husband rose she lay a while, dreaming. Slowly a glorious joy filled her. She was married! She was no longer only her parents' daughter. She was the Lady of Duart. She sighed in delight at the delicious possibilities for revenge . . . And her husband—her handsome husband—would back her . . . But no. Regretfully she dismissed dreams of dungeons and torture. It must be done politely, for she was a great lady now. She had a position to maintain, as her mother kept reminding her. And after some thought, she knew exactly how.

The next days were filled with meeting her new relatives, feasting, and listening to interminable songs praising her beauty. She didn't believe a word of them, of course. Not really . . . She was busy, and astonishingly happy. She never knew how often Lachlan looked at her and thought of a slenderer, more elegant figure. But one day a visit to Glensanda on Loch Linnhe was planned. Elizabeth, knowing her mother was a bad sailor, cried off at the last moment, claiming she was tired—she was surprised at the laughter that raised—and as she expected, her mother took the chance to stay behind with her.

Standing on the battlements waving the galley goodbye, Elizabeth looked down—down the wall, and then down again. Lord, she'd not realised the cliffs were so high! On the hillsides all around, the sun-dazzling orange of the bracken against the black of the heather startled the eye. Fishing cobles were scurrying about the Sound like water beetles, black dots on the deep blue. The hills to the west and south, and over the water to the north, were Maclean land; it was pleasant, rich land, and would soon be hers! The long, low island of Lismore away to the east was Campbell ground, and the great fortress of Dunstaffnage out of sight beyond it on the mainland. She wasn't so far from home, and help if she needed it . . . But she wouldn't. This was her home now.

It was time. She turned courteously to Bridhe. 'Lady Bridhe? If you have leisure, I'd be grateful if you would kindly show me the castle?'

At once the countess's nasal voice arose behind them. 'Aye, and not before time, we'd best see right round the place. There's a deal needs clearing out, and we've to decide where to start.'

Mother, dear mother, she knew already exactly where she'd start!

Bridhe, treated with charming deference instead of Lady Campbell's arrogance or Marion's former insolence, declared herself delighted to guide the young mistress. They clambered back down the ladder and visited all the little rooms in the top floor to a steady stream of disparagement from the countess. The bower they knew well already. It was a large, old-fashioned nursery-cum-workroom, with piled baskets of wool and two looms at the far end. The lasses carded wool or span whenever they had nothing else to do, just as at home.

At home . . . Here was home for her now. Not for ever . . . Well, maybe . . . Elizabeth felt a thrill now, instead of a chill, at the word 'husband' . . .

By the hearth lay two cradles. One babe was Catriona's. No-one had said whose the other was, but from the tone of their glances Elizabeth guessed he was her husband's—she glowed inside at the word. She'd find out soon.

The three ages of woman, Seumas Ban thought, greeting them in the hall; the plump young mistress, her harsh-boned mother, and old Bridhe, softly wrinkled like an old pear. He showed them the huge chest, far too heavy to lift, with the silver cups and plates for special occasions. Not as much as at home—at Inveraray, Elizabeth thought, but more than she had expected.

As they moved on, the countess constantly and caustically criticised the small rooms, the narrow corridors, the dirt, the cold, the lack of all civilised amenities. Elizabeth listened intently, till she could practically see steam puffing out of the ears of Seumas Ban and Lady Bridhe. The time had come!

She stopped dead. Her mother jolted to a halt just before bumping into her. 'Mother,' she declared firmly, 'I feel I would prefer your absence.'

Her mother gaped unattractively, turning a blotchy red to match her gown.

Elizabeth cast one happy glance at the dawning delight on the other two faces, and continued with the joyful work. 'I pray you remember, dear mother, that it is I who am Lady of Duart. You arranged it for me. Indeed, you insisted. You will recall?' Let her remember that night too! 'I know I have much to do and learn, but with the able assistance of Lady Bridhe and Seumas Ban, I feel quite capable of running the household to my husband's satisfaction without your interference.' But with your expert suggestions in mind, ha-ha!

Childishly elated, she saw her mother's fury growing and her hand rising to strike. Let her try it! She almost welcomed a pitched battle, and her fists clenched. But Bridhe stepped between. 'Very well, my lady!' the countess snapped. She swung on Bridhe. 'Do you advise her, then. You'll find her not so well-tempered as she might seem!' She stalked off like a scarecrow in a rage.

Elizabeth took Bridhe's hand. 'I thank you for your support, lady,' she said, gasping slightly. 'I was afraid for a moment that she'd strike me.'

Bridhe beamed at her. 'Afraid? No, no, my dear! I'd have scratched the eyes from her head, countess or no, before she laid a finger on you!'

Hard tried not to giggle with triumph, Elizabeth leaned tremulously on Bridhe's shoulder, and let the old lady comfort her. From now on, she knew, she couldn't set foot wrong. Her mother, defeated, would be away home as soon as she could. And Bridhe and Seumas Ban would make it plain to everyone that the new mistress had their approval. It had been a grand few minutes' work.

That same day, before the galley returned, Bridhe told her the story of the strange baby. They were looking through a box of embroidery threads when the child started to cry. Elizabeth turned and lifted him. Strange how warm she felt with him in her arms. She rocked him gently while Bridhe told her the story, and she felt a confusion buzzing in her head. This was Alan; Alan Mac Lachlan Maclean. Her husband's legitimate child and heir, for a handfast marriage was valid while it lasted. She had, after all, expected something like this. A fine, vigorous man like Lachlan . . . But only his heir till she had a babe of her own. Well; that would be as soon as she could manage it.

She felt a hot urge to strangle the child, but controlled herself. No. Better to be good to him—be specially good to him. It would put her husband in her debt. And he was a fine wee lad. She wished he'd stop crying . . . She tucked him carefully into his cradle, smiling, very aware of the warm approval of the women round her, and suddenly found the cradle rocking under her hand. She jumped back with a startled squeak, but Bridhe laughed; and then she saw the little girl who had slipped in under her arm to comfort the baby.

'That's Luch, Elizabeth Roisin,' Bridhe said. So that was to be her by-name—the Rose? Not bad, she thought . . . She had missed some of what Bridhe was saying. This lass had been the first cause of Eachuinn Odhar thinking of an alliance with the Campbells? Dear God, who would ever have thought, looking at the insignificant scrap, that she could affect the world more than a dry leaf? She'd need to get the lass a new dress—she was a fair disgrace . . .

This Marion woman, though. Should she make a fuss? No. Time enough for that later, if need be. Lachlan would be glad of her understanding. It was before he wed her, anyway. And it was the woman had cast him off; she knew him well enough already to realise how much that had hurt his pride. Marion was living in a hut up on the moor. With a little luck, the bitch would die in the winter. Should she stop the lass from taking the food up to her? Again, no. She wanted to be loved for her kindness, and that would spoil her reputation . . .

No, she decided. She'd do nothing. She had nothing to fear from Marion.

By the next evening, she was of a different mind.

A great drive of deer had been organised for the wedding guests. The ghillies had been gathering the herds into the area for days. All the clan from six to sixty were up on the hill before dawn, ready to drive the deer that would help feast them. John and Muriella, who was an excellent archer, were eager to be out at the butts. Elizabeth herself hated exercise, but her husband's company—her husband! she shivered in delight—and escaping the glowers of her mother in the castle were well worth a ten-mile ride. Hector could entertain the countess for her, for this once!

It was a gorgeous golden day. They all shot well; even Elizabeth slew a deer, loosing too high at a stag and accidentally killing a hind beyond it. She accepted their praise, sharing a private smile with her brother, who knew her too well to be fooled. Nobody was killed by a panicked deer or a stray arrow to spoil her happiness. But as they headed triumphantly home, a scree slid under the hooves of Muriella's garron, which fell. When they helped her up, blood was streaming from her face and hands, and although Muriella made little of it, Elizabeth insisted they had to bathe the scrapes.

'There's a hut over there, past those beehives.' John Campbell pointed, and Elizabeth was leading Muriella towards it before Lachlan could stop her. Well, why not? Let Marion be reminded of what she had cast away. The clan held back politely as he swaggered down after the others into the sheltered hollow.

Marion came out of her hut at the noise, straightened, and found herself staring into Lachlan's eyes. She froze, but almost at once gathered herself. She welcomed them politely, sat Muriella down on a stone by the fire, gave her warmed water to clean off the blood. She did not look at Lachlan again. 'I have a little mead, if the lady would care for it?' she offered.

Muriella, more shaken by her fall than she had expected, was glad to sit for a while. 'You are kind,' she said. 'A cup would be most grateful. What is your name, wife, that I may know whom to thank?'

Wife! Marion's face and smile were angelic. 'I am Marion Maclean, lady. They call me Marion Aluinn.'

'And with good reason,' Muriella agreed pleasantly. She whispered to her husband, as Marion stooped gracefully into the hut, 'Did you ever see such beauty? That hair, and those huge eyes! Who is she, Lachlan? Lachlan?'

He blinked, and came to himself with a start. 'Oh—oh, just a lass, Lady Muriella. A witch, some say.' He avoided his wife's eye.

Elizabeth was finding it hard to breathe. Marion Aluinn, in a hut. Dark chestnut hair. And her husband couldn't take his eyes off her. God! Dear God!

Muriella laughed. 'A witch? I could well believe it. Eh, John?'

Her husband smiled, coming back rather more smoothly than Lachlan from his own thoughts. 'She's no more beautiful than yourself, my dear. She's too thin. But if she was dressed and fed—'

'That has been a stylish gown. And a gold chain, in such a poor place!'

Yes. Yes, indeed. And Elizabeth knew who had paid for them.

Politely, Muriella hid her curiosity as Marion returned and offered her a horn cup. 'My, but that's good!' She sipped appreciatively.

Marion refilled it for each of them. She came last to Lachlan, and for the first time since he had startled her raised her head to look him in the face. 'I have but the one cup, sir,' she murmured, 'but you are welcome to share of it.' He flinched. Elizabeth's heart was turning cold. Lachlan was standing quite still, gazing at Marion, who stared right back at him, head high, challenging him. Not another word was spoken, till he tossed back the mead in one gulp.

Noticing the stiffness, Muriella chattered on to cover it. 'Is it not excellent, Elizabeth? It should soon find you a husband, lass!'

It did. Oh, it did. And it may find him for her again. The sweet drink was sticky in Elizabeth's mouth. She swallowed desperately, feeling sick.

Someone touched her hand. She looked up with a start. Her

brother John was smiling warningly down at her. 'Brace yourself, lady of the Campbells!' he murmured. Of course he would know the gossip—he always did. 'Half the Maclean clan is watching.' Tautly, she forced her mouth to smile, her head to lift, her tense shoulders to slacken. He nodded approval. She should have known he would notice, and be there to support her. Her husband —there was no glow now—had clearly forgotten he was wed to her; the link between him and this woman was almost visible.

Slowly Lachlan moved to the side, to where he could see his two wives, one on his left, one to his right. Both looking at him, smiling. One dark, slender, vital, exciting; one mousy, dumpy, childish, politically useful. Oh, Dhia! He knew which one he wanted, then, now, still, always.

Suddenly he relaxed. He was daft! As soon as the Campbells were away, he could have both. He could come up here every day! His wee wife would keep the castle warm for him, down there, and Marion would welcome him up here, for food and warm clothing. And the pleasure of his company, of course! For they both loved him!

He was out of date there. Each of them had loved him. Once.

Marion's great eyes were gleaming. The hook was still in the fish . . .

Elizabeth's solid little spine had stiffened to iron. Not for ever . . .

On the way back, Elizabeth's husband, in high spirits, tried joking with her. Disappointed by her dull response, he moved away to talk to Muriella.

'What will I do?' she asked John, beside her, in an anguished whisper.

'What do you want to do, my dear?'

'Kill him! Kill them both!'

'But not until you are mother of his heir. That's your position safe.'

'But until then? How can I cope?'

He smiled that charming, sardonic smile. 'A nettle stings if you brush it lightly, dear sister. Grasp it firm, you go unharmed. And it can make a good soup, if well cooked.'

She considered, the confusion and anger slowly clearing from her head. 'Aye, John. Aye. And who feels sorry for the nettle?'

'That's my fine sister again!' he approved her. And when her husband cracked another joke, she found she could laugh with the rest.

They didn't notice Farquhar, walking just behind with the hounds, watching them carefully and listening very intently for their half-lost whispers.

Two days later, rather sooner than was polite, Lady Campbell was cold and distant as she and her daughter kissed formal good-bye; Muriella Cawdor was warm and encouraging; John's smile hid a deeper one. Elizabeth saw them off with a sense of loss, and heartfelt relief. She had things to do.

It was nearly noon. She watched her husband and his dallta head off along the path that led to the clachan, and then on beyond it, up to the moor. He might have waited an hour, she thought, and returned briskly to the kitchen just as Luch drifted in for the soup. 'Wait you! Luch, is it not?' Elizabeth's tone was pleasant enough. 'Is that the soup for—' she had more difficulty than she'd expected in saying the name—'for Marion Maclean? I'll come with you.'

There were a good few raised eyebrows as she marched out with the lass. She smiled to herself. There would be more when she came back.

The weather had changed to cold, steady rain. As they tramped up the hill, Elizabeth's hair started to soak and drip down her neck, under her silk-lined hood. She was panting. That dratted child never seemed to hurry, but slipped along like a cloud shadow, faster than you'd expect. At last there was the hut, crouched near its grove of hives. And squatting in what little shelter there was beside the door, just where she'd expected him, Farquhar Neas.

It was no part of her plan to rush in on them. She picked her way gently down to the door, nodded pleasantly to Farquhar and bent under the lintel, to find her husband sitting by the tiny fireplace, watching Marion turn a hare on a spit over it. They looked up, a touch too surprised. She took a deep breath to steady herself. 'God bless the house! May I enter, lass?' The lass was not much older than herself, but not a married woman. Not now.

Luch knelt beside Marion with the soup. With four of them in it, the hut was crowded. Elizabeth, smiling, settled on another rounded stone and stretched her hands to the warmth. They waited warily for her to speak. 'Dhia, the year's coming to its ending at last, I fear. Are you not soaked through, husband?' With the least little stress on 'husband', she leaned forward and wifely felt his shoulder that twitched under her hand.

'What are you doing here, Elizabeth?' he demanded.

'I might be asking you the same thing, my lord.' They stiffened. To giggle would be childish, and spoil it all. 'But I see you're on the same errand as myself.' She gestured towards the roasting hare. 'Charity. Christian kindness. Kind it was of you to bring the lass solid meat in this cold weather. Turn the spit, now, lass, or it will be burning.' She smiled as they relaxed a touch. 'But you must not think it is only to bring you charity that I came. I have a thing to ask you, Marion Maclean.' They tensed again as she paused. 'Your mead. I have to agree with my good-sister that it was exceptional.' She could have laughed at her husband's struggle to hide a strange mixture of emotions.

Marion bowed. 'I thank you, lady. It is the herbs I add. I never told—' she hesitated before making the mistake—'told anyone exactly what they were.' She quirked an eyebrow, starting to enjoy the risks of the moment. 'It seemed to me that it did not please you greatly when you first tasted it.'

Elizabeth shrugged, maliciously apologetic. 'I fear I was paying you little attention. But it was much to my man's taste, I could see.'

At the seeming-innocent jab Lachlan suddenly leaped up, forgetting where he was. He walloped his head on a beam. Lumps of turf thumped down on them and into the fire. Farquhar, listening outside the door, dived in, knife drawn, and was nearly trodden on by his half stunned dallta.

'Dhia, Lachlan Cattanach, it's clumsy you are! You've not hurt your head, have you, my dear? And what are you after, under our feet, Farquhar Neas? Out, now!' Elizabeth chased him back into the wet again with no compunction. 'Lachlan, sit you down again

125

and see have I not got a grand idea. Sit, sit!' He sank down, head awhirl with more than the knock.

Luch fished the worst of the earth from the soup bowl and offered it to Marion, who didn't notice. Her eyes, and Lachlan's, were on the plump, round lass smiling so confidently in the firelight. How could such a guileless young face be anything except honest?. 'That's better. Now. I came all this long way, Marion Maclean, to ask you to be coming back with me to Duart.'

'What?' Lachlan was half-way up again before he remembered and ducked. He looked wary, like Marion; but then he started to think what this might mean for him. His wife, inviting his ex-wife to come live with them! She couldn't know, of course! And she loved him so much, and was so innocent, she didn't dream a beauty like Marion's might draw him away from her. He glanced at her draggled hair beside Marion's flowing curls, and started to grin.

It was just as Elizabeth had expected. She forced kindness into her voice. 'I need you—we need you, Marion, to make our mead and ale as good as yours.'

Lachlan eagerly approved. 'Dhia! Why did I not think of that, then? Elizabeth, it's a fine suggestion, that!'

'It is my duty and my pleasure to attend to your welfare, husband,' she smiled. 'I hope to take care of you thoroughly.'

'I'm sure you will, my dear!' he praised her. She smiled the more as he preened and kissed her hand gallantly. The conceit of the man!

Marion was studying Elizabeth carefully. To give herself time to think, she dribbled some sea water onto the hare from a half-pot, lifted thankfully from the clachan rubbish heaps; and looked at it and round the hut afresh. Dhia, was this what she was reduced to? Two months of cold, loneliness and hunger had changed her, and not just by making her thinner. She was harder, and more self-controlled. She could wait for her vengeance. She'd do almost anything to get away from here, especially with winter coming in. But what was in the mind of this fat wee lass? More than mead, for sure.

Elizabeth was smiling at Lachlan. Something—some wryness in her lip—caught Marion's attention. That was no look of innocence or ignorance. The little wife knew exactly what she was doing. Jealousy, then. Hurt pride. So why invite her into the castle? To push her down the cliff? It could be, so. She'd need to be careful. But she could maybe turn Elizabeth against her husband. The two of them could even end up working together against Lachlan. That would be a good joke! And then ... Anyone could fall from a cliff, even great ladies ...

If she'd known, little turning was needed.

Within two breaths, Marion made up her mind. Whatever the Campbell lass planned, she was too young, soft, inexperienced. Marion could match her! She smiled sweetly at Elizabeth. 'My lady, it's happy I'll be to accept your gracious offer.' Lachlan's smug look spread her lovely smile even wider. 'May I invite you and your lord to share my meat with me before we leave?' She waved a hand round the bare hut. 'As you'll see, it's a great pile of belongings I have to carry with me, and the hare can travel easier inside than outside us.'

They all laughed heartily. Every one satisfied, and looking forward eagerly to future developments, they cut up the hare and called Farquhar in.

He had been listening carefully. What in the devil's name was the Campbell lass up to? And her speaking so close with her brother, just after she'd seen Marion the first time! As he knelt down by the fire with a hare leg to gnaw, Farquhar Neas studied her again. And Marion. They were each one plotting something against his dallta, he'd swear it. Lachlan would heed no warning, of course. He thought he was irresistible. Always had. No, it was for himself to protect his dallta, as usual. And that he'd do.

An odd thought came to each one of the four as they chewed; they were sharing a meal, eating meat and salt together. By the laws of hospitality, they should be bound by the strictest rules of honour, custom, decency, each one to help and preserve and defend all the others.

And each of them smiled, publicly and privately, and looked at the rest, and thought what fools they were.

Luch drank the soup.

The Birth of an Heir

'Didn't I tell her myself, Eachuinn, who Marion is!' Old Bridhe was distressed. 'Why should Elizabeth Roisin be asking her to come here?'

'Never fret yourself, Bridhe!' Hector was laughing on his stool beside his grandfather's chair. He was in better spirits and colour now, for he had been out walking several times with Luch since she had gently persuaded him to dress and go to the wedding. 'I'm thinking your rose-like Elizabeth has a right sharp thorn or two. We'd best be remembering she's a Campbell, so she's not born a fool. She knows what she's at, whatever it is. It's in my mind, grandfather, that Lachlan may rue the day he called in on Marion Aluinn again!'

'But why—

'Leave it, Bridhe!' Eachuinn Odhar's voice, though weak, was firm. He was sitting by the window, wrapped in his great plaid, his head twisted to one side to ease the wound in his neck. David Beaton poulticed it every time he could get the old man to stay at peace long enough, but as soon as it started to heal Eachuinn would be up and about, restless, until the deep puncture festered and broke out again. 'Leave it, now, I say! The lass has set her hand to something. We'll find out soon enough what it is. If she expects you to treat that bitch politely, then you'll do it.'

'Polite!' Bridhe spat into the rushes. 'I'll be polite. There's nothing more cutting than politeness, if it's used right! But how will Lachlan handle a wife that knows what he's at, and has a great clan of powerful relations at her call if she's ill done by, then?'

'I've warned him I'll give Argyll his head on a plate if he causes any trouble.' Eachuinn Odhar plucked absently at his bandage.

The thought came to them all; 'While you live, Duart!'

Hector broke the silence. 'It should be interesting to see!' he commented.

His grandfather sighed with silent, deep relief. Ten days before, the lad couldn't have said that. And he was clean and tidy now, and civil, and could even crack a joke. It was the wee lass had changed him somehow, God bless her.

In ten angular jerks and a trip Ranald rose from his seat in the corner by Luch to open the door for Lady Bridhe to leave. Nodding her thanks, Bridhe asked, 'How is Ruari doing, then, Ranald? Is he up and about yet? Good, so.'

Hector grinned. 'He's fine now, Bridhe. We visited him yesterday. You'll mind it was pouring rain? Ranald was first in the door, the water fair drip-dripping off him, and shakes himself like a dog. The water sprays off him that his mother's screaming at him for soaking us all. 'D'you think it might be raining soon?' he says.' Ranald grinned sheepishly as they all laughed.

Luch smiled, and Bridhe saw her. 'Well, lassie! And are you happy that you've no need now to be traipsing away up the moor every noon-tide, eh?'

Luch considered, as she always did, and slowly nodded.

Bridhe patted her gently on the head. 'Aye, you're a kind lass. You're still carrying your baby, I see. Is he well?' Luch gathered her bundle in more carefully and nodded again. 'Will you come then and get a cup of milk for him?' It was a game in the bower, for the cup would be returned empty after a while, but no-one ever saw where the milk went. Luch looked over at Hector for his smile before bowing grave thanks.

Entering the bower, Bridhe stiffened as she felt the resentful hush. Marion was kneeling by the cradles, hugging her son, tears rolling down her face. Elizabeth, watching, felt an unexpected sympathy for her, remembering how she had felt herself, with baby Alan in her arms and him not even hers. But the other women noted that Marion's face was unbroken by her weeping.

Elizabeth glanced up. 'Lady Bridhe! I have been wondering where Marion Aluinn could sleep.' One eyebrow lifted to quell a snigger. Her face, still chubby with puppy-fat, was unexpectedly stern and demanded equal seriousness from all of them. 'I wish her to sleep in here to tend her child. Will you see to it? She can share a mattress with one or two of the others.'

Bridhe realised that Hector was quite right; the Campbell lassie was no fool. 'I'll do that and welcome, Elizabeth Roisin.' She looked round. 'Jean. And Catriona.' Jean, the toughest and nastiest, nodded grimly; her brother had died at Arivegaig with Catriona's husband. 'Aye. You'll both share now with Alan's mother, over by the cradles.' And she'd not rise and slip out unnoticed!

Marion looked up, the tears still welling beautifully. 'I thank you, Lady Bridhe,' she whispered. 'Your kindness—when I have behaved so badly—'

'Now, Marion Aluinn! You'll not be lonely here,' Elizabeth said briskly. 'And if anyone bothers you, you'll let me know. Anyone at all.' She glanced round. 'All of you note that. You'll keep Marion constant company, and if she is—bothered—' her light voice paused just enough to give the word extra significance —'you will tell me. At once. Whoever it is. You are hearing me?'

Gathering their satisfied nods and muttered agreement, she smiled and whisked out. From malice or revenge those women would stick to Marion tight as nits in her hair. Now she had to let her husband know, oh-so-artlessly, that she had set a guard on Marion that he couldn't break without scandal. And let him—let all of them—think that was all she had had in mind!

As the winter passed, Elizabeth found, rather to her surprise, that marriage agreed very well with her. Seumas Ban and Bridhe ran the household as they had done before. She could order all the alterations her mother had mentioned, but tactfully. At first it went slowly, but in December Luch could tell the bees, warm in their straw wrappings, that an heir was on the way. From then on Elizabeth's whim was law. Wine? Spices? Dishes? Carpets? Silk threads for tapestries? Panelling? Shutters? She could have asked for the moon, and seen the clansmen climb on each other's shoulders to reach it down for her. Hugh—poor Hugh—was seldom thought of. She had a fine, strong man, power that she'd never had before, respect and position as Lady of Duart. And she specially enjoyed the extra malicious thrill of her husband's frustration.

Marion worked hard. Whenever she was free from the brewing she hurried up to the bower to spin with the other women. She never tried to escape from their constant supervision, avoided both Lachlan and Farquhar like lepers, took sly slaps and pinches in silence, made much of loving her son, and could, they discovered, tell a story to make a corpse laugh. Slowly, in spite of their enmity, the women of the castle let her make a place for herself among them.

She became Elizabeth's companion, rather than servant, to their mutual surprise. They sat often at their sewing, discussing mead and medicines and men. As they laughed together, enjoying the unexpected sharp play of minds, their liking deepened. Not to friendship; each knew that the other would see her dead without a qualm; but to respect and a queer, unstated confederacy. Although they never spoke directly of Lachlan, each knew the other's mind; though not as well as she believed.

Marion even helped Elizabeth gain a touch of style. She turned her from pink to soft blue and grey-green and gold, to the satisfaction of everyone with an eye for colour. She brushed the girl's long, rough locks five hundred times, morning and evening, till they started to shine, uncomplaining when her arm ached. It was hard, but better than the hut.

Her greatest pleasure was to pass near Lachlan, see his deep breath and his head turning to follow her, and retire as if unnoticing, straight to the company of his wife. Whenever Lachlan sought Marion, he always found both of them, close as praying hands, murmuring together, and raising their heads to smile sweetly at his frustration.

Once, he ordered Marion to come with him; Elizabeth set a hand on her wrist to detain her. 'But I need her here, husband. I am sending some recipes to my father, the Earl of Argyll,' to remind him. 'Marion is helping me. Have you any message I may pass on to him?'

What would Argyll do? Maybe nothing, but . . . Marion Aluinn was not—not quite—worth the risk. He whirled away, not looking back. He'd done so once, and seen them writhing in silent laughter. He never turned again.

The situation he found himself in was a source of much amusement to the rest of the clan too, but also considerable tension, for a frustrated Lachlan Cattanach was an unchancy man to encounter. Not a few men lost teeth because they had met the big man at the wrong moment. And that winter, if Eachuinn Odhar was sick and Lachlan was judge, the accused quailed. A many men were hanged who other years might have escaped with only a whipping.

Hector spent the winter learning how to cope with his blindness. He had a staff, long and slender, to aid his unsteady feet, and Luch and Ranald never left him. He walked and walked, in fair and foul weather, pretending that he was training the young hounds to stay at heel; and did so. But his real reason was that he was blind; he was crippled in a land where a man's worth was judged mainly by his physical ability.

He had some pleasures. He enjoyed handling Glic's pups, that Luch, alone in the castle, was allowed to lift from their dam's teats and set warm and wriggling in his hands while they were as blind as he was himself. He studied with Father Patrick. With Donald Crubach's help, he played the harp and sang, and started again to compose songs and poems. Elizabeth, and Marion of course, heard him practise, and were kind enough and wise enough not to admire too uncritically, but to give fair, helpful comments. He played in the hall some evenings, and took pride in their applause. He was naturally unaware of Lachlan's scowls. Elizabeth and Marion delighted in them.

But often, away up alone on the moor, Hector would break from Luch's hand and run across the rough ground till his blind feet tripped and he fell crashing, to lie striking his face and fists against the rock, snow or heather, screaming in despair and hatred and cursing Lachlan, Farquhar, Elizabeth, Marion, his grandfather, Ranald, Luch, the whole world; and himself most of all.

Luch, of course, told nobody about these hour-long outbursts; except the bees. More than once, though, she slipped in close and slid his dirk from its sheath, in case he should use it against himself. If anyone came near, Ranald would wave them away. The clan quickly learned what he meant, and in pity and love allowed Hector privacy for his lonely suffering.

The children helped him find a better cure, too.

Ruari's work started again in March. Most of the over-wintered hives had survived, with the help of bread soaked in ale every couple of weeks, and now they were unwrapped, one or two at a time in case of a late frost, and set up in sheltered corners. Ruari had recovered well, but tired easily and needed help even more than before. Mairi complained, wishing that Ranald was still at home, and Ranald repeated the need to Hector; who thought about it, and then started to come down himself with the youngsters. The new interest gave him the en-couragement of success, to help him over the worst of his terrible despairs. He learned quickly with his sharpened hearing to distin-guish the exact hum that said a hive was too hot, or near swarm-ing. And facing the fear of the bees helped prove to himself that he was still a man.

Eachuinn Odhar had his ups and downs, but more downs than ups. It was Lachlan Cattanach who started the Beltane fire for Clan Gillian that Mayday, and later, in the sacrifices of ale and blood to the old gods of the sea and the fields, Lachlan led the clan again. The chief was slipping steadily away.

Lachlan travelled widely that spring, trying to escape Marion's poisoned sweetness. Building a new lymphad; hunting; fighting —a wee private raid or two for cattle from the Camerons, nothing serious; other girls; even whisky by the barrel could not blot her out of his mind.

'Lachlan Cattanach,' Farquhar said sternly one day, 'will you for God's sake be either forgetting the lass, or letting me carry her away up the hill for you? If she just vanishes, Elizabeth Roisin can say what she likes, but there's nothing she can do! If I'm caught, I'll say I was lifting her for myself.'

The new galley was sailing into the Sound of Mull after its sea trial. Lachlan himself was handling the thick steering oar with casual strength, hauling steadily to keep the lymphad's head straight across the wind. The shipmaster was down by the mast, ready to lower the cross-spar with its square sail, and the crew were flexing their muscles and setting oars in the rowlocks to slide out for the turn up against the wind into Duart Bay.

'Don't tempt me!' Lachlan muttered. 'She'd find out, and she'd cry insult to her father. And my own father, damnation take him, he'd not support me. The old man's lost all his spirit this last year.'

Farquhar sneered at him. 'He's not alone, then, Lachlan Cattanach! For what would you have done this time last year if a lass had been held back from you like this? Dhia, every girl's fair throwing herself at you from Ardgour to Jura. Why make such a fool of yourself over this one? These two! I have to tell you, my heart, the whole clan's laughing at you, mooning about like a weaner calf seeking its dam.'

'Laughing!' The thick steering oar bent as Lachlan heaved angrily at it. It was the truth, and he could not stand it. 'Let me see them laugh, just—' The sailing master called up to him to take care, but he paid no heed.

'It's not likely that you will see them, for who would be foolish enough to be laughing before your eyes? Or mine? It's behind our backs I'm hearing the sniggers. You do not do me justice, my dallta, for what you do reflects on me also, and they laugh at me with you because you let a wee Campbell lassie put a petticoat on you!'

With a roar, Lachlan let go the rudder and leaped at Farquhar. They crashed from the raised platform at the stern, down among the feet of the rowers who hastily jumped out of their way. The shipmaster raced to grab the rudder as the ship swung broadside-on to the swirl of the tide, shouting to his men to hold the ropes, but they were distracted by the fight and the sudden tilt of the deck, and lost their grip. The spar and sail clattered down, burying under the heavy red canvas both the sailors and the men fighting.

By the time the shipmaster had practically blasted the sail off them with his cursing, the tide was carrying the lymphad sideways up into the mouth of the Sound. Oars were thrust out, and the ship got under control. The brawl was not. Lachlan was still snarling and kicking when they uncovered him, and they nearly broke his fingers trying to unfasten them from Farquhar's neck.

'Lachlan Cattanach!' The shipmaster's bellow and a wallop on the head from a daring sailor finally pierced the berserk rage. 'Will you let go, now, or you'll kill him! Your dallta! Your milk-brother, you great fool! Let go!'

The big man suddenly collapsed like a wet parchment. He and Farquhar sat on the deck side by side, panting and groaning. Deep sobs were shaking Lachlan, and abuptly he swung round to clasp Farquhar in his arms, the tears streaming down into his beard. 'Farquhar! My heart! I near killed you! Pray you forgive me!' He held his foster-brother away from him to get a good look at him. 'Speak to me, then, Farquhar! Tell me you're not dead!'

'Leave me get a breath of air, and I'll do that!' Farquhar croaked. He coughed painfully, and swallowed with care. 'Dhia! You've a grip like the father and mother of all lobsters, Lachlan Cattanach! But kill me—never, my heart!' He was more upset at having caused this worry to Lachlan than at the near-strangling; and it hadn't once ocurred to him to draw his dirk to save himself.

Lachlan rolled to his feet. 'Duncan Rua! Why did you not stop me?'

His shipmaster was too angry to be daunted. 'Stop you, is it?' he roared, his hair less red than his face. 'Tell me how a man can stop you, so, and you in your rage! Dhia, you near sent us all to our deaths! Look you there, Lachlan Cattanach!' Only a few feet from the side of the ship a sucking swirl dimpled the water ominously. 'Was I the fool who let go of the rudder when the ship was on top of the rock there? If the wind had been stronger or the tide just a touch faster it's broken on it we'd be this minute! Will you make a habit of running your galleys on the rocks, then? For if so, you can be finding yourself another shipmaster, for it's not me that will stand responsible for your mistakes! Do that to me again, Lachlan Cattanach, and I'll heave you overboard!'

Lachlan was near heaving the shipmaster overboard, but he knew he'd been wrong. He must control himself! He could not bring himself to apologise. Instead, he tried to make a joke of it. 'Will you so, Duncan Rua? And yourself dead with me, then, for killing your chief!'

'Hah!' Duncan Rua snorted. 'Not my chief yet! And I'll not kill you! I'll maroon you on the rock there at low tide, for the waves rising to take you! Two fathoms deep it is at high water. And it wouldn't be me, so, that killed you, but God himself, for if he wanted you alive, sure he'd hold back the tide for you like Moses and the Red Sea!'

Farquhar staggered to his feet to attack, but Lachlan held him back. He put a supporting arm round Farquhar's shoulders and grinned at the men rowing only hard enough to hold the ship steady. 'Do you expect God to hold back the tide for us to float here all day, then, or do we turn in to Duart?' And knowing he'd gone a bit too far, and glad enough, now his fright and anger were fading, to have faced down Lachlan's temper and Farquhar's knife unharmed, Duncan Rua was satisfied to grin back, and turn aside to work the ship.

In July young Catriona was wed again, and she took her child to her new home with her. To everyone's relief, including his mother's though she never said so, Marion's year-old Alan was taken off by his fostermother to be reared at her father's home in Killundine. In the suddenly-peaceful bower, Elizabeth looked the old cradles over carefully.

'They're too small,' she stated firmly at supper that evening. 'One will do fine for his dallta, Lachlan, but I'll have a new one made for your heir. A fine big one, of oak, with a carved band on it to say "Dominus mecum, dominus sum".'

'Eh?' Lachlan spat out some gristle, and wiped his beard on his sleeve. Elizabeth sighed gustily at his table manners—or lack of them.

'If the Lord is with me, I am the lord,' Hector translated. 'I'd not wish to argue, Elizabeth Roisin, and we ourselves know that the Macleans sit on the left hand of God Himself, but Abbot Kenneth could be objecting that a claim to actually be the Lord sounds a touch excessive.'

'And what does he know about babies? Or about the Macleans, either?'

'Or about the Campbells, then?' her husband sneered. 'Is the Maclean motto not good enough for you, that you must needs be inventing one?'

Elizabeth frowned. Then she saw Lachlan flush, Hector's mouth twitch and eyes all down the tables exchange glances. 'What is it? I don't just recall—'

'Virtue Mine Honour.' Bridhe's voice was dry. Marion,

sitting where both Elizabeth and Lachlan could see her well, bit her tongue not to laugh.

'Ah.' Elizabeth sat back against her cushions. 'You are right, husband. That is what I should have chosen from the start "Virtue Mine Honour". Of course! How suitable! I thank you for setting me right, my dear.'

Eachuinn Odhar started to laugh. He wasn't often out of his bed now, and David Beaton had said privately to Bridhe that it was only determination to see the baby born that was keeping the old man alive. But now, propped in his high-backed chair, he cackled with a malicious glee. '"Virtue Mine Honour", eh? It suits you, Lachlan! Heh, heh!' He stopped, coughing harshly, but as he sipped at the medicine Master Beaton held to his lips he was still grinning.

Angrily Lachlan turned on Hector. 'Well, master scholar! Hector Odhar, they're calling you now, I'm told, for that you can scarcely be called swift, nor my father brown, with his wisps of hair like dandruff! Sing to us now, some of your Latin, maybe, and give us the benefit of your great learning!'

To keep the fragile peace Hector agreed. Ranald fetched his harp, and he sang a story of a great selkie, one of the seal people, who loved a land maiden but warned her that if she took their son away from him, the baby would kill him when he grew up; but in fear that her child would become a wild selkie himself she stole the baby and reared him inland as a normal man. His selkie blood called him back to the sea, though, and he became a sailor. And one day he came across a huge seal and killed it, never knowing that it was his own father in his seal form.

As the clan clapped Hector's fine performance, Lachlan cast glowering looks at both Elizabeth and Marion Aluinn. One had already borne him a son; one would do so soon. But neither of these brats would kill him!

On a hot August night, Elizabeth gave birth to her baby. It was an easy birth, for a first time. As Hector had judged, she was the right shape for it.

Bridhe lifted the baby, slipped a magic coral and rowan-berry necklace over his head and walked sun-wise round the bed three times for good fortune, before taking the child down to the hall to present him to his father, to Eachuinn Odhar and the clansmen assembled. 'It is a boy child, whole and healthy, Duart!' she announced proudly.

The old man, propped in his chair for the first time in over a month, laid a trembling hand on the babe's head. He turned his eyes to Donald Crubach. 'Declare for me,' he whispered, 'this is Eachuinn Mac Lachlan Mac Eachuinn Maclean. I accept him as heir of his father after me to Clan Gillian.'

As the bard repeated the welcome to the cheering crowd, Lachlan, Hector and all the rest drank to the health of young Eachuinn Og. They gave him his first meal, of bread for the body and purifying salt for the immortal soul, and cheered as his tiny red face puckered at the taste and he yelled lustily. The beacon was lit, and answering bonfires spread the happy news throughout the Maclean lands. There would be feasting for many nights.

Bridhe smiled down at the baby as she panted up the stairs again. 'Come, then, my hero, come and we'll settle you with your milk-mother.'

Eachuinn Odhar closed his watery eyes to shut out the din, smiling dimly. 'I've seen him, I can rest . . . Damn Lachlan . . .'

Elizabeth lay in her bed, tired and sore and feeling astonishingly energetic, smiling up at Marion who was brushing out her hair. 'I am mother of the heir . . .' She started mentally composing a letter to her brother.

Marion smiled sweetly down at her, glanced across at Alan's old cradle, and thought, 'Now it comes, my lady, eh? Well, we'll see . . .'

Three days later Abbot Kenneth himself christened the baby.

At the feast that night, Eachuinn Odhar lay back in his chair and shocked them all. 'Father Abbot, it's not worth your while going back to Iona now. For in a day or two days you'd just be returning the weary road for the funeral mass.' They all glanced at each other in dismay. The Maclean was laughing at them. 'Don't look so mournful! I've had a good long life—well, a long life, eh, Father Kenneth?—and I'm not right done yet. I'm going to see to it that my sending-off is as I want it. There's not many Maclean chiefs have had the chance!'

Within an hour his bed was moved down to the hall, so that

everything was under his own eye. He had them set up his bier at the end of the hall, draped in black velvet, and its handles tasselled in black and gold. The black velvet canopy hung above it had to be renewed. 'Hell mend all moths!' His great oak coffin that had been ready for him for years was set up like a cupboard at the head of the bier, fresh lined with red and gold damask, its silver handles polished bright. 'You'll use my wolfskin coverlet for mortcloth. I killed the wolves myself in my young days. Bridhe, put a black fringe on it for me.'

His armour was polished. 'Sharpen that claymore, you idiot! I'll not have any man say I was ever afraid of a sharp edge in my life!' The Maclean coat of arms was repainted on the funeral banners and his shield. His best red velvet saddlecloth was re-embroidered with gold thread. 'Aye, it'll be a grand show!'

'David Beaton! Have you oils and spices for my embalming? You'll need plenty, this time of year, or I'll stink out the hall. Ranald, tell Ruari to bring up sixty pounds of wax for black candles, and for the cerecloth. And he's not to leave a bee-sting in it to prick me!'

The Maclean tomb at Kilpatrick was cleared of leaves and rubbish. His father's body that had lain in the great lead-lined stone coffin there for forty years was reverently removed and buried below the flagstones inside the chapel, which was hung with black, and the old man was told that all was ready for him. 'Huh! I should hope so! What else does the priest get paid for?'

He called up Mairi Ban and her friends from the clachan, to rehearse the coronach, the song of praise and mourning that would follow his coffin. 'Louder, wives! Sing out! It's not you had an arrow in your throats!'

'Seumas Ban! How much black cloth have you? Dhia, that'll never drape the mourners and the flags, let alone the hall and the kirk. Get another five—no, six hundred ells. Not silk, though— I'll have no skimping, but there's no need to be outrageous.'

His shroud of silver brocade, one of the pair that had been his wife's first task after their wedding, was aired. 'Fine work Margaret aye did. I'll see her soon. And Lachlan's mother too. God help me between them, eh?'

Bridhe and Seamus Ban consulted him about the amount of

drink that would be needed, and were told to double it. 'My lykewake's to last ten days, mind, and if there's not a good fight or two, I'll be back to haunt you!'

There was a constant stream of visitors. 'Come to pay your last respects? Can I take a message to your late wife, eh?' David Beaton, shaking his head, said that the interest was keeping him alive, and his mind was clear.

Lachlan Cattanach's was not. His father was dying, and he himself on the very point of becoming chief of Clan Gillian. He had two fine sons. When he was Maclean of Duart, no-one could keep Marion from him any longer. He had every reason to be happy. And yet ... Somehow, in those last three days, the loathing he'd developed for his father faded. The old man, facing his death with such courage and dry humour, deserved respect. Or even love, maybe.

At the last, Marion and Elizabeth brought their babies for the old man to bless. Abbot Kenneth exchanged a wry glance with Father Patrick at Eachuinn Odhar's words. 'I give you my blessing both, bairns. And what good it may bring you God alone knows!' To the young women kneeling by his bedside he spoke seriously and kindly. 'Elizabeth Roisin, Marion Aluinn. I have the same word for each of you. When I'm gone, just mind you, in your scheming, that neither of you, nor Lachlan, is a fool. God keep you in mind of your souls as well as your bodies.' As they rose and stepped back, they both were surprised to find their eyes pricking.

'Hector.' The painful tears seeped slowly from Hector's bandage, and his grandfather reached out a trembling hand to wipe them away. 'No weeping, so! Now take care of that wee lassie Luch. It's in my mind she's of greater importance than she seems. God preserve you, my dear, dear lad.'

'God save you, grandfather,' Hector choked.

'Maybe, man, but he's left it a bit late, eh?'

The old man beckoned Lachlan last. He was very weak, but the spark was still in him. 'Lachlan. What the devil can I say to you I've not said before?'

The big man snorted with sudden laughter. 'Your blessing, father?'

140

'Oh, aye, you can have that and welcome, for what it's worth. I've no doubt you'll need it sore, with two women in your house. No, I'll offer you no advice, for you'd rather be damned than heed it.' He drew a deep, gasping sigh. 'Man, do you know what I'm thinking? There's a grand bit ham I can see on the tables down there. I could be doing fine with a wee taste of it.'

Abbot Kenneth's praying hesitated for a second. He stopped altogether as Lachlan solemnly shook his head. 'No, no, father, we can't be cutting into that ham. That's for the lykewake.'

Father and son exchanged looks, in better temper with each other than they'd been for years. Together they started to laugh, the deep chuckle and the dry whispery cackle rolling past the monks, who returned with a start to their praying; past Bridhe, Elizabeth, Marion, Hector and his young attendants, the women, clan officers, nephews, cousins, clansmen great and common, clustered weeping at the death-bed of the man who had been chief for the whole life-time of most of them.

And then only the chuckle was left.

A New Chief

Salt, bread, and a green turf were placed on Eachuinn Odhar's breast, and his hands clasped on his claymore hilt over the wolf-skin coverlet. The whole hall was hung with black cloth, the window slits covered, and the flicker of the torchflames and the black candles round the bier the only light.

The clan were greeted and offered hospitality in silence, till at sunset the lykewake started. Lady Bridhe, weeping, led the first dance with Lachlan. Slow Donald Crubach harped and fast, sad and merry, guiding the dead man's soul from this world to the next, ten nights from nightfall till dawn, the clan dancing and singing, giving thanks for their chief's life, lamenting his death, and rejoicing that they survived.

Eachuinn Odhar's ghost had no reason to return in disappoint-ment. There were several fights, and a man danced drunken off the cliff to his death.

John Campbell of Cawdor arrived, to be met by Lachlan and Elizabeth in front of the bier. Bowing, he greeted Lachlan form-ally. 'Duart!'

Suddenly, for the first time, the reality of the title flowered in Lachlan's heart. In the dark hall he almost glowed in exultation.

'My father, Archibald Campbell of Inveraray, Chief of Clan Diarmaid, Earl of Argyll, Lord Lieutenant of the Isles, regrets that by reason of attendance on King James he cannot come himself, but sends his condolences to yourself and your clan. Eachuinn Mac Lachlan Maclean was a man of excellence, a hero, fit heir to his heroic father . . .' The eulogy was long and flowery, as was expected.

He moved to happier things. 'Argyll congratulates you on the birth of your son and heir.' Lachlan's smile did not flicker; Elizabeth's position must be secure. Lady Campbell had sent some satin for Elizabeth. Pink. For Lachlan, there was a quarter falcon, and for Eachuinn Og a silver rattle and a handgun, heavier than the baby himself. 'But he'll grow into it, Duart!'

Lachlan, busy admiring his little cannon, nodded. 'Convey my thanks to Argyll for his princely gifts!' Proudly he put out a foot to the rockers of the new cradle, and the baby awoke and started to yell lustily. As one, the men rubbed the back of their necks in dismay. Elizabeth nodded to her women to pick up the cradle, and took the chance to leave them to their talk.

'Men!' Bridhe laughed, yawning as they returned to the bower. Elizabeth beckoned to Margaret, the wetnurse, who set down her own baby in the old cradle and soon had young Eachuinn feeding quietly. Bridhe smiled. 'Aye, he's taken to you, Margaret. And your Calum's a fine laddie. They'll do well together.' She sighed. 'I'm for my bed. And you too, lass. We need sleep, or we'll never dance this night through.' She looked sideways at Elizabeth. 'Marion stayed down in the hall.'

Elizabeth nodded absently, her eyes warm on her son. Then she realised what Bridhe had said. Marion. Yes. It was starting now . . .

Eachuinn Odhar's funeral was not shamed by drunkenness; at least, nobody dropped the coffin. Lachlan and Hector led the procession of three thousand black-cloaked mourners down to the chapel and three times sunwards round it to keep the chief's spirit safe in his grave, while the women wailed the coronach.

That night, at the funeral feast, Elizabeth's eyes slid aside under lowered lids. During the last ten days, the watch over Marion Aluinn had had to be relaxed. There she sat, in her usual seat, never lifting her eyes towards Lachlan and his wife and their guests at the high table, but smiling secretly, more like the cat that stole the cream than ever, and Lachlan was fairly radiating satisfaction. 'Aye, I thought so,' Elizabeth said to herself. 'The pair of you have met, and you're making your own plans. Well. So am I, my dears.' She was especially attentive to her husband, under Farquhar's twisted smile.

John Campbell leaned forward to speak to Elizabeth. 'Sister,' he said kindly, his eyes gleaming, 'You look tired. Paler than usual.'

She followed his lead. 'I do feel wearied, John. But then, with so much worry so soon after the birth of my son, it's only to be expected.'

'Muriella told me to offer you this tonic, which she herself has found excellent. One drop each day, in water or wine, will help you recover your strength. She warns you against taking more. It is most powerful.' As he handed Ranald the brown bottle to give to her, he wondered just what she was planning to do with the potion. Was it for Lachlan? Or Marion? Or both? Quite a lass, his wee sister!

Elizabeth controlled her expression with some difficulty. She'd not expected this! But yes, it was sense. They'd all heard, including Marion, that it was dangerous, and that she'd not asked for it. Oh, clever brother!

Suddenly inspiration came to her. She remembered the old man's warning; if she actually killed Lachlan, or Marion, with John's 'tonic', her soul was damned. But if she only tricked Marion into thinking she planned to; and if Marion then accused her of attempted murder, and she proved the accusation was false; then surely Lachlan would have to cast Marion out! Or kill her! Her own conscience would be clear, and her soul safe. How Lachlan would suffer! And with all done so openly now, no-one could suspect her of plotting anything.

She missed the tilt of Farquhar's head, and Marion's, like cats hearing a mouse scratching. They'd had the same thought; a tonic? Dangerous? I wonder . . .

Next day, Lachlan Cattanach was installed as chief of Clan Gillian. On the ancient sacred stone in the hills he stood alone, small but not insignificant in a white tunic among the riot of colourful banners and plaids. The sennachie recited his ancestry, proving his claim to the Chiefship. Then, exalted and over-whelmed by the majesty of the occasion, in unexpected humility, absolute pride, total sincerity, Lachlan took his oath before the whole clan; 'I promise, here in the place of my father and his fathers, that as they were so I will be; a loving father to Clan Gillian, a faithful and just leader in all things.'

Three days later, while the women were all up on the battle-ments with Elizabeth, waving farewell to her brother's galley, Marion slipped away, combed her hair, smoothed her best green dress and ran down to meet Lachlan returning from the shore. In the middle of the yard, before all his men, he swept her up in his great arms, hugging and kissing her. 'Marion! Thank God he's gone! Dhia, I've hungered for you, lassie!'

Luch, leading Hector up just behind him, stopped dead at the sudden fierceness of the grip on her shoulder.

'Careful!' Marion scolded, laughing. 'Mind my gown!'

'To hell with your gown, lass! And to hell with care, too! I've held back far too long!' He was shouting, holding her high against his chest.

'But your wife—'

'I've told you, I'll not set her aside. I'll not start a war over you with the Campbells. But she'll not care now she has a babe to occupy her. She'd better not!' He laughed, triumphantly, in the laughing crowd round them.

She pretended annoyance. 'Will you put me down, you great bear!' He tossed her higher. 'Lachlan! What do you mean by me, then? Am I to be your mistress?'

'Why not? No more brewing, eh? You get on well enough with her. Let her take you as a maid of honour—maid of honour! That's good, eh? But I'll see you have your own room. Aye, and your own maid! I'll keep you both happy!'

Hector came to himself. 'Luch, up to the bower! Hurry! Ran-ald, run, tell Seumas Ban to offer them wine, keep them in the hall till I warn Elizabeth!'

The bower women flocked excitedly round their mistress, ex-claiming, sympathising, swearing to tear Marion's eyes out, but she cut them short. 'If any one of you as much as lifts an eyebrow at Marion, she'll be out of here before she can lower it. If it is for anyone to object to Duart's—arrangements, it is for me; and if I say nothing, then neither will you.'

'But the insult—' Bridhe began. 'Do you not care, then, Elizabeth Roisin?'

Elizabeth's stare scorched the old lady to silence. 'I am still mistress here. Marion Aluinn is—is a guest. Show loyalty to me by obeying me, and not her. If she gives you any order, tell her—politely, mind!—that you will ask if it is my will.' She sighed, rather theatrically. 'I fear it aye will be, but we can make the gesture.' They nodded agreement, muttering their support. 'She will be treated with polite respect. Mind me, now! Thank you, Hector Odhar; pray you send me Seumas Ban. I also have arrangements to make.'

When Marion followed Lachlan into the bower a little later, half defensive, half smugly triumphant, no-one leaped at them to scream abuse, or complain, or toady. The spinning and weaving and gossiping seemed to be going on as usual. The pair exchanged glances, taken aback. They must know, surely?

Elizabeth looked up smiling from the window seat where the two lasses had so often gossiped over their stitchery. 'Marion! I've been waiting to see you! Husband, a word before you go out, if you will!'

They walked warily down the bower, seeing now the determination with which everyone was being absolutely normal. A hush grew; all ears turned to the window. Marion's eyes met Elizabeth's in open challenge for the first time. 'Lady, my lord Lachlan Cattanach wishes me to have a room of my own—'

'And I'll have no argument from you, Elizabeth Campbell—'

'It is done, Marion Aluinn.' Elizabeth's voice was angelically gentle, but it stopped Lachlan better than a shout. 'My husband and I have moved into the great bedroom, as is fitting. I've told my own maid to prepare our old room for you, and attend you there. And from now on I wish you to join my husband and myself at the high table. A chair has been set for you, on his left side.'

It took their breath away.

As Lachlan hauled his jaw off the floor, Elizabeth turned to him. 'I am weary, husband, and busied with our son. I fear I cannot see to your comfort as a wife should. While I am unwell, I thought you might perhaps find pleasure in the company of Marion Maclean. She has been most useful to me these past months. I pray you do not deny me, but allow her to attend you in my place.'

There was a stifled snort of laughter as the women saw what Elizabeth was doing. All the signs of favour Marion had been planning to demand were already provided; a generous, charming gesture to a lowly servant lass from the Lady of Duart, rather than hated tribute dragged in triumph from a defeated rival.

Lachlan stared at his wife for a long minute. She bore his gaze fully, smiling up at him, blandly enquiring. 'Does it displease you, my lord?'

He was almost lost for words. He had been ready, almost eager, for a screaming match, to insist, to shout, to beat her if necessary. Slowly, though, he also understood. Saving her dignity—well, why not? He eased his shoulders, slightly disappointed not to have had the grand row, slightly peeved that she wasn't going to fight over him, but also relieved. 'Aye, well. No, I'll not object.' He cleared his throat. Dhia, there was more to this lass than he'd thought! She even looked better than he remembered.

His two wives smiled at one another, slanting hazel eyes meeting round, innocent blue like a silent clash of swords. Marion's lips were twitching, in spite of her fine triumph being spoiled. 'Dhia reward your generosity as it deserves, lady,' she whispered. 'I shall attend your lord most willingly.'

'I'm sure you will, Marion. I promise, I am not finished with you yet.'

Lachlan was grinning at them. 'Dhia, I'm a lucky man, that has two such beauties!' he beamed. He sensed an awkwardness in the air, but well, it was only to be expected. When two women had to share a man they both loved, there was bound to be a bit of roughness till things settled down. Better leave them to get on with it. Treat them equally, and they'd not be jealous. He kissed his wife's cheek, and Marion's. 'I'll see you both tonight, my dears!'

He strode out, clapping Farquhar on the shoulder as he passed him at the door. 'Come on, man! It's all turned out better than I'd have dreamed!'

147

Following his dallta down the stair, Farquhar sighed in sheer disbelief. The man was so dense whiles, you'd think his head was a pine knot!

Elizabeth suddenly realised she was about to burst. She smiled at Marion. 'Forgive me, Marion, but I must go—' where, for God's sake, to get away from all the eyes?—'to speak to Hector.' She marched out like an invading army.

Marion curtseyed regally and respectfully as she passed; glided after her, paused as the door closed, chuckled at the babble that rose behind it, and sighed in delight, eyes closed, before walking along to her—her own!—room.

Luch was changing Hector's bandage when Elizabeth stormed in, flung herself face down on his bed, bit into his new sealskin coverlet to muffle her screaming curses, and hammered it with her fists as if it was Marion's face. Why didn't certainty of future revenge console her for present insults?

It was half an hour before she could sit up, picking the last hairs from her teeth, her eyes swollen and her skin unattractively mottled red, and tell Hector what she'd done. He was sympathetic and approving. 'Aye, Lachlan could never resist her serpent tongue. I suppose there's nothing else you can do?'

'Little, I fear, Hector.' Elizabeth absently accepted a hot, damp cloth from Luch. 'I'll not risk losing all I have by trying open defiance. I haven't controlled myself to accept what I must, to throw away all power to refuse what I can.' She sighed with pleasure as the cloth soothed her eyelids.

'Have you any?' he asked. 'Power, I mean? Will your father not—'

'My father? Hah!' But he knew nothing of the scenes in Inveraray, of course. 'Father wouldn't lift a finger for me! But while I pretend acceptance, I can stay mistress of Duart, and Marion second to me.' She dried her face on the towel Luch offered, and at last noticed the child. 'Thank you, lass.'

'Be careful, Elizabeth! Your baby Eachuinn Og is the only soul stopping her own lad becoming the next chief.'

She patted his hand reassuringly, pleased that he'd seen it without her having to bring it up. 'I'll watch out, never fear. And with your help—'

148

'Mine?' The young man's laugh was bitter. 'But whatever I can do, I will.'

She looked over at him with real affection. She was quite glad she hadn't married him; he was a nice lad . . . But soft. 'You're too good to me, Hector.'

'No, I swear it. And for Luch. She sees everything, but no-one ever sees her.' He reached a hand out to Luch, who swayed so that his fingers landed on her shoulder. 'Will you swear too, Luch? To help Lady Elizabeth if you can?'

Luch considered long enough for Elizabeth to start frowning. This girl was looking at her as if she could see right down to . . . How dare the dimwit stare like that, as if she had a mind to make up! For the first time, she felt uneasy. Not her brother's sardonic glance, not Marion's sly subtlety, not Farquhar Neas's distrust, certainly not Lachlan's confident stare, disturbed her as much as the wide, unblinking gaze of those large dark eyes. What could she say? Her own eye fell on the brown-shawled bundle by the bed. 'And my child, Luch. My baby. Help him too.'

The relief she felt as Luch finally nodded was quite ridiculous.

From that night on, Lachlan sat at table with a wife on each side of him, relaxed and happy. Elizabeth and Marion smiled too, especially when they caught each other's eye. The women supported Elizabeth; the men began to cluster again around Marion. Farquhar Neas watched them all carefully.

Elizabeth took the 'tonic', one drop every night in wine. At first she had a slightly upset stomach, but that passed. Marion regularly poured Elizabeth the wine, but never went near the shelf where the tonic was kept. One day while removing the empty cup she dipped a finger into the dregs. Good! She knew the bitter taste. One drop daily cleared the skin. Three drops caused vomiting. Eight drops could kill. Aye, that was it. Elizabeth must be waiting till enough time had passed for folk to grow careless. Then Lachlan, and maybe Marion too, would have an unhappy 'accident'. So clever, the Campbell lass thought herself. But there was a cleverer . . . She must watch out, she told herself; only eat and drink if she was sharing the dish with others.

Marion didn't notice Elizabeth's glance on her as she set her tongue to her finger, nor the tiny smile the Lady of Duart wore for the next few days, even when she wasn't in company.

Halfway through September, Marion decided she must move now, before Elizabeth beat her to it. Lachlan dead, and herself driven out again, wouldn't suit her at all. Elizabeth dead was what she wanted, and Lachlan alive; wed to her for choice, though it didn't matter greatly. Then his heir, that repellent brat Eachuinn, would die too. Babies did, so easily. How tragic! She smiled. And after that, she'd dance at Lachlan's lykewake as soon as she could manage it, assured of her position as mother of the next chief of Clan Gillian.

So one day when the women were heading down for dinner she waited behind. It took only seconds to pour some of the liquid from the brown bottle into one of her own, and refill it to the same level with water. As she stowed her little flask away in her belt pouch and glided swiftly down to enter the hall on the heels of the rest, she imagined dear Elizabeth Roisin's expression when she realised she'd drunk the poison she had meant for her husband!

Eight drops would kill? To make sure, she used half her phial, that same night. It wasn't hard to pour the poison unseen into the cup as she filled it with wine for Elizabeth. No-one paid any attention. She set the cup down by Elizabeth as usual, and retired to her sewing without a backward glance.

At last Elizabeth called for her tonic, and added one drop carefully. With her usual smiling grimace for the bitter taste, she sipped . . . and sipped . . . Marion could scarcely breathe in her excitement.

As the maids began laying out their mattresses for the night, Elizabeth winced and laid a hand to her stomach. At once Marion was eagerly there. 'Is something wrong, Elizabeth Roisin? A pain? You feel sick?'

'No, no, thank you for your kindly care. Something I've eaten, most like.'

All that night, Marion listened for a moan of pain, a cry for help. There was nothing. Next morning, Elizabeth rose as usual, set the maids their tasks, smiled serenely. Marion slapped her maid sore for nothing at all.

What could have gone wrong? The fat wee sow had drunk enough poison to kill a horse, and thought it was something she'd eaten! Dhia, she must have grown used to it, taking a little regularly! Marion bit her fingers in vexation. Oh, why had she waited so long? And there was worse; the next time Elizabeth tasted the tonic, she might well realise it was too weak. What could she do? How could she turn Lachlan's mind so much against the lass that he'd even risk a feud with the Campbells to get rid of her?

Suddenly, laughing, she held up the little bottle, still half-full of liquid gleaming in the sunlight, and kissed it in delight. She was being just too clever! She only needed to tell the truth! Well, nearly.

With Farquhar Neas, four ghillies and a fine deer, Lachlan rode back from the hill that golden noontide, singing happily, the hounds strolling at their heels. But near the chapel, Marion Aluinn ran out from the bushes, calling, 'Lachlan, I must have word with you. Private word.'

'What is it, Marion? Is one of the babes sick? No? What, then?' His brows raised at her agitation, Lachlan leaped down. 'Farquhar, give Iain the dogs' leashes and stay. The rest of you go on. Away, now!' He turned to Marion, drawing her down the side path to sit on a tombstone. 'Come, Marion, come along here. Now, sit down and tell me. Has Elizabeth been uncivil to you?'

'Uncivil?' she screamed at him. 'Hah! That's scarce the word! Your wife's planned murder! I found this flask hidden in my room. It's some of the tonic John Campbell gave her! It's poison —poison for you, and I to be blamed for it!'

Hector was just returning from the hives up on the moor. Luch trotted behind him, for by now he knew every track round Duart and marched jauntily along, seldom needing his staff. Ranald was gambolling ahead like a colt as usual, for he felt confined inside Duart's thick walls and liked to stretch his legs outside. As he ran and turned his somersaults, he kept up a stream of comment and jokes. 'There's Marion Aluinn at the chapel track stopping Lachlan, sir! They're sending on the ghillies. I wonder what she's wanting with him there, eh?' He chuckled. 'Will I sneak up on them and find out?'

'You?' Hector laughed in his turn. 'You couldn't sneak up on a dead cow, my lad! You'd trip over your big feet and scare the beast back to life again!'

'I would not, so! Silent as mist on the moor! I'll show you!'

'Ranald! Don't be a fool!' Hector called, laughing, thinking little harm, but the lad was away. 'Ach, the foolish laddie! If Lachlan catches him spying, he'll skin him alive! Come on, Luch, a bit faster. We'd better save him!'

Suddenly there was a shouting ahead. Ranald yelled, and stopped abruptly.

'Dhia! If he's harmed my lad—' Hector started to run, reckless of falling on the rough path, seeking the turn-off with his staff.

Luch caught hold of his plaid and tugged him aside, to stumble to a halt among the broom and hazel. 'What is it, so? Is the lad here?' He bent down to feel the ground around his feet. As they crouched there, hooves clattered galloping towards them, heading for the main track. 'Lachlan?' Hector called, starting to stand up. She dragged him down again.

Lachlan was roaring, 'God damn her! Ah-agh! I'll tear her to shreds! I'll gut her!' The threats faded with the hoofbeats up the path.

Two other voices were raised on the other side of the bushes. One was sharp and vicious. 'And why should I be caring, Farquhar Neas? If you're that set on saving her, go you after him and hold him back—if you dare!' Farquhar cursed her and raced off up the track after his dallta. 'Let the Campbells avenge her death, then! If the clan suffers, what should that be to me? Did any of them care for me when I was suffering?' she screeched after him.

Hector gasped in fury, and thrust forward past Luch. 'Elizabeth! He's going to harm Elizabeth! Marion, you bitch! Where are you?'

Marion jumped at the sudden uproar in the bushes, and barely dodged his blind clawing. But after a moment's alarm she simply stepped aside among the bushes, and walked quietly away, sneering in triumph; for what could he do?

'Dhia! I must stop him!' He started towards the castle, but Luch tugged at him again. 'What is it?' he demanded. 'We must save Elizabeth! Saints, I forgot Ranald! Dhia, I'll never get there in time!' The answer came quickly. 'Luch! You stay and find Ranald. I know the path. I'll send help back!' His staff swinging before his feet, he hurried off along the track.

Luch stared after him, shook her head in dismay, and scurried off. She found Ranald easily, lying under a bush where he had thought he was hidden. A wound in his side was pouring blood, and there was a huge lump on his head, but he was alive. She was bathing his head with holy water from the chapel font when David Beaton and men from the clachan arrived to carry him home.

'Will he live, so, saints guard him?' old Ruari begged, as Mairi wailed.

'Aye, aye, man, be easy. The knife sliced along a rib. It's not serious, nor the bump on his head. A bit bandage and a day's rest and he'll do fine. But it's as well I was in the clachan. The lass hasn't said what happened? Hector raced by me so fast . . . Well, come up to the castle with me, and we'll find out.'

When the three of them panted up the track, they found Duart in an uproar. One of the guards fairly leaped on David Beaton and shoved him into his infirmary, where Hector lay unconscious, a deep gash in his scalp. 'Master Beaton, thank God you're back! See what he's done to Hector! And Elizabeth Roisin—ach, Dhia! It's crazed he is!'

Lachlan had stormed into the hall, shouting for Elizabeth. 'Well, Elizabeth Campbell!' he roared at her. 'Has your brother made you any more gifts, then?'

She stared up at him. 'What are you talking about, Lachlan? Husband! What have I done, to put you in such a fury? Has my brother harmed you somehow?'

Lachlan laughed harshly. 'Harmed me? No, wife. Not yet. But it was only a question of when! See you here!' He held up a small bottle. 'You know this?'

Her voice was nearly steady. 'No, husband.' She suspected, though. Here it came . . . She only had to demonstrate her innocence, and that was so easy . . .

He struck her staggering backwards. 'I'll tell you, then! It's some of your "tonic" from your brother! That was so powerful you should only take the one drop at a time! Hidden away in

Marion's room! And why?' He hurled a stool at her, knocking her to the floor. 'I'll tell you why, wife of mine! To poison me! That's what it was for! And have Marion Aluinn blamed for it!'

Elizabeth writhed among the rushes on the floor, holding her side where the stool had hit her, appalled by the speed and uncontrolled, uncontrollable violence of his anger. 'No, Lachlan! It's not poison!' she denied desperately.

'Why, then? Why hide it there?' His face was scarlet, his voice hoarse, as his temper rose again towards the berserker rage.

'I didn't!' Coughing in pain, her rising anger overcoming her terror, she struggled up. She must convince him! 'I swear it's not poison!'

'Liar!' One fist seized her shoulder, the other held the bottle before her eyes. 'It was hidden! Hidden under her mattress! You venomous bitch! Viper!'

At each word, the fist holding the bottle punched her, and she screamed in pain and rage of her own. 'And if I had planned to poison you, had I not reason? Taking another woman into the house, to my insult—'

'Reason?' he howled. He dropped the bottle and seized her neck in both hands, shaking her violently. 'Reason, to kill me? Your husband? Your master—'

At that moment something hit his back. He raised his head, not loosening his grip, but turning from the woman scrabbling with her nails at his hands. Hector struck blindly again with his long staff, shouting, 'Stop that! Monster! Murderer! I'll stop you!'

He succeeded. Lachlan dropped Elizabeth to collapse among the rushes gasping; but only to turn his rage on Hector. He grabbed the end of the staff and tugged it from Hector's grasp, laughed wildly, raised it and smashed it down to break across the young man's skull. Then he dropped it and pounced, drawing his dirk. 'Ill-trained pup! It's I am Duart! Raise your hand to me, would you?' He dragged Hector's head up by the hair to cut his throat, as if he was a deer, while Hector lolled unconscious and helpless in his grasp.

There was a dull thud. Lachlan's eyes glazed, his knife clinked among the rushes. Hector slid down, unmoving. And Farquhar

Neas dropped the butt end of Hector's staff with which he had stunned his dallta, and caught him as he fell.

He stood looking down on the three at his feet. Dhia! What a carry-on!

The steward came slowly up behind him. 'Farquhar Neas! How could you do that? Thank God you stopped him, but— what will he say? What will he do?'

Farquhar glanced sideways, his twisted smile growing. 'He'll do as he pleases, same as always, Seumas Ban.' Killing Hector would have solved a problem, but he knew his dallta wouldn't thank him for allowing it to happen like that. He'd be angered for a while; well, let him. Farquhar beckoned some of the men. 'You two, carry Hector Odhar out to the infirmary, and send for David Beaton. You four, carry Lachlan Cattanach up to his room. Careful, now. And you—throw the Campbell woman in the dungeon, to await Duart's judgement.'

Before the story was done, Hector was stirring under the doctor's hands. 'Has Duart gone clean mad, Master Beaton?' Ruari demanded.

'God knows,' Master Beaton snapped. 'But I know this, with the temper Lachlan Cattanach has, the lad had better not be under his hand when he wakes. Ruari, I'm sorry to put it on you, and you not well, but can you hide him?'

'There's nothing wrong with me, so! Aye, I'll find the lad a place.'

As Ruari and Luch half-carried Hector down the track David Beaton looked at the folk round him. 'Where is Hector, then, and Farquhar Neas seeking him?'

They exchanged glances. 'Hector Odhar?' said an old wife. 'He left a while back with that Luch lass. But I didn't see where he went.' They nodded.

So. That was one safe, for a while, anyway. Thanking them, Master Beaton went in to see to Lachlan and Elizabeth.

In fact, Hector went no farther than Ruari's own bed next to Ranald's. They lowered him onto it, groaning but struggling to think. 'Luch? Are you there? Go and see can you help Elizabeth Roisin. Find out what's happening. You mind you swore you would help her, Luch. Luch? Where are you?'

Mairi was hysterically wailing. 'The house will be burned over our heads!'

Ruari was swearing at her. 'Will you be silent, saints hold your noise! The lad's here now, and your only chance is if Duart doesn't come to hear of it, so you'd best shut your mouth, woman!'

It was left to Ranald to answer Hector, sitting up dazedly, holding his aching head and ribs. 'Sir, she's away this good while!'

Hector sank back on the heather pile, his head spinning, a noisy darkness swamping his mind. Of course Luch had gone already. She'd see to it . . .

Quest for a Baby

It was late that evening when Lachlan Cattanach came down to the dungeon. The door's creaking and the light of the crusie lamp he carried wakened Elizabeth, dozing uneasily on damp, stinking straw. David Beaton had been turned away. Two of her ribs felt cracked, and she'd lost a tooth. Dhia, and remember the reason for the last night she had spent like this . . . She stiffly pushed herself up to meet Lachlan's eyes, peering in the tiny light amid the darkness.

After a long minute, Lachlan broke the silence. 'You loved me.' His voice was flat, not complaining, not scolding; just tired.

She swallowed painfully. 'I did. Till I found you loved her, not me.'

He nodded. 'I thought I could keep you both happy.'

'You were wrong.' No bitterness, no anger; just a fact.

Wearily, 'Aye.' A long pause. He sighed. 'You planned to kill me.'

'Who says so? Marion? Remember how she tried to trick your father.'

He drew a deep breath of annoyance. 'Don't deny it, Elizabeth. You hid away this poison to blame Marion.' He was holding out the phial.

'No,' she started to argue again. 'No, it's not poison! Test it on a dog—'

He hurled the little bottle out to tinkle on the stones of the passage. 'No! I'll not hear you!' He controlled himself again as she slumped back. 'No,' he repeated more moderately. 'Don't deny it, Elizabeth, or I'll grow angered again and strike you, and I'm not wanting to. Aye, so. You planned to kill me.'

Dully, she kept trying. 'Or her? Think of that, husband.'

He thought, but shook his head. 'Either. It makes no matter. Did you know Hector tried to help you? Struck me with his staff. The lad has courage, and him blind. I'll maybe just forget it, for him. But I can't let you live.'

'Kill me, and my father will call out Clan Diarmaid against you.'

'Not for a wife who tries to murder her husband.'

That was true. 'Then bring me to trial, before the king!'

He shook his head. 'Why waste time? It's I am judge here, and I judge you guilty. Besides, I've no wish to tell all the world the story of my life.'

She did her best to sneer. 'No, indeed! Admit before a court that you took another woman in beside your wife? You'd be excommunicated.'

He smiled slightly. 'No, no, that's not what a man gets excommunicated for. But I'd not wish my clan and yours to be at war over you. I find there's a difference between leading fighting men, and the whole clan. I'm responsible . . .' He sighed again, deeply. 'I can't let you live. But I'll not kill you.'

It took a moment for her to understand. With an effort she sat up straighter. 'What, then, Lachlan? A nunnery?'

'As good as death to you, eh? No. A man said to me once that he'd set me on a rock at low tide, for God to save if He pleased. Farquhar Neas will set you on that same rock and leave you to God's mercy. Fitting it is, for the Maclean shield bears a rock. God himself will kill or spare you, not I.'

'I see; you can swear your hands are clean. And all for Marion's lies—' At his expression, she sighed wearily. 'No. So, then. It's she who wins.' It almost didn't matter any more . . . 'Will you send me to my Maker unshriven?'

'No, Elizabeth. Elizabeth Roisin; a rose with a poisoned thorn. You are, after all, the mother of my heir. I'll send you Father Patrick.'

'You're graciously kind. Husband.' He could carry a message . . . Where?

His irony matched hers. 'You're welcome. Wife. But he'll stay in that cell till you're gone at dawn. Who would dare help you, anyway?' Her shoulders sank. He looked at her long, regretfully. 'Goodbye, Elizabeth Campbell.'

'One thing, Lachlan Cattanach Maclean!' At the sudden urgency in her tone, he paused. 'Do you set a good guard on my son, your heir. For when I'm gone, Marion will be in charge of the bower; and Eachuinn alone standing between her Adam and Duart. I'll not beg, but I warn you; care you for him!'

He bit his lip, and went out quickly, locking the cell door behind him.

The motionless little shadow crouched knee-low in the dark angle of the passage outside drifted silently after him. And when Farquhar Neas, a swelling on the side of his jaw, for Lachlan had indeed been angry, went out to rouse a couple of fisher lads, she wafted unseen through the gate behind him.

She scratched at the hut door for Mairi, still sniffling, to let her in. Ruari, in the light sleep of age and worry, woke quickly, but it took some time to rouse Hector to a blurred attention. 'Don't whisper so, lassie! What? A rock at low tide? What rock?' She shrugged. He put out a wavering hand towards where Ruari hovered. 'We must save her. Row out after them and lift her off.'

'You can't! You're sore hurt yourself, and my father's heart's bad—you can't ask him to take such a risk! Not for a poisoner!' Mairi was desperate, her voice rising. 'You might never find her, and he might die on the way! Or you'll both be drowned by the waves! And we'll all suffer if Lachlan Cattanach finds out! We'll be exiled from the clan, to starve! You ask too much! Too much! Is it not enough that Ranald is hurt? What more? In God's name—'

Ruari patted her hands, clasped shaking before her mouth. 'Hush you, Mairi Ban. Should I—should any man stand by and see murder done, and call himself a man afterwards? And murder this is, for even if she's guilty, she's had no trial. Someone must help her. And the lad here can't go—'

In his bed, Ranald could bear it no longer. His grandfather wasn't fit to row far. And Hector Odhar couldn't go alone. 'Why not, grandfather?' As they turned to stare, he blushed. 'No, mother, I'm no hero, but I must! My side's fine—just a deep cut. And the bump on my head—I've had worse a dozen times.' Well, that was true. 'And you'll be spared my daft tricks for a while!'

Ruari argued, and Mairi Ban wept; but this was the only way, and at last his grandfather accepted it. His mother fell to a silent, hopeless resentment.

Hector simply sat. A roaring in his head drowned his thoughts. Drowned. Aye, that was . . . drowned . . . Elizabeth . . . he had to try . . . something . . . a rock . . .

About two hours before dawn Ruari and the lads crept down to the shore. Hector stumbled and staggered down the track in spite of Luch's arm round him to support him. It was Ruari and Ranald shoved the coble off the mud. Ranald scrambled in fairly briskly, trying not to show the pain the deep gash over his ribs caused him, or the buzzing in his head; but Ruari had to help Hector in. 'No, lass, there's no room for you and her both.' Luch stood back unhappily.

'Come on, then, sir! Get out your oar,' whispered Ranald. Hector just sat.

'Dhia!' Ruari prayed. 'He's dark of mind as well as eye! With that blow to his head!' He put the oar in place, and nudged Hector's hands with it. 'Take it, Hector Odhar!' The slack hands grasped the oar shaft, but his face was blank.

The old man shook his head. 'Ranald, my lad, it's you must be master of the boat, not him. Act like with the bees. Go slow and careful, and tell him all the time what to do. Keep on telling him. Thank God it's calm. And the mist will hide you.' He hoped. 'They'll not wait to see her drown. When they're well away, you can go in to rescue her. Take care, now, for you can't rely on Hector to help you.' Dhia, he thought, the lad can never do it! He'll die! They'll both die! I'll never see him again!

But as if he heard the thought, Ranald grinned cheerfully.

'Aye, aye, grandfather, I've been out with you often enough! I'll manage! We'll do fine!'

'Stay with Hector, so, and look after him! God and all his saints guide and protect you, and bring you back safe to us, my heart! On you go, now.'

He thrust out the boat sliding over the still water. Ranald, drawing a deep breath, whispered, 'Row, sir! Row, now! Set your oar in the water and pull! That's it, now, sir! Pull steady!' Obediently, Hector bent to the oar. Ranald cast one relieved grin back to his grandfather. 'Quiet, now, Hector Odhar! Row!' they heard him whisper as the little boat faded into the haze of moonlight.

'Dear God! Save him to us!' Ruari's voice was a breath.

Luch looked up. More than Ranald needed saving . . . Wordless as always, she put her arm round Ruari's waist. He leaned on her heavily as they trudged home.

An hour later Elizabeth, gagged as well as bound, was pushed down the steep path and into the boat. She had no chance to escape, or scream for help, or plead with them. And she felt so sick and sore . . . God have mercy on her!

Out across the Sound. As they rounded the point, strange echoes of their oars started whispering behind them in the pearly mist. The brothers rowing muttered about ghosts, and Farquhar had some trouble making them go on.

At last they found the rock, low in the water. The sailors stopped rowing, but the echoes went on for a second or two. 'What was that?' one man muttered.

Farquhar sneered. 'Nothing. Waves, or a seabird, maybe.' The men held the boat steady while he hauled Elizabeth out, forced her to sit, and tied her down. He stood back and studied her—no, not her; the ropes—and nodded. 'She'll not poison anybody again.' It was his only comment. He climbed back into his boat. Avoiding her eyes, the men took to their oars again, and faded into the mist.

Elizabeth had never been so cold. Not just physically cold, but chilled to the heart by his indifference. The waves were already washing round her. She tugged, not in any hope; and found it in vain.

The ghostly noises started again. She shook her head. Foolish; she was thinking the waves were whispering her name.

Suddenly she raised her head. It was true! Someone was calling her!

It was another agony. She tugged and writhed, but the ropes were well tied, tight and wet, rigid against her soft fingertips. She kicked and cried against the gag, but the splashing and her moans were lost in the sound of the rising waves. Ranald's voice and the noise of the oars came and went, tantalising and tormenting, within a few feet of her invisible in the mist.

They didn't find her till the tide was rising to her shoulders. Ranald cast one resigned look at Hector's blank face, tied the boat's rope to his waist and made a wild, splashing leap onto the rock now hidden underwater. He ducked under to cut her free, and then he lifted her and scrambled her and himself into the coble as it crushed its barnacles off against the rock.

They drifted a good while as they recovered. At last, trembling with cold, Ranald forced his knife through the cord still tying Elizabeth's hands. 'Steer us, lady, for we'll not can row straight, the state we're in.' He was exhausted by the rowing, the tearing ache of his wounded side and head, and the strain of guiding Hector. 'We'll take you over to Lismore. Your father's men will send you safe to him at Inveraray from there. And he can see to Hector. You can see he's sore hurt for your sake. What will your father do, think you?'

Elizabeth was rubbing her mouth and wrists, sore from the bindings; easing her side, her cramped arms, her shoulders. She shuddered, with wet and chill and relief. 'Dhia, I'm more worried about what my mother will say!' She tried to laugh, to show spirit, to thank them. She burst into tears.

There was a bitter silence about Duart Castle for a day or two. Father Patrick prayed ceaselessly. Lachlan drank sullenly in the hall or escaped the tension by going hunting, Farquhar watching over him constantly.

Marion looked sweetly after old Lady Bridhe, who had taken to her bed, ignored Eachuinn Og, and made no open display of either sorrow or triumph. Her hard-learned restraint had its effect. It surprised even her how few days it took for the clan to decide that after all, the Campbell woman was a poisoner. It was wrong of Duart, they admitted, to kill her without a proper trial; but then, what man would be reasonable, and his wife trying to murder him?

Marion moved to Lachlan's right hand at the table, and he was expected to wed her soon. She was impressed by the way he had dealt with Elizabeth. It seemed there would be no war with the Campbells after all. Never mind; it maybe hadn't been a good idea anyway, when her own son was to be next chief of Clan Gillian. The word was firmly spread; the Lady Elizabeth had gone out rowing with just her maid. The overturned boat had been found next day. A tragedy, to hide a scandal. And woe worth anyone who hinted any other story.

No-one was surprised that Hector Odhar had fled; only that he'd left that Luch lassie behind. Wherever he had gone, it was the lad Ranald Gorach had led him. Mairi Ban was wailing her woes to the world, for the man whose boat they had taken was claiming its value from Ruari. Hard pressed he was with the work of the bees, too, poor old man.

Dawn and dusk Luch worked beside him, helping him with the first of the honey harvest, but when she was free she went in and about Duart as before. The women were pleased, for the babies were quieter when she played with them and settled them after their feeds. Soon they noticed her as little as ever.

The fiercest deerhound bitch, Borb, had another litter; just one pup this time. She made her bed in the corner at the foot of the hall stair. No-one cared to take the risk of trying to move her; they just walked wide of her. If Luch was leaving the castle at dinner-time, she would pause to soothe her and let the serving lads slip by easy with the dishes from the kitchen.

Ten days after Elizabeth had vanished, a boat bearing the yellow and black Campbell colours brought Lachlan a letter from Argyll himself. The big man laughed softly as Father Patrick read it to him. 'Joins me in my sorrow at Elizabeth's death, does he so? A tragedy—but then, if she would go boating alone, who can be blamed that she met with an accident? An understanding man, Archibald Campbell. But he asks me to carry her body to

Inveraray for burial with her family. Mourn our loss together, he says, eh? Well, now.'

Marion was leaning gracefully against his high chairback. 'You can aye take a coffin, Lachlan. One body's much like another, and I doubt if he'll be unwrapping the cerecloth to examine it too closely,' she murmured, smiling at Father Patrick's futile glare. Left alone with the brat—what good fortune!

Lachlan pondered for a moment. He didn't have to go to Inveraray. He could find a good excuse for refusing. It would be a grand joke on Argyll, though; one he'd hate to miss if he could arrange it.

But the warning Elizabeth had given him about Eachuinn Og and Marion remained in his mind. He grinned up at Marion's glowing beauty above him. 'Well, lass, I can scarcely take you. Tactless, eh? And I don't like leaving you alone here, with Elizabeth's friends remembering her. Or Eachuinn Og, in case Argyll tries to kidnap him. Remember Muriella Cawdor! But I know what I'll do, to ease my mind. I'll leave Farquhar here to watch you. Both.'

Her smile froze for an instant above his head. Did he suspect? He couldn't! Surely? It took all her control to relax and laugh at his fears. He wouldn't change his mind, though, and she couldn't argue too much.

'Now, where can I find a fine coffin, fit for my dear wife, eh?'

'There's but one that I know of, my lord. Lady Bridhe had hers made the same time as your father's. I'm sure she'd let you have it gladly.' Well she knew it would near break old Bridhe's heart to part with the coffin she'd kept ready for the last forty years. It might even kill the old bitch! 'And for a body, there's aye the Campbell maid, the handless lump. She might tell.'

He shook his red head. 'Marion, you're behind the news. She's wanting to be wed on the piper. She's safe enough.' Twice over, he thought with an internal grin. 'No, I'll just take a weight, if no-one dies in time.'

No-one did; so, two dawns later, Lachlan Cattanach's lymphad carried away Lady Bridhe's fine coffin, holding a sack of damp sand wrapped in a cerecloth.

When they heard where Lachlan was going, Mairi Ban had

hysterics. 'If Ranald and Hector are alive, where'll they be now? Inveraray! And he'll find out all about us! Dhia, why do they not send us word! They're dead! Oh, let them be dead so that Lachlan Cattanach never finds out! Dhia, what am I saying?'

Ruari had a hard time of it to keep her quiet. 'Will you be stopping that wailing, saints preserve you! I'm sure they're not dead. And Argyll may well stop Lachlan somehow.' Kill him, he thought, and felt a dreadful mixture of emotions. Rage, that a Campbell might consider doing such a thing to a Maclean—Maclean of Duart! Grief and worry for his grandson. Hope that they were dead, almost, as his daughter had done, for that would save them all from Lachlan Cattanach's anger. And guilt for the hope. His heart was thundering to shake him. 'Ach, Mairi Ban, Mairi Ban! We must just wait and see what happens!'

Luch scarcely noticed his state, for she was distressed by another matter entirely. Words echoed in her mind. 'I trust you with her . . .' 'Help my baby too . . .' She cuddled her old bundle in its faded brown shawl, fiercely, deeply protective. Lady Elizabeth's baby—her baby—a baby was in danger.

The afternoon of the day Lachlan left, she slipped like a breath of air in through the gates and up to the bower. Farquhar was squatting already beside the cradles. The orders he'd had were quite clear. He hated being parted from his dallta, but this was the first sign of sense he'd seen in him for months. After the babies were fed, Luch played quietly with them as usual, hushing them to sleep as was her gift while the women prepared to go down for dinner.

No-one realised that she took a little longer than usual to lay Eachuinn Og back in his cradle. No-one noticed her wrap her tattered brown shawl round a living baby, and lay him down gently. Nobody saw the love and regret on her face, as the soft plaid blanket was folded round an old doll with a sadly worn face, and carefully tucked deep under the hood of the fine, carved cradle. Not a soul, not even Farquhar Neas, only three feet away, his mind and eyes on Marion, dreamed that the baby that she lifted from between the cradles, the shawled bundle that was a natural, accepted part of her, without which she would

165

have seemed strangely mis-shapen now to them, was no longer the wood and straw dummy she had carried for so long.

When Marion rose at last, Luch drifted out invisible among their skirts, a brown-wrapped baby as usual in the crook of her arm.

The lads were dashing across the yard through blattering rain to serve the meal. She slipped into the corner beside Borb, who cocked her head to have her ears scratched as the lads dived into shelter and up the stair with their platters. Luch looked at the one puppy, curled up fatly asleep by his dam. A thought stirred . . . She gently lifted him and tucked him into the folds of her plaid. Borb rose, curious but unalarmed, and followed her pup. They walked quietly into the courtyard and past the guard, who wondered vaguely where the hound was off to in this wet weather.

Farquhar was left alone in the bower, pacing up and down the long room. A lad brought him a platter and a bowl. 'From Seumas Ban's own hand, he said I was to say.' Farquhar nodded. He would refuse anything from Marion's hand. One of the babes, the milk-mother's child, cried restlessly; he squatted between them and rocked both cradles, till the crying died away. The other baby, the one he was concerned with, lay at peace.

He rose and stretched as the women returned. 'Aye, Margaret,' he nodded to the wet-nurse. 'Calum cried for a minute there, but he's settled again now.' She smiled her thanks, and settled with the others to their eternal spinning and gossip. Marion Aluinn, with Lachlan away, had the lads of the guard fair drooling over her . . . Set a hook in every man she saw, eh? . . . Lady Bridhe was wild angry at losing her fine coffin, and it not even used yet . . . The afternoon passed pleasantly into twilight. Farquhar even smiled once or twice.

At last, young Calum stirred. 'Come away, then, my fine laddie!' his mother laughed, lifting him. It was rare for her to have the babies one at a time to feed, and she enjoyed it. When her lad was fed, changed and handed cooing to one of the women to play with, she took a drink of ale, yawned, stretched to ease her back and reached down into the carved cradle. 'Dhia, Eachuinn Og, what a grand sleepy-bye you've had, my chieftain, my hero—'

She screamed, and the dummy flew into Farquhar's arms as she fainted.

At that moment Marion opened the door, saw what Farquhar was holding, and her quick brain jumped to the answer while he still gaped. Luch! She'd taken the baby! She clipped the ear of a lad who had come running at the scream. 'Go you, saddle me a garron. And call me a dozen men for a guard! Run, fool!' Shoving him towards the stair, she swung on her maid. 'My cloak! Dhia, what a snail! You should have gone in that coffin!' She snatched up a plaid lying on a chest, but took a second to sneer at Farquhar Neas. 'And what will Lachlan Cattanach say, that his heir is reived from right under your nose?' She pattered away down the stair just as the first of the folk started up it.

Farquhar followed her, but too late. Marion, pushing out, heard the shouts behind her. He was trapped by the shouting, questioning crowd packing up the narrow spiral stair, and as he tried to shove through, someone fell, creating a total jam. In seconds she was across the courtyard, calling several of her young admirers behind her. A garron was being led out. She must beat Farquhar Neas to the child! She scrambled to the saddle and charged off down the path, with her followers racing behind still unsure what had happened.

'To Ruari Beeman's!' she shrieked, wild with exhilaration. Clattering through the dark, plaid flying, clutching at the saddle, ducking her head for the lashing rain, she prayed she might get there in time. Just one little ten seconds alone with the baby, and he'd be dead, and Luch blamed. Or if that failed, she'd be the baby's saviour; she could send Farquhar away as useless, and who would wonder if the baby died soon, after the lass had misused him?

One of her lads burst open the door of Ruari's hut. Mairi screamed in terror. Ruari, rolling off his bed, blinked dizzily as they seized him and hauled him upright. There was no sign of Luch.

'Search!' Marion ordered. 'The brat may be hiding in the thatch or under the hay in the byre! Find her!' She turned on Mairi and Ruari, and demanded, 'Where is Luch?' They didn't know. 'Luch! She's stolen Eachuinn Og! In this rain, she must be in shelter! Where, you fools?' Her voice screeched with tension; Farquhar Neas must be close behind! In fury, she tossed down the leather sacks of honey, the first cakes of new wax. One fell into the fire and flared up. Marion's mud-splashed face, lit from below, was a demon's. 'Don't dare defy me!'

Mairi Ban was hysterically furious. This was the evil wife that they'd driven out last year! 'I know nothing! Nothing!'

Ruari, gasping already with shock and fright, was equally determined. 'I'll not tell! Never! Even if I knew, and that I don't!'

'Aye do you! And you'll tell. Willingly or not!' She stared round the hut; then picked up a stick from the fire. 'Angus! Hold the old man firm!' She held the flaring branch to Ruari's face. As his lips drew back in fear, Mairi Ban screamed. 'Where is the lass Luch? Where is she?'

'We don't know!' It was Ruari who gasped it. 'She didn't come in tonight! How should we know where she is? Mairi! We don't know!'

In desperate defiance, Mairi screeched, 'True it is! We don't know!'

'Then guess!' Marion held the flame to the old man's face again. 'Where is she? She'd not lie out in this weather! Where is she? Where?'

And where was Farquhar Neas?

Try a different way . . . Marion turned to Mairi Ban, held struggling and shrieking, and took her trembling hand. 'Come now, wife. The child has stolen the son of her chief. You know how crazed she is about babies. Who knows what she'll be doing to poor Eachuinn Og! Shame be on you! Traitor to the clan!'

Mairi Ban was sobbing. Her father was suffering, and his heart not strong. It tore at her! But tell this wife? Luch would never harm the baby—

'You'll tell me, wife. For if you don't, I'll blind him—and burn down this house!' Ruari's beard was singeing as the flame approached again.

Lose her father as well as her son? And her home? Mairi whimpered.

With a huge effort, Ruari spoke. 'No! We don't know . . .' His head lolled.

'We must find the baby!' Marion's shrill voice insisted. 'She stole him, and we must get him back! Tell me, and your father will live. Save the baby!'

Baby. Save the baby. Mairi started to sob again. 'I don't know! I don't know!' Marion raised the burning branch again, and suddenly Mairi's nerve broke. 'No! Stop! There's but the one place she'll be!' Marion was smiling, nodding, approving. 'The old shieling! Where she took you!'

As Mairi sobbed, Marion felt an unexpected jolt at her heart. She'd quite forgotten that this child she was pursuing was the one who had helped her, the only one who had helped her, when she herself was in sore need.

She thrust the thought away. She'd no time for that now! 'Come on, lads! Leave him!' Ruari was dropped into Mairi's arms as she wept in shamed defeat.

The clan had gathered outside, roused by the screaming; angry, waving torches. She had no fear of them now. 'Eachuinn Og's taken! Stolen! It was that Luch daftie! The beeman's hut on the moor! That's where she's taken him!'

Her excitement spread and stirred them. 'We'll save him!' Half the clachan started to run. Laughing to herself she kicked her pony up the path with them. In the confusion of a mob, as she'd once told Lachlan, anything could happen.

But where was Farquhar Neas? All the way she looked round for him. But nowhere did the light of the many torches gleam on that tall, fair head.

At last, there was the little hut. Dhia, how well she remembered it! The sheltered hollow, with the grove of bee-skeps on their rocks; the burn, running full into the flooded pool; the low, crumbling thatch toppling onto the last scraps of the peat-stack. She slid down, panting in excitement, and waved the men to surround it. Then she called out. 'Luch! Come out! Bring out the baby!'

There was a pause. She laughed. 'She's hiding! She's afraid— small blame to her, the wee bitch! Wait you, I'll fetch her out!' Alone in the hut, with just that child and the baby . . . It was her chance . . . She ducked eagerly into the hut.

The fireplace, the heather bed-pile scattered by sheltering sheep or foxes, a couple of old straw skeps. No child. No baby.

She dived out again. 'Search the rocks! Check among the hives, there! Seek over the moor, under the whins, every bit of shelter! She must be here!'

They scattered, beating through the soaking whin, up the burn, among the hives—with care, as the bees murmured sleepily—all around the hut. At last they gathered again, their torches guttering out in the rain. 'Not a sign, Marion Aluinn. She must be away on the moor. We'll fetch the dogs in the morning.'

'The hounds won't chase her!' Marion protested.

They eyed each other, till one called, 'They'll seek out the child, though! Borb and Glic will find him for us, and her with him!' That thought settled the matter for them, in this wet. Dripping, they set off back down the track.

Balked and furious, Marion stared at the little hut. There was something eerie about it; maybe it was just her conscience . . . 'God damn you!' she snarled, she didn't know at what; hurled herself onto the garron and whipped it to a risky gallop down the dark path. Her men shrugged, and trotted after her.

Luch rose quietly from the scatter of peats by the hut wall. She'd been out of the way of tripping feet there, in plain view if anyone had noticed her, but of course no-one had. She lifted away the half-dozen peats that had camouflaged the hound beside her, quiet as usual under her hand. The puppy lifted head from its dam's teats, whimpering at the cold stab of the rain.

The little girl was tired and worried. Instinct had guided her so far, bringing her away up here, making her hide the baby and the hound as soon as she saw the line of torches still miles away down the track. But she didn't know what to do now. She bent to drink at the pool while her slow mind waited for the answer to the problem to emerge.

And suddenly a tall, thin figure loomed over her, his mouth even more twisted than usual, and said 'Well, lass? Where is he?'

He didn't hurry her. He knelt beside her, dipping a palmful of water for himself, while she recovered from the fright. But after a while he asked again. 'Eachuinn Og? Where is he? You had to keep him in shelter, in this wild weather. And not far off, neither. Where is he, Luch? We have to get him to safety, away from

Marion Aluinn.' He took her trembling hand gently. 'Luch, I know you have no love for me. But this baby is the son of my dallta. It's my own right arm I'd cut off to save him. Where is it you have him safe?'

He didn't know she had heard him, the night they returned from the raid. She knew about Hector, and Ewan. And Ranald, and Elizabeth . . . But Hector and Elizabeth had asked her to save the baby . . . He wanted to save the baby too . . . Unreasoned and slow, a balance in her mind tilted and settled.

Luch rose. She didn't turn, as he'd expected, towards the moor, but walked in among the beehives. Right in the middle, where the men had been searching five minutes before, going gingerly and quietly as she'd known they would, she lifted a skep from its base. Tucked in a warm, cosy little ball in the sweet straw nest, Eachuinn Og was sleeping soundly.

Farquhar suddenly sat down on a rock and started to laugh. He wasn't used to it, and his laughter at first creaked like a floorboard; but after a while he got into the way of it. He threw back his head and roared till he slid off the rock and banged his head on it and laughed still.

Luch stood by him, sheltering the baby from the rain, rather puzzled. She didn't see what was so funny at all.

Inveraray

Just before dawn there was a scratch at Ruari's door. Mairi whimpered in fear, but opened. When Luch slipped in with the baby, an enormous deerhound at her heels, Mairi's jaw dropped; when Farquhar Neas followed, she drew breath to scream. His knife, glinting instantly at her throat, silenced her.

'Woman, shut your mouth and the door,' he hissed. She did so, trembling. Luch had run to the old man trying to rise from the narrow heather bed in the corner. Farquhar motioned him to lie quiet. 'Lie still, Ruari, and rest you. A brave man you are, so, and due all honour for it. How are you?'

Ruari eyed him distrustfully. 'Well enough,' he muttered. 'I'll live.'

Farquhar looked surprised. 'Why are you afraid? Oh—that knife I put in Ranald ten days back? He was lying hidden. My dallta has a hot temper—' Aye, you might say so, thought Ruari—'and a many men have been seeking harm to him. But I saw your lad as I threw, and changed my aim. Or he'd be dead now.'

'I should be thanking you, maybe?' Ruari whispered ironically, but Farquhar took it seriously.

'No need, man. I've aye used a knife handy, cutting and throwing. It's just a skill. I'm damned if I'd go near your bees.' He nodded, coldly friendly of eye. 'The men were speaking of your silence, and your courage. Duart will hear of it, and thank you himself, in spite of your daughter's weakness.'

Ruari frowned. 'I've been at her already for giving in—'

'I'll be bound you have. But no blame to you for it. We came to say that, just, and let you know your wee lass is safe, and the baby.' He grinned his twisted grin as Luch rubbed Ruari's hand in mute sympathy. 'She'd not leave without seeing that you were well. I've never known a lass as determined with as few words! But I'll not be risking the babe hereabout any longer. I'm for Iona with him, and your lass to care for him, to stay with the nuns there till Lachlan Cattanach returns. She'll feed him here while I rouse a couple of lads. We'll be away in an hour, and safe by sunset. You can be sure Duart will reward you for the pain you've suffered for his heir's sake.'

Not even the hound heard the stealthy feet that had paused outside the door, and now crept away, to run up the track to the castle.

Farquhar slipped out, while Mairi Ban wailed in a whisper that she'd no milk in the house, what would they do when the baby cried, they were ruined . . . And then fell silent in horrified amazement.

Luch knelt by Borb, settled in a corner with her pup. The wee lass laid the baby in beside the wriggling puppy in the warm grey-white curl of the hound's belly, and as he squirmed and started to grizzle she turned his head in towards the full teats. Nuzzling, grunting, he searched for the milk he could smell, as he had learned to do on the moor earlier; and she supported his head while together the two young things drank their fill, snortling in shared annoyance when hair tickled their noses. Borb's vicious snake head weaved above them, deadly and motherly, her long teeth gleaming as she licked the baby and her own pup with equal tenderness. Luch gazed blankly at Mairi Ban's flapping hands and mouth. Surely this was only sensible?

When Farquhar came back for her they were ready to leave again. 'God bless you, lassie, and all the saints bring you safe back to us!' Ruari prayed as Luch lifted the baby and the pup. It was so short a time since he had said farewell to Ranald . . . But sure God would take care of them all.

173

They coaxed Borb into the coble and climbed in after her, and the lads pushed off. If the last trip they had made came to Farquhar's mind, he didn't mention it. As they rounded the headland close in below the castle, shouts arose. A group of folk were running down from the gate to the boats by the shore. Farquhar peered over through the grey light. 'Marion Aluinn herself, and a dozen men! Pull, lads! What has she said to them, that they're all after us?'

He seized the spare oars, set them in the rowlocks and added his sinewy strength to speed the coble through the water, close enough in by the point to hear Marion's sharp words. 'Haste you, haste! Dhia, what spell has that witch child cast on poor Farquhar Neas! God send he's not going to drown the baby like its mother! Oh, hurry! Heave!'

She scrambled into the skiff to take the tiller as the young men launched it, but not knowing the water she steered wide of the headland. They avoided the rocks, but had to fight the strong current further out that Farquhar's lads had dodged. By the time both boats were heading east across the Firth of Lorn, the larger boat was well behind. However, with eight rowers against three, it soon began to overtake the coble. Marion drove on her men urgently. She must surely get hold of the brat this time! And then a slip, and over the side, for it to drown, or die of chill later. After all her effort, she was due a little luck!

Nearer, and nearer; and at last almost in reach—but Borb was standing, snarling viciously, her forepaws on the stern of the coble. Farquhar yelled, 'Keep off! Come within ten feet and she'll take your throats out!'

They knew it was true. It held them for a while, while the two boats struggled farther east; but again Marion's boat came in to the attack, two guards in the bows, swords poised to strike Borb down as she leaped. They strained at the oars, gathering speed to ram the coble.

Suddenly Farquhar dug his left oar deep and pushed instead of pulling. The coble twisted to one side. Marion automatically pulled her rudder, for the skiff to follow. Two of her oarsmen, taken by surprise, missed their stroke, the skiff lurched wildly, the men in the bows tottered, and one fell overboard.

'Row!' Farquhar urged his panting oarsmen. 'She must pick him up!' In fact, they gained a fair bit, for Marion had to be forced to wait for the man overboard, and wasted time in argument. They pulled well away, while Luch crouched in the stern of the coble nursing the baby.

But only too soon the skiff was catching up again. Marion's eyes were blazing with triumph. Farquhar shipped his oars and drew his dirk. 'Now, lass! Hold Borb's collar till I tell you!' he told Luch. 'If she leaps over at them they'll just kill her in the air. But if I can guard her till we can get in their boat, she'll have good foothold, and the lads can slip you off while we keep them busy. Dhia! The murdering bitch—and I'm not meaning the hound!' Grinning sideways, he poised ready to fight.

Luch touched his arm, and he looked round, forward, for the first time in a good while. Not far ahead, a long lymphad was creaming south across their bows. The pennons were black and yellow. He slapped a hand fiercely on the gunwale of the coble. 'They're Campbells! Dhia, I never thought to be glad to see a Campbell galley!' He stood up, waving the end of his plaid and shouting.

For a moment he thought they'd not been seen, but then a hand waved to him, the near oars dug in and held for the turn, and in a fast twist the lymphad swung in between him and the skiff racing after them, like a greyhound after a hare. It halted dead in the water in a well-trained swirl of foam. Its white oars rose to rest smooth and efficient as the wings of a swan, and its archers leaned casually over, grinning, arrows nocked, to make certain that everyone accepted their shipmaster's invitation to come aboard.

As Farquhar lifted Borb up to the deck on one side, and Luch scrambled aboard, careful of her precious burden, Marion was helped up on the other. Glaring, she straightened her gown and headed towards them. But the great hound, teeth flashing, drove her back; and then a smooth voice cut in. 'Well, now! Is this not a great pleasure! I scarce could believe my eyes, Marion Aluinn, when I saw your marvellous hair in the skiff there! I was up at Cawdor till some days back, when my father sent me the news of my poor sister's unhappy fate. Aye, so. And called me to come down to meet Lachlan at Inveraray. But I swear, I had no hopes of such intriguing company! It should be a most interesting meeting!' John Campbell smiled benignly on them all.

A huge square box was Inveraray Castle, seat of the Earl of Argyll. Less impressively placed than Duart, but still strong, at the end of Loch Fyne under a pleasant shelter of hills. Luch came to it on horseback, riding safe in Farquhar Neas's arms from their landing at Taynuilt through the awesome Pass of Brander, aye clutching her baby, a real, live one now, in her arms. She rested alert and watchful while Argyll's boatmen rowed them singing across Loch Awe, and a fat, friendly Campbell wife fed the baby. John Campbell firmly refused to allow the hound to do so, 'For it's the MacGregors are sons of dogs, lass, not the Campbells—or the Macleans!' Then she was mounting again, stiff and sore, for the long haul up and down Glen Aray, Borb loping behind.

In all this time, John had contrived that Marion Aluinn had exchanged no word with them; nothing but long, reflective stares. Luch found them hard to bear, for she was unused to being constantly watched. When he noticed her discomfort, Farquhar smiled like a sneer, but took care to keep aye between them, to give the wee lass shelter from the burning cold hazel eyes.

The cavalcade arrived at the castle in late afternoon, just as the Maclean galley, which had taken two days on the sea voyage, appeared down Loch Fyne.

Luch was led trembling up to the women's room and warmly welcomed. 'Come away in, lassie! Oh, the bonny lad! My lady, see your fine big grandson!'

The countess sniffed. 'God, is this what my grandson has come to for a nurse? Is he well, Morag? Good, so. Find him a decent shawl, for God's sake. Who let that dog in here? Get it out. And put the lass down to the kitchen.'

Suddenly she was thrust brusquely aside. Her daughter Elizabeth pushed in among them, careless of her mother's dignity and her own, and snatched the baby from Luch's arms. 'My baby! He's well? Oh, thank God! That bitch didn't kill him after all! Dhia, lass, was it you who saved him? I'm ever in your debt! Oh, Eachuinn, Eachuinn Og, my darling!' And Elizabeth hugged the child, a quite unexpected, almost unbearable surge of love and relief bursting over her like a wave, till she sank down on the floor in a sobbing, laughing, exclaiming whirl of pink wool. The baby, alarmed by the violent movements and emotion, started to wail, but Elizabeth simply laughed and wept and hugged him the more. The bower women stood watching, cooing and murmuring in delight at her happiness; and even her mother started to smile stiffly.

Luch gaped at Elizabeth for a long moment, till it started to dawn on her what the lady's presence meant. She looked round, a smile growing. Her great eyes lifted, dark and beautiful, and the maids were surprised by the change in the dull, miserable-looking child. Her tired face brightened, almost glowed with joy at the sound of feet racing down the passage outside.

Ranald bounced off the doorpost as he dragged Hector in too fast for safety. 'Luch! How did you get here? How's my grand-father? What's happened? What's this about a baby?' He dived at her, questioning, laughing, shouting, grabbing her and shaking her in excitement till the pup, still tucked in her plaid, squealed. Borb leaped snarling to its rescue. The maids jumped aside, screeching. Hector yelled to know what was happening. Ranald, shouting, tripped over his own feet as he tried to grab the dog's collar and fell over Elizabeth, who screamed. The baby wailed, and Luch dropped the pup in front of Borb and ran to help her darling. In the middle of the uproar the countess stood like a rock, her glare nearly as fierce as the dog's.

At last, though, Borb calmed down to a grudging, suspicious acceptance of Hector's hand. The countess chased the lads out. 'Get that brute into the kennels, Ranald Gorach, and don't dare let it loose again! Hector Odhar, you can see the child later, and get your news from her. She's tired out, and sore from the journey. Leave her be. The earl will wish to speak with you about the arrangements for this evening. Away with you, now!'

Lady Elizabeth herself oversaw the women as they tended her baby and the lass who had saved him. In half an hour they were both fed and bathed, warm and comfortable in cots in the bower. But Luch, uneasy at all the attention, slipped from her bed as soon as they turned their backs. When they looked for her in alarm they found her crouched by the baby, sound asleep, and Eachuinn Og holding fast to her thumb. Elizabeth smiled, and whispered to the women to slip a mattress under her without waking her, and let her be.

Marion was very impressed by the standard of service. A maid to fetch her hot water, cloths, food and wine, a comb, a mirror even . . . When she returned to Duart she'd do the same . . . If . . . Of course she would return!

When the maid told her Argyll would receive her later, and left her to rest, she tried to go out. The door was locked.

Controlling her urge to rattle it and scream, she sat down. She could explain everything. There was no proof against her. None! Her stomach was churning. Dhia, she'd not felt like this since waiting for Lachlan Cattanach to return from that raid on Arivegaig.

Farquhar was made welcome in the castle guard-room. But when he tried to leave, 'No, no, friend, there's no need for you to go now!' called the guard captain. 'Argyll will call you in an hour or so when your dallta arrives. Sit down, man! Do you play the bones?' His knife hadn't been taken; he wasn't a prisoner . . . But a score of alert-looking Campbells were grinning cheerfully between him and the door. Farquhar smiled twistedly back, and set himself to skin them at dice. At which, incidentally, he failed.

Draped in black, the piper playing a lament, the Maclean lymphad eased in to Inveraray quay. Lachlan Cattanach, the same black plumes in his bonnet as the month before for his father's funeral, firmly composed his face to stern grief as his men carried the beautiful coffin ashore. With Donald Crubach and his guard, all black-cloaked, he walked in solemn procession up through the township behind the box. By God, he was enjoying the joke!

The Campbells were doing the exact same thing.

The street was full, many folk with their plaids thrown over their heads in mourning. Sobs, sniffs, moans of grief sounded all round. It struck Lachlan how odd it was that weeping sounded like smothered laughter. He was rather surprised; he'd not thought his little wife could be so loved by her own clan. Or was this unmanly display of emotion just another sign of Campbell inferiority? He was hard put to it not to smile at the crowd of mourners falling in respectfully behind his own men.

In the great hall of Inveraray Castle, Argyll waited a step in front of his tall sons, Colin and Archibald, John of Cawdor and Donald, all richly gowned and furred as suited the mournful occasion. The earl spoke flatly. 'Play me for a fool, will he? We'll see who laughs. Now mind my orders. I expect you all to act well.' His sons nodded obediently, settling their faces into solemnity. Under his cold glance the guard ranged round the walls stiffened. The two-foot blades of their long Lochaber axes gleamed in the torchlight.

The great doors opened, and the bier was carried in and gently laid on a trestle ready covered with black velvet. The chief of Clan Gillian, in silence, bent to embrace the shoulders of the chief of Clan Diarmaid. The currents of mingled comedy and tragedy swept strangely, strongly round them all.

Lady Campbell and a group of ladies, mourning veils hiding their faces, gathered round the coffin, sobbing. Again Lachlan observed how much the noise resembled stifled laughter. After a while the countess, face rigid as her back, led them, still wailing and hiccuping, to stools set ready at one side.

Then the earl turned to Lachlan Cattanach standing beside him, and put his hand on the coffin, his podgy face absolutely serious. 'Duart,' he said, his voice stern and dry, 'I pray you tell me exactly how my daughter met her end.'

What, no word of welcome? Well, it was understandable. Lachlan braced himself, and took a firm grip of his expression. Dhia, he was near splitting! But he must remember, this wasn't the old fool he looked; this was a Campbell. He sighed deeply. 'No man can say, Argyll. After her baby's birth Elizabeth was—disturbed. She could scarcely stand the company of anyone, even myself.'

One of the Campbell sons spoke up. 'Was there none of her women who could help her?' His father cast a warning eye on him. 'Your father's sister, Lady Bridhe? Or we have heard something of a Marion Maclean?'

Lachlan's nerves tightened a touch. What exactly had they heard? Pass over it quickly. 'Aye, Marion was one of Elizabeth's women. And good friends they were. But even she was less welcomed than she had been.' They nodded, apparently satisfied. 'The September heat also irritated her, and the castle—she said she felt imprisoned. And one day she and her maid—that same loyal girl you sent with her, Lady Campbell—' that should keep the old bitch from complaining, if anyone was likely to upset a boat it was that handless lass—'they took a boat from the shore. No-one noticed them; they just slipped away. That was the last time any man set eyes on my poor Elizabeth Roisin alive.'

He also laid a hand on the coffin, facing his father-in-law in apparent honesty. 'I beg you, my lord, do not open the coffin to see her face. It was some days before she was found.' Marion would be proud of his acting, he thought, his head drooping artistically, his lips trying to escape.

The earl cleared his throat. His face was unreadable. 'Duart, I honour your consideration for me, in the midst of your own grief.' Hah, if you only knew! Lachlan thought. The earl's tone did not change. 'If it is true.' What? Lachlan nearly choked. 'It is whispered in my ear that you killed Elizabeth.'

Dhia, who had dared talk out of turn? Lachlan straightened in outrage, eyes flashing. 'Set the man who says that before my face, and my sword will prove him a liar! Argyll, I do solemnly swear to you here as God is my judge that when I last saw Elizabeth she was alive and in good health. It was by the will of God alone that she died.' And not a word of a lie . . .

Argyll's deep-pouched eyes rested a long time on the young man before him. At last he nodded and gestured to a page. 'It is only right that you should meet your accuser,' he agreed. Lachlan tensed. Who could it be?

The side door opened, and two young men entered. Ranald was on his best behaviour, clean and recently tidy, well warned to keep his feet and grin carefully under control. He led in Hector, frail compared with his burly uncle, but well recovered again, and braced against this meeting. They moved quietly forward to stand before the coffin.

Lachlan thought fast. Of course it would be Hector! How should he cope? Flat denial? No—a careful part of the truth. He'd learned that from Marion. Attack! 'Well, Hector Odhar? I should have expected to find you here, I suppose. No Maclean house would take in a man who raised his hand against his own chief, but here you could claim refuge for defending the lady who was

180

nearly your wife.' Lachlan cast one glance down the hall behind him. His guard, all fighting men, were already alert for trouble. Pretending unconcern, they casually eased their muscles and blades, and eyed the spearmen round the walls and the Campbells behind them. Which would be the best door to fight towards?

Hector's head was lifting in surprise. 'You admit it, then?'

'Admit what? How can I answer, when I don't know what you've said?'

A carved chair was brought forward and set to the side of the coffin, facing down the body of the hall towards the surrounded Macleans. Argyll swept his dark red robe of state round him, and seated himself. Suddenly the hall was a court of justice.

Damn it, Lachlan thought, this was supposed to be a joke on Argyll! What had got into him, to try such a daft laddie's trick! But he had no time for such thoughts just now. He needed all his attention to pull himself out of trouble. Here, in his own castle, Argyll had the right of pit and gallows, as Lachlan had in Mull; to imprison or hang any man who displeased him. And the killing of his daughter was likely to displease him a good deal.

As Hector and Lachlan faced each other before the coffin, John of Cawdor stepped forward beside his father like a lawyer. 'Hector Odhar has brought us a strange tale, Lachlan Cattanach Maclean,' he said in a neutral tone. 'He tells us that the day before our sister drowned, you accused her of poisoning you. And then you tried to strangle her. It was in defence of her, he says, that he struck you.'

If that was all they knew . . . Lachlan laughed, then shook his head. 'Forgive me, Cawdor. I forget myself, that my wife lies here. The tale Hector has told you is half-way to the truth.' He turned respectfully to Lady Campbell. 'My lady, I did not tell all the truth, for I wished to spare you this pain. But now that the word has been spoken, it must come out. Aye, your daughter did indeed plan to kill me, with a dangerous potion that your son here brought for her, to use as a tonic, he said.' And that should keep him from pressing too far . . . 'A phial of this "tonic" was found hidden in the room of—' no, don't say it—'of one of the servants, who tasted it to discover what it was, and recognised it as a poison. Why should it be hidden there, except to kill me, and accuse the servant of my murder?' This was truth, and it showed in the anger and betrayal in his voice. Argyll exchanged glances with his sons and wife.

'I admit, my lord, I was angered. Would you not have been? In my anger, I struck her. I admit it, here before you all. But I ask you again, my lord, you and your sons, here in your own hall; in all honesty, say which of you would not have done so? To a wife who was trying to kill you?'

The sudden tension, as he spoke of hitting their sister, their child, faded as they thought ... Well, true enough ... And remember the night she'd thrown a spear at her father ...

'It was then that Hector arrived. He may indeed have thought I meant to kill her.' That was a nice touch of generosity. 'For that reason, I will forgive him and accept him back to Duart.' And that disposed of Hector's story!

Then he turned to a lie. Enough truth was enough. He had no wish to start a feud with the Campbells—and especially not here and now, when he was so badly placed for it. 'I locked her in a room apart, until my temper had time to cool. And in the morning, she had gone. Her maid, I think, let her out, and they tried to flee together. I lied to you, to save your feelings.' Could any bard craft a better tale, then? A poor story, to hide a good one that was embarrassing, and no-one would look for a third beneath ... One last stopper on any questions ... 'I cannot think that she would have tried to take her own life, in guilt and fear. No, that was not her way. She may safely be buried in hallowed ground.' And if Argyll did question it, he risked having his daughter—well, his daughter's aunt-in-law's coffin, but he didn't know that—buried on a headland far from any house, unblessed, unholy, accursed. He'd surely never dare risk such a tragedy—such a disgrace to his clan. So, now, what next?

But there was to be argument. Lachlan's anger rose as Hector spoke slowly. Almost regretfully. 'No, Lachlan. You lied indeed, but not in that way. You sent Farquhar Neas to set her on a rock to drown.'

Dhia, they had it all! Whose tongue had been flapping? As Lachlan started to bristle, John of Cawdor gestured to Ranald to draw Hector aside. 'Aye, a most serious accusation. But we will return to it later, with your permission, Hector Odhar. Tell us, Duart, have you any evidence that it was the truth that you were told? About this poison?'

Lachlan stared, thrown off balance by the changes of angle. 'I told you—the potion was found hidden!' What was all this about?

'In whose room? Who told you about it at the first?'

Why not tell the truth? 'My wife's maid of honour. Marion Maclean.'

'Marion Aluinn? Aye, so.' He turned inquiringly to his father, who nodded. 'Would it not be as well, think you, to ask the lady herself?' He lifted a hand.

Lachlan drew a deep breath of shock as the side door opened again and Marion was ushered into the hall, her gracious smile and graceful curtsey to the earl very nearly hiding her nervousness. 'Marion Aluinn, in God's name how did you come here?'

She almost sighed with relief at the sight of her man, and not just Campbells. 'I was trying to save your child, Duart.'

'What?' He came right up to her, gripping her arms. 'What has happened? Where is my son?'

Suddenly annoyed, she tugged to free herself. He had another son, after all! 'Your heir Eachuinn Og, my lord, is somewhere in this castle.'

He whipped round. 'What? What devilry is this? How did you seize him?'

'Seize?' To his fury he noticed amusement in John's tone, and all round. 'Nothing of the kind, I assure you, Duart. Indeed, your foster-bother Farquhar Neas, who had both children in his care, actually called to me for help in saving them from this lady.'

'Both children?' he yelled. 'You! What have you done?' He shook her violently.

'Nothing!' she snarled back at him. 'That brat Luch stole the baby from under your precious dallta's nose, and I went after her! To save him! And then I saw Farquhar Neas taking him away in a boat and went after them—'

'And what if you had found them? How long would my son have lived then? Elizabeth warned me about you! No, you didn't know that, did you? And another thing you didn't know! I told

Farquhar Neas if harm came to my child through you, to kill you. Aye, I did so! So you can be glad you didn't catch them!'

'Can I so? After all I've done for you, Lachlan Cattanach, you'd rather have that damned baby than me!'

'Aye would I! My heir!' They had both forgotten the people around them, listening silent and intent to the growing, revealing fury.

'I can give you a dozen to take its place!'

'Not my wife's child!'

'Dear God! Its mother tried to kill you, and you killed her! I'd think you'd be glad to see the back of it! I was your wife—and I will be again!'

'Never!'

'Never? After all I've done . . .' Her mouth opened, and stayed, as her mind noticed the listeners; and went back over what she had said; and her stomach shrivelled into a hot little iceberg. Then her rage burst out again. 'Never, is it? Well, so, my lord, there's no call for me to keep your secrets any longer, is there?' Lachlan's own jaw dropped, as she swung round to her enthralled audience. 'Argyll! You ask what happened to your daughter? I'll tell you! He killed her! Lachlan Cattanach Maclean of Duart! He murered Elizabeth Campbell, your daughter! Hang him!'

As Lachlan drew his dirk John Campbell's sword was already out, the flat of the blade against Lachlan's wrist knocking the weapon from his hand. 'None dies here save at Argyll's order! Or the killer hangs!' he snapped. The guards seized the dirk fom the floor, and their axes forced Lachlan back against the coffin, away from Marion's frightened defiance.

'Bas no Beatha!' one of the Macleans shouted, ready to do battle. Their blades rasped out to face the long pointed axe-heads swinging down all round the hall. The Campbells behind them reached for their swords also. If the fight once started, the Macleans would die, but so would many of the Campbells.

The women screamed, but Argyll was already on his feet to prevent bloodshed. 'Let no man move!' His voice, used to overbearing the unruly lords in the King's Council, cut through the uproar to hold them still for long enough to hear him. 'Men of Clan Gillian, you have heard this grave charge laid against your chief. Will you wait in peace to hear the evidence, and bear witness to your clan of my judgement?'

Against all the spears . . . Donald Crubach, their spokesman, gestured behind him for them to put away their knives and swords for the moment, and bowed. 'The justice of Clan Diarmaid is well-known.' But not praised. 'We will surely report it to Clan Gillian, and the world.' The warning was there; either do justice, or you must kill us all to keep it quiet. Not that that would worry a Campbell . . . And Lachlan was guilty. No word spoken, they all knew to be ready, and watch for a better chance.

'Now, woman.' All eyes turned again to Marion. 'What have you to tell us?'

A Lady of the Macleans

Recovering from her fright, more beautiful in her anger and fear than ever before, Marion didn't hesitate. 'That man, my lord. Lachlan Cattanach Maclean. He killed your daughter.' Lachlan, guarded by the spearpoints still, twisted a corner of the black cover on the coffin as if it was her throat. She smiled in triumph. 'Before he married your child, he was hand-fasted to me—'

'I know. Yourself, you broke the contract.'

'Aye, but he loved me yet. But he wed her—your daughter. And cast me aside. I hated him for it!' It was plain, in her snarling face and voice. 'But he still loved me, and as soon as he could he took me in beside her as a second wife.' She didn't notice that they weren't surprised or shocked by the news. 'And when she planned to poison him—'

'That is true, then?' The earl's tone was sharp as her own.

'Aye, Argyll. I swear it, on my hope of Heaven! But I found out, and told him. For I thought he would kill her, and marry me again. And then—' a hint of caution stopped her—'then I'd be Lady of Duart again, at least! And it worked, for he near strangled her, and he ordered Farquhar Neas to take her—'

'This is the same Farquhar Neas that my son John found with the children? He is outside. Fetch him in.' The lad by the far door turned to obey.

'Aye, my lord, Lachlan Cattanach's dallta! He'd do anything for his milk-brother, anything at all. He took your daughter out in a boat to a rock and bound her, and left her there for the tide to take. So that Lachlan Cattanach could swear he didn't kill her, God did.'

They nodded, consideringly. Lachlan Cattanach had sworn just that. 'But this was done at the orders of Duart himself?'

She nodded eagerly, triumphantly. 'Aye—Agh!'

There was a black knife hilt sticking out from the base of her throat.

Farquhar Neas stood still amid the screams, as Marion clutched at the long knife. He could do little else, for there were a dozen spears levelled at him, and his dirk was now gone. He watched, they all watched, for a long minute as she tried to pull it out; tried to speak; turned towards Lachlan, and fell slowly, without grace, to knee, hip, elbow, shoulder, to sprawl at his feet.

Lachlan was staring, paralysed like the rest, standing above her as she clutched at his shoes. Then he knelt and took her hand. She gripped his big fingers and shook them, gazing into his eyes, mouthing, straining to speak; but her desperate grasp failed, and her head rolled back on the paving.

Lachlan slowly raised his head to look at Farquhar Neas, but Farquhar was not looking at him. He had gently shoved aside a couple of the long axes and walked over to kneel at Argyll's feet. In pride, not submission.

'It was my doing that your daughter died, Argyll. When I heard how she had tried to kill my dallta, I punished her for it. Duart knew nothing of it till after. He had no hand in her death, and so I swear to you. It's myself alone you must hang for it. And for killing that woman there, in your hall of justice, to put an end to her lying. I did it for him. As God is my witness, Duart is innocent. It's I that am the only guilty one.'

'No!' Lachlan had pulled himself heavily up, leaning on the coffin. 'No! Farquhar Neas—' Pushing aside the wavering spear-points, as his foster-brother had done, he stumbled stiffly across the three or four paces between them. 'For me? You say you killed her for me?'

The tall, fair man rose also, to meet him. 'I killed both of them for you, Lachlan Cattanach,' he said clearly and steadily. 'My dirk at your service, my life between you and harm, my heart.' Mouth twisted, eyes level, he never glanced at his own knife, still red with Marion's blood, as Lachlan lifted it from where he held it hidden in the folds of his breacan-feile and drove it straight and fast into his dallta's chest.

The two men sank together to the flagstones. Lachlan held Farquhar's body in his arms, hugging it tightly, silent sobs tearing at him, his face pale and contorted with a dreadful grief, his tears rolling unheeded.

There was a cry from the silent rows of women. One of them ran forward, to kneel by Lachlan and set her arms round him, helping support Farquhar's weight. The big man lifted his eyes blankly over the body to the woman; focussed; and started to tremble. 'No—no! Not you! You're dead!'

'Aye, so?' The Earl of Argyll rose from his chair to look down on them. 'May I introduce you to the lady? Your dead wife, Duart! And who's in the coffin, then?' He started to laugh, jeering. Alone, in a dreadful stillness.

John Campbell turned above them, the living and the dead, to stare coldly at his father. 'Is the masque finished, then, Argyll? Did we act well enough at your direction? But who is there applauding?'

The scornful comment stopped the earl's laughter dead. The silence, the uneasy glances, showed him his clan felt he had acted coarsely, in a way not fitting for a gentleman. His dramatic comedy had turned to sudden tragedy, but in his excitement he had not changed the speech he had planned as its climax. Sullenly, with an unaccustomed flicker of shame, he sank back to his seat.

After a while the countess broke the spell of shock, and ordered the bodies straightened decently. Lachlan knelt stiffly as his arms were loosened from Farquhar's corpse, and the two people he had loved most were laid before the mockery of the coffin; and then suddenly he heaved to his feet. 'Where is he? My son Eachuinn.' He cast a driven, desperate eye round at them, and kept on shouting. 'Dhia, who can I trust! I will see my son. Eachuinn! Eachuinn Og!' The Macleans started to fidget uneasily again, recovering from their surprise.

As the spears pressed around Lachlan to hold him back Elizabeth, in pity for his anguish, ran from the hall up to the bower. She reached in to lift the baby from his cradle. Luch wakened with a start and struggled to her feet, alarmed by the rush. 'Aye, come you, then, lass! You aye come in handy.' Flustered and upset, the child followed her pattering down the stair again.

'Who are you, Duart, to make demands here?' Argyll was bellowing.

With Eachuinn Og in her arms, gurgling in astonishment at being snatched from his sleep, waving a tiny starfish hand, Elizabeth walked steadily forward through the spearmen surrounding her husband, setting aside the sharp steel to hold out the child. 'Here is your son, Maclean,' she said quietly. 'Our son.'

He seized the child, looking ready to hurl himself at them all to escape. The baby, frightened by the jerk and the fierce clutch, started to squirm and scream. He paid no heed, but drew a deep breath to brace himself and swung to face his enemy. But Argyll's threat was not physical. Not immediately.

'Well, are you satisfied that we've not murdered him?' The earl's tone was caustic. 'Have we your permission to proceed?'

'Maybe not now, father,' John of Cawdor suggested. He felt a sympathy, not for the first time, with Lachlan. A fool, of course, who thought only with his fists; but straightforward. Unlike his own father. Too much taste for the dramatics, Argyll, he thought in irritation. And see what came of it!

'Now.' Deeply shocked, Lachlan could bear no delay. Violent death, at his own hand, he was used to. But this was different. 'Get done with it.'

'Aye, so.' The Earl of Argyll settled his furred gown smoothly, once again Lord Lieutenant of the Isles, in dignity and power. And then hitched forward and swore. 'For God's sake, quiet that squalling brat before it deafens us!'

Elizabeth reached for the child, but Lachlan snatched him back. 'No! Not to a Campbell!' Elizabeth felt like screaming herself, to match her baby. In another moment her father, insulted and angry, would order the soldiers to grab the child, and what would Lachlan do then?

Behind Elizabeth Luch was biting her lip. Her baby was in

trouble. She forced herself to slip forward through the crowd of soldiers and reached up to tug shyly at Lachlan's breacan-feile. He leaped round defensively—the baby screamed and wriggled wildly again; but when Lachlan saw who it was, his face relaxed, and he reluctantly, gratefully released the baby to Luch. 'Are you here too? Aye, I'll trust him to you. You see to him, lass!' he muttered.

'I'll trust you . . .' The spears shifted to let her pass, head down, heart singing, to the side of the room, all eyes on her; within a minute the wails stopped; within another minute not a soul remembered she was there, and she could nurse her precious baby and watch, as usual, unnoticed.

The earl leaned back, solemn and stately once more. 'You slew a man here before my eyes, Duart. Murder in my own hall. The penalty for that is death.'

Lachlan was standing alone now in the centre of the hall. His vast energy was exhausted, after the horrors of the past hour. He was almost glad to have it over with. His head was bowing in acceptance when he felt a movement at his side.

Hector had stepped forward and also was bowing to the earl. 'I have a word to say, Argyll.' The earl's hand was raised to stop him, but Hector, of course, didn't see it. 'As a Highlander, you know how deep is the bond between foster-brothers. Duart has been driven by a grief he could not bear, into a grief he can never lose. Argyll, no punishment you can give him will hurt as much as the memory of the deed itself.'

'May I speak also, father?' Elizabeth found herself moving to her husband's side, not looking at him but aware of his puzzlement at her action. It was little greater than her own. The earl eyed his daughter carefully, but she took extreme care to be respectful. 'Pray you remember, my lord, that Farquhar Neas had just killed a woman, here, before you. His life was forfeit. He was of the Clan Gillian; the duty was Duart's, to punish the crime. Can you hang him, my lord, for saving you the trouble of doing so?'

That wasn't why . . . Coming slowly back to himself, in considerable amazement Lachlan opened his mouth to put her right, but winced as she stepped aside and a high heel ground into the instep of his brogans.

A whisper hissed behind his shoulder. 'Be quiet, now, sir! It's at saving your life for you they are! Hush!' Ranald was amazed at his own daring.

'H'm.' The earl rubbed his chins. 'Aye, well. If we leave that aside, for the moment, then, there still remains the charge of attempting to murder my daughter.' He lifted an eyebrow at Elizabeth, standing protectively beside her would-be murderer. 'Or have you a plea in extenuation of that as well?'

Hector bit his lip; Lachlan was about to mention a little matter of poison; but Elizabeth looked surprised. 'Extenuation of what, father? We all heard Farquhar Neas confess he had tied me to the rock without my husband's knowledge. He alone was guilty.' Again Lachlan prepared to speak, to defend his dallta, and again she stood on his toes, under cover of her long skirts.

'What?' Her father frowned. 'That's not what you told me last week. Emphatic, impassioned you were, so, about your husband's brutality.'

Elizabeth was prettily shamefaced. 'I must confess, father, that when I first was brought here I was confused. Hysterical, even. I fear I exaggerated.'

'Indeed? As I recall what you told me he said to you—'

John cleared his throat. 'In law, sir, hearsay evidence is not admissible.'

The earl's eyes narrowed. 'Aye. But in a trial—'

Most respectfully, Elizabeth interrupted him. 'I believe a wife cannot give evidence against her husband. Is that not so, my lord?'

He studied her. What the devil was she up to now, the vixen? 'Not exactly. She may do so if she wishes. Do I understand that you do not wish?'

She still did not look at Lachlan, who was eyeing her in deep distrust. 'No, father. I cannot—I will not—bear witness against my husband.'

Lachlan suddenly felt a surge of life again. Hector helping him? And, for whatever reason, his wife? Dhia, the world was upside down!

Argyll considered carefully. His son John, whose opinion he respected, was clearly for Duart; and Hector Odhar; and even his daft daughter. What to do, then? How best to make use of his advantage? Hang him anyway, rear the brat himself, and so rule Clan Gillian? He'd have to kill all the Macleans here as well. Including Hector, who had saved Elizabeth. His own clansmen would support him, and John would keep his mouth shut even if he disapproved, but Elizabeth would create seven different kinds of trouble. The poisoning scandal—what was the truth of that, anyway?

He reared angrily to his feet. 'Do you all take me for a fool?' They stiffened satisfactorily. 'Lachlan Maclean, for murder and attempted murder I could hang you here and now! And by God I should! But—' he lowered his voice for effect, as the Macleans farther down the hall tensed for action—'but I'll offer you one chance. Take it, or die!'

Lachlan glanced round. Elizabeth shrugged slightly. She knew no more than he what her father would say. At his father's shoulder, John nodded. Whatever it was, it would do no harm to hear it.

'What had you in mind, Argyll?' asked Hector.

Argyll's tone was suddenly mild. 'A fair offer.' Oh, aye? they all thought, instantly even more wary. 'Duart may return home—on conditions.'

Lachlan was driving his brain to work again. 'Conditions? You mean—my son as hostage?'

Elizabeth's expression would have scared off a thunderstorm. Then by pure willpower she cleared her face, and moved forward to kneel reverently before her father's chair, charming and appealing, hands clasped as if in prayer. He knew what she was going to say before she said it. 'My lord of Argyll, you are a great and just lord. I beseech you, as you hope for mercy from the Lord of all mankind, have mercy on me and my baby. On my knees, father, I beg you humbly, forgive my husband and release him, and my son, to return freely to Duart and praise your justice to all of Clan Gillian.'

He was hard put to it not to laugh. Lying little bitch! He knew the hell she'd raise if he said no! But it gave him an excuse to pay the debt he owed Duart for his lapse in manners. Besides, generosity now might bring better results in the end than force. Friendship, rather than hatred . . . Aye.

He tut-tutted in shocked reproof. 'Would I do any hurt to my dear daughter's child? Your son may go freely back to his own home.' She relaxed, sighing deeply. Genial and friendly, everybody's favourite uncle, he smiled like a podgy shark. 'You'll bring him back here when he's seven or so, Duart. For a bit court polish, eh?' As Lachlan, scarlet with humiliation, bowed agreement, the earl added smoothly, 'And you'll take back Hector, as you've already said, and swear to consult him about all matters to do with the clan.'

Lachlan pondered. 'I owe him a great deal—'

'Hah!' The earl snorted scornfully. 'You owe him your life, Duart. If he'd not saved Elizabeth off that rock, and spoken for you here, you'd be up on my gibbet this minute as an example to all wild Islesmen that the sovereign rule of law must be obeyed!' John hastily controlled his eyebrows. Sovereign rule of law? Aye, when it suited him . . . 'Well? Do you accept?'

The lad would advise him well, for the good of the clan. And he could slip a lot past a blind man . . . Lachlan was getting back to normal fast. He suddenly thought of another possible demand. Prevent it—now! 'In gratitude I'll do more. I name Hector Mac Eachuinn guardian to my son, to rule Clan Gillian till he is grown, if I die.' He nearly smiled at the earl's annoyance.

'I'll return only if it's your own wish, Duart!' Hector spoke strongly, touched by the honour Lachlan gave him.

'It is indeed, lad!' Lachlan hugged him warmly, and he hugged Lachlan back, grinning freely and openly, accepting his uncle as chief at last.

'And last of all, you will take back with you your wife Elizabeth.'

'What?' Lachlan yelped. 'But—After what she did? And what I did? How can you expect us to live together again?'

'Politely.' The earl's voice was cold. 'She's to be treated well, with all due respect.' He'd not keep his daughter in Inveraray for the next forty years, her fights with her mother driving him daft. God! Not another day if he could help it! 'You have your choice; take her with you, or hang!'

'Take back a wife that's tried to kill me?' Lachlan protested.

Elizabeth flushed. 'I did not, so, Duart! What proof have you?

And have I not been trying to save you here? Does that count for nothing?'

Lachlan's face was still mutinous, and he shook his head in determination.

John did his best, coming down to speak privately to them, an arm confidentially round Elizabeth's stiff shoulders. murmuring so that his father couldn't hear. 'Look, man,' he argued, 'it cancels out. You say she tried to kill you. Well, it wasn't right, what you did either—my apologies, sister—what you didn't do; but we've all known worse. And most of us done it. If father's willing to let it pass, and so is she, why not you? You're no worse off than many a couple.' Hector snorted his disbelief. 'Well, maybe a bit; but you can manage. Father thinks to use her to control you. You must see it. But how much control he'll actually get—that's for you to work out between you. Take her back—and then tell him to go to hell!' He returned to his place, smiling faintly under his father's cynical eye. They knew each other very well.

'I can't. I can't!' Lachlan said to John's back.

She took his sleeve and turned him towards her. 'Lachlan, you are my husband. Have you no word for me myself, instead of talking through John?'

There was a pause. The audience around them stood silent, listening.

'Why—tell me, Elizabeth, why have you been helping me?'

She looked down, away from his gaze. 'I don't know. I just—I don't know.' It was true, much to her annoyance.

Her husband shook his head. 'How could I trust you?' He sighed. 'Could we ever have happiness again, Elizabeth? As we had before?'

'Did we?' she asked, rather coldly.

'We were happy enough, surely!'

'Dhia, what a man's thought! You were happy, sure, but who else? Not I. Not after you saw Marion again. Nor her, seeing me in her place. She'd have found some way of destroying me, and our son after me. She was set on it. It just happened to be that story of poison.'

He looked at her in a weary disgust. 'Ach, Elizabeth! Is this

194

not the time for truth? John, Hector, tell her not to deny it. I held the bottle in my hand.'

'But what was in it?' she demanded. 'I asked you then how you knew it was poison. I told you to test it on a dog. You wouldn't let me speak. But now I tell you again, it was not.'

He shook his head and sighed. 'Don't lie to me.'

'If I had it now I would drink it to prove what I say!'

He snorted in near-laughter. 'Easy said, wife, when you're not likely to be called on to do it. Before God, I wish I had it here, to try you. We'd see then whether you spoke truth or not.'

He broke off at a gasp around him. Luch, forgotten as always by the wall, had slipped through the throng and was shyly holding something up to him.

'What's that?' He bent to take the little object, then straightened with a shout of amazement. 'Dhia—it's the bottle itself!' He held up the small green glass bottle, with its carved wooden plug. 'Where did you get that?'

Elizabeth's breath caught. 'In the dungeon. You threw it out the door . . . I heard it fall—but not smash . . . She must have been there.'

Ranald cleared his throat bashfully. 'Hector Odhar sent her to spy—er—find out what was happening, sir.'

'Was that it? Were you in the passage outside, lass?' Elizabeth asked. 'And you picked it up? And kept it? Why?'

As usual, Luch had no answer. She shrugged, looking down. It was pretty . . . and she had vaguely felt it was worth keeping . . .

Hector laughed. 'My grandfather said on his death-bed the lass was important. A wise man, so. Well, Elizabeth? Will you drink it, and prove your words now?'

Lachlan, Hector, John, her father, the Macleans, the Campbells, the whole crowd watched to see how she faced the challenge.

If she drank it, and lived, and so was proved innocent, she would return to Duart free of all stain, to a husband full of remorse, to wealth, rank, power.

If she refused, they would know she was guilty. Her husband might decide to take her back, but could beat her, chain her up, starve her to death as a proven murderess. And for his pride's sake, her father, who had supported her when nothing was proved, would refuse her any help.

Or a guilty woman might prefer to drink, and die swiftly. Which would suit everyone just as well.

Luch's tiny, vital part had turned the evening's drama on its head. The wife was no longer the wronged innocent, and her husband the villain. It was no longer Lachlan Maclean who was on trial; suddenly, it was Elizabeth Campbell. They all waited, even her father, to find out the truth.

Elizabeth gazed levelly round, facing the greedy eyes, the excited faces. She drew herself up slowly and regally, a natural actress, making the most of the dramatic tension. She glanced at Luch. 'This is that same bottle, lassie? Untouched? Will you accept that, Lachlan? Aye? So, then.' Swiftly, casually, she uncorked it and drank it down. 'Ugh! Bitter it is, so. But only a tonic!' After the grimace at the taste, her face was sweet and forgiving.

Of all there, John of Cawdor was most taken aback by his sister's action.

'It was true, then! It wasn't—Dhia, Elizabeth!' Lachlan slid to his knees before her. 'Elizabeth, God forgive me! And you forgive me too! I truly thought—but I see now it was all Marion's lies and scheming!' He hesitated, and went on with some difficulty. 'Your father wants me to take you back.'

'Aye. I know it. But what do you want?'

He shrugged a shoulder. 'Does that matter to you?'

She had to restore his pride, for both their sakes. 'Aye. For I'll not return unless you ask me. You, not him. It's you are my man.'

He drew a deep breath. 'Elizabeth Campbell, can you find it in you to come back to me? I know it'll be hard, after what I've done, but we can try—'

She leaned away from him a touch, to study his face. 'I'd be your wife? Your only wife? Undisputed Lady of Duart? And you'll never distrust me again?' To each, he nodded; and she leaned forward to take his head in her arms. 'Oh, Lachlan. Aye, we can try, husband!' The thrill at the word was there again.

Over his shoulder she saw her brother smiling, and beyond him her father wreathed in smug complacency. And her own heart was filled with joy too.

Dhia, the clever, scheming wee bitch, John thought in admiration as the celebrations erupted round him. She'd watered down the bottle long ago, to trap her rival Marion into making this accusation, and prove it false. When her husband wouldn't let her prove her innocence, just sent her to her death, it must have been a right shock to her! Maybe she'd be less devious in future. But he'd not bet on it. A lass to treat with care, this one!

As Lady Campbell commanded wine to be brought for them all, her husband gestured to the bodies lying silent, but not forgotten. 'Carry Farquhar Neas back to the Maclean galley, in the great coffin. And throw the other—'

But his daughter stopped him. She also owed a debt. 'No, father. Lachlan, she parted us—but she brought us together again. We will take her back in the great coffin. She deserves some respect—some dignity. Let her go in state to her rest.'

Her husband was puzzled. 'Why, Elizabeth? Why this regard for her?'

She looked down at Marion's face with satisfaction, and compassion, and not a little guilt. It could have ended so differently ... 'I've finally beaten her. In spite of her beauty, and her schemes. But I'm sorry she is dead. Truly sorry. I thought I'd rejoice, but— I'll miss her. And she loved you.'

'No, you're wrong, lass. It was hate she had for me—like you.'

'No.' She didn't explain who she meant. 'Love. That was why she turned against you. As I did. But love doesn't die so easily. Even in the end she betrayed you only when you finally rejected her. But when she was dying it was you she turned to, because she loved you. And she knew that beyond all, you loved her. Aye, Lachlan, you did. That was why you took the knife and—' She stopped. She had opened the worst hurt; she had to go on. 'Poor Farquhar. He gave his life for you, to save you from my father, out of love and loyalty. And for nothing, for I was alive. I aye feared him, but—what a waste.'

'Aye,' he whispered. 'Dhia! How did it all start?'

Ambition, she thought, and greed, and love; hard drivers all three. 'Farquhar—we will lay him with love in a plain man's

coffin, and the clan will bury him with honour. But Marion—'
She sighed. 'She loved you . . . I can't find it in me to hate her, or
blame her—not entirely. Everyone else will loathe her, curse her.
But . . . Let her have the great coffin. It's little enough, for the
mother of your firstborn son.'

'You're generous. She'd not have done the same for you, Elizabeth Roisin.'

'Indeed? Then should a lady of the Macleans decide her actions
by what any other woman would or would not have done?'

'A lady of the Macleans? You do truly accept me again, then?'
He turned to her, and took her in his arms.

Hector heard the approving coo of the crowd round the un-
heeding couple. 'Ranald! What's happening?'

'Sh! They're hugging and kissing, sir. Like a snake with a frog.'

'Dhia, what a way to put it!' Hector sighed in satisfaction.
Lachlan would make a good enough chief for the clan. In a way it
was even a relief. He could get on with his learning, and play a
good part in the clan without the full responsibility. 'Get me a
glass of wine, Ranald, my throat's dry. And don't spill it over me
—Dhia, that's my best shirt! Will you ever learn!'

Lachlan held his wife close for a long time, while around them
the chatter and cheering rose in relief and excitement. But when
the men at last lifted Farquhar and Marion, he left her and followed them out, head bowed.

Best leave him to grieve in private, for a little while. Elizabeth
watched him go, his own men falling in behind him. She was
surrounded by a swarm of friends and family congratulating her
on her innocence. They'd known all the time, of course . . . She
was glad when her brother John touched her arm to offer her
wine. She took it gratefully.

'Well, my dear.' In the din, no-one could hear a word they said.
'I believe you'll do well enough together now.'

'I think so too, John.' A gulp of wine helped stop her trembling.

'But keep Marion Aluinn in mind, eh? She did you little harm,
in the end, and much good, with her desperate attacks on the baby
. . . That was what turned Lachlan from her . . . And proved to
father that you weren't lying. Not entirely, anyway. Aye,' he
smiled rather grimly at her surprise, 'he had that in mind, too.

Don't look so shocked, my dear. I've told you before—he's no fool, Argyll.' He glanced down at her. 'A thought for you. The flask—it was Marion who gave it to Lachlan? Tell me, dear sister, how did you know that she hadn't added anything to it? That it wasn't really poison? Then if he had tested it . . .'

Her jaw dropped as she suddenly realised what could have happened. 'Or if I had drunk it, and she had . . .' Her hand went to her throat in horror at her escape. 'Oh, John! I might have . . .'

He smiled. 'Aye, my dear. Something to consider in future . . . But she didn't, and you didn't. So now you have all you wanted, eh?'

'I am alive. And she is dead. I have my husband—all to myself,' she said thoughtfully, recovering her self-possession. 'My baby, safe at last. Freedom from mother again—Dhia, her and her damned pink! And she's not forgotten—something I said. Position.' Elizabeth nodded, and finished her wine. 'Aye, John. I have it all now.'

He looked at her quizzically. 'Love?'

She considered it seriously. 'It well may grow. Now that it has no rival.'

'But what about Hugh—Hugh—What was the idiot's name?'

'Hugh?' She frowned for a moment. 'Oh, Hugh! Hugh . . . Des —Despainter? Despoins, that was it! Ach, John, that was long bye. When I was a child.'

'Hah!' Unusually for him, he laughed out loud. 'And how old are you now, grandma? Seventeen?'

'Near eighteen, sir!'

He smiled again. 'You're older, my dear. And wiser, maybe.'

She changed her mind about making a joke of it. 'I hope so, John.'

'One thing, Elizabeth—'

'Aye?'

'What happened to the—er—the rest of the tonic?'

Her smile was brilliant. 'Why, dearest brother, I poured it away.'

One sardonic eyebrow rose. 'Forgive me, dearest sister, if I say I don't believe you.'

'Why, John Campbell! To suggest that your own sister—a lady

of the Campbells—would tell a lie!' They laughed gently together.

'I do hope, sister, that Lachlan Cattanach does not allow his eyes to wander again,' the tall man said thoughtfully.

'So do I, surely, brother! Or a lady—of the Macleans—might well be sore displeased.' She glanced round. 'Now, where's that child—she aye vanishes—Luch! Luch!' She gradually became aware of a movement at her elbow. 'Ah, there you are, my dear! Father's calling me. Take Eachuinn Og up to his cradle again, lass, I'll come up in a while. And do you stay by him, for it's you has saved him. He's as much your baby as mine, now! I know I can trust you with him.'

John looked after her as she moved away, smiling graciously. Did she realise how much she owed the child? Without Luch, Marion would have triumphed. Elizabeth would be dead, and Lachlan, and Eachuinn Og, and possibly Hector too. The clans would have feuded, maybe. Like his sister once before, he wondered just how such a dim scrap of nothing could be so vitally important to the world about her.

Luch drifted invisible as usual through the crowd and up the stair to the bower, dreamy with joy. 'You saved him . . . as much your baby as mine . . . I trust you with him.' She nursed her baby in total content. Nothing else, no war or peace, no love or hate, no life or death mattered to her. She noticed them as little as others noticed her. This was her love, her life; just this, her own baby. Her real, live baby. Her trust, her quest, at last fulfilled.